TRAIL OF POISON

M.J. RICHARDS

Available from M.J. Richards

The Emily Swanson Series
Next To Disappear
Mind For Murder
Trail Of Poison
Watch You Sleep

As Malcolm Richards:
The Devil's Cove Trilogy
The Cove
Desperation Point
The Devil's Gate

Standalone
The Hiding House

Sign up for the author's New Releases mailing list.
www.malcolmrichardsauthor.com

Storm House
This paperback edition 2019

ISBN 978-1-9993384-9-7

Previously published as *Cold Hearts* in 2016

For more information about the author, please visit
www.malcolmrichardsauthor.com

For Casey

TRAIL OF POISON

1

EMILY SWANSON RANG the doorbell then sucked in a nervous breath. What was she doing here? She looked up at the house. It was a large but not sprawling affair, with latticed windows and white walls. The drive, which was wide enough to hold several cars, was currently empty, while a towering, evergreen hedgerow smudged out much of the quiet, suburban street.

Seconds passed. Shrugging off her backpack, Emily removed the letter that had arrived a few days ago, and checked the address: 112 Ford Road, Epsom, Surrey. She pressed the doorbell again.

Above her, the Friday morning sun was bold and bright. After an overcast July and a rainy August, September was turning out to be uncharacteristically hot. Closing her eyes, Emily took a moment to enjoy the warmth on her skin. When she opened them again, she saw a woman smiling at her from the doorway.

"Diane Edwards?" she asked.

"You must be Emily."

She was led through a carpeted hall and into a spacious kitchen at the back of the house.

"Please sit down." Diane Edwards gestured to the table and chairs in front of the large bay windows. "I'll make some tea."

Emily smiled politely and turned to view the rear garden. An expanse of vibrant lawn, which was bordered by colourful flowerbeds, stretched into the distance. A copse of trees stood at the far end, watching over the house. Beneath the table, Emily's knee began to jig up and down. She wondered if it was too late to make her excuses and leave.

Diane returned with the tea tray. She was somewhat older than Emily's twenty-seven years, perhaps in her mid-forties, and where Emily's hair was blonde and fell just above her shoulders, Diane's was jet black and cut short. As she turned the cups over and reached for the teapot, she offered Emily a slight smile.

"You must forgive my quietness. It's not often I invite strangers into my home, especially in such unusual circumstances."

Emily untangled her arms and placed her hands on her lap. "I'm a little nervous myself. And a little surprised."

Diane eyed her as she poured the tea. "At my proposal?"

"Mrs. Edwards, I—"

"Please, call me Diane. Sugar?"

Emily shook her head. "I should probably make it clear before we go any further that my being here isn't an agreement. I admit I'm curious, but I may not be qualified for what you need."

Diane slid a cup of tea toward Emily. "That's understandable. Perhaps if I elaborate on the details of my letter it will help you to form a decision." She flashed a nervous glance across the table. "My husband, Max, worked as a sustainable development manager for a big chemicals company. You may have heard of it—Valence Industries. It was his job to find new ways for the company to be more environmentally friendly, or at least that's my understanding of it. The chemicals industry doesn't have the best reputation when it comes to the environment, which is why Max took the job in the first place.

"He'd been actively involved in green issues for as long as I can remember. Even back when we first met, he was always off on one protest or another, occasionally getting himself arrested. . ." She smiled sadly. "Part of Max's remit was to nurture partnerships with various environmental charities. He'd been working for months on a project to bring clean water to parts of the world where there was none. The project was to launch with a fundraising gala. . ."

Diane gazed through the window at long ago memories. When she spoke again, her voice was quiet and controlled. "The official consensus is that Max attended the gala in London in May of last year, then spent the night in his hotel room. When he didn't show for breakfast the next morning, his colleagues went to look for him. His room was empty. The bed hadn't been slept in." She paused again and clenched her jaw. "He was found by tourists early the next morning, washed up on the bank of the Thames."

"I'm very sorry for your loss, Mrs. Edwards." Emily's teacup was frozen in mid-air. She set it down on the saucer with an accidental clatter. "Your husband drowned?"

"My husband was an alcoholic," Diane said matter-of-factly, as if describing her late husband as a keen golfer or a lover of antiques. "Max's drinking almost ripped our marriage apart more times than I can count. Each time, I packed his bags and left them on the doorstep.

Each time, I brought them back in. That may sound very weak of me, but I understood that, like any addiction, alcoholism is a disease. Besides, despite everything, I loved him." Her expression hardened. "The coroner's report revealed that the alcohol levels in Max's bloodstream were so high that if he hadn't drowned first there was every chance he would have died from toxic shock. But before that night, my husband had been in recovery for almost ten years. That's why you're here, Emily—to find out why, after ten years of sobriety, my husband saw it fit to suddenly drink himself to death."

Emily cleared her throat. "No offence, Mrs. Edwards, but are you certain Max hadn't been drinking without your knowledge?"

"When you've been married to an alcoholic for twenty-three years you get to learn all the tricks and the lies. You find all the hiding places in your home, the garden shed, the car. Oh, I'm sure if Max had been tempted to drink, he could have tried to hide it from me. But I say *try*, Emily. My husband wasn't the kind of alcoholic who could drink a bottle of vodka then do a day's work. He was the kind of alcoholic you stepped over in the street."

Emily felt a surge of pity for the woman. Alcoholism didn't just destroy the person doing the drinking.

"If he was back to his old ways prior to that night, he wouldn't have been able to hide his guilt from me," Diane continued. "He tore our marriage apart. I should have left him. But I stayed. And he knew that. He *knew* that. Which is why he found the strength inside him to stop drinking. He did it himself, you know. Oh, he tried AA, but all that higher power business didn't agree with him. Max was not a follower of organized religion or spirituality. He believed in nature."

Emily leaned back on the chair and let out a steady breath. "Mrs. Edwards—"

"Diane."

"Sorry—Diane. . . Wouldn't you be better off pursuing a more professional route with someone more qualified? The police perhaps, or a licensed private investigator."

Emily tried to look away but found her gaze inexplicably drawn back to Diane. It was as if all the woman's anguish and desperation had created a magnetic pull.

"The police saw my husband's death as an open and shut case. An alcoholic gets drunk, falls into the River Thames and drowns. The ruling: death by misadventure." Diane hesitated, terrible memories drawing shadows across her face. "I read about you in the newspapers, about what happened at that retreat. And then again last month, with the Doctor Chelmsford trial."

Emily's shoulders stiffened. In an instant, she was back at the courthouse, standing in the witness box as she answered question after question, and desperately avoided Doctor Chelmsford's snakelike gaze. He would now spend what remained of his twilight years behind bars. *Good,* Emily thought. It was a fitting end for a monster who had preyed upon the sick and the vulnerable.

Unhappy about where the conversation was headed, she stared into the cooling contents of her cup.

"I read about what happened to you in the past," said Diane. "Losing your mother, then what happened with that boy. What was his name?"

"Phillip."

"Yes, Phillip. And I thought, here is a woman who understands the pain of not only losing a loved one, but also the humiliation of having her reputation destroyed. And yet, here is a woman who has risen above it all, who is good and kind, intelligent and resourceful, who is determined. I wrote to you because your story spoke to me. And I believe you can help me, Emily. I believe you can help me understand what happened to my husband."

Quiet draped itself over the table. Emily was momentarily elsewhere, her mind replaying the events of the last two years like scenes from a film.

"I don't think I can help you," she said at last. "I wouldn't know where to start."

Diane stared at her with pleading eyes. "I can help with that. And of course, as I mentioned in my letter, you'll be paid for your time."

"I'm just an ordinary person who happened to get caught up in an extraordinary situation. Or two. I don't have the skills or the resources that would be needed."

"Please, Emily." Diane was leaning forward now, her hands clamped together in a silent prayer. Most of her calm demeanour remained, but quiet desperation was oozing through the cracks. "You know what it's like to wake up each morning and wonder why life can be so cruel. You know what it's like to have all the happiness, all the joy snatched away from you. Something happened that night to take my husband away from me. I know our marriage was tumultuous at best, but I loved him. I need to know what happened. I need to understand why he did what he did."

Emily drew in a breath. Her shoulder muscles tightened as she felt the woman's anguish flooding the room.

This house is like a mausoleum, she thought. Diane Edwards was trapped inside; a living ghost doomed to repeat each day in a never-ending cycle of grief. Emily wanted to help her. She did. And the money would certainly help now her savings were almost gone.

It was just that she didn't know if she *could* help. She was not a private investigator. She was Emily Swanson, the shamed ex-teacher fated to spend the rest of her life atoning for her sins.

"Last Friday would have been Max's fiftieth birthday," Diane said. "I was going to throw him a party."

She locked eyes with Emily, transferring her grief. In that instant, Emily knew she could not refuse.

2

THE CALL CENTRE hummed with voices. Emily's return train to London had been delayed, making her uncharacteristically late for her afternoon shift. As she headed past the network of desks, she saw movement from the corner of her eye. Carter West was waving at her. Her pulse raced. She quickly waved back, then ducked into a long corridor. Quiet resumed. Emily headed into the archives; a small, cramped room at the back of the building filled with shelving units. Pulling a notebook from her bag, Emily ran a finger down a list of reference numbers, then scanned the color-coded ring binders on the shelves.

Two minutes later, she sat in a poky office in front of an old computer, typing information into an onscreen template. An open ring binder sat on the desk. The sad face of a teenaged boy stared up at her. Emily had been volunteering at the missing persons charity, *Lost,* for just over two months. She'd been offered a variety of roles but had settled on volunteering as an archivist. The charity had thousands of missing persons case files on paper that needed to be checked and entered into their electronic database. It was a repetitive task, but Emily found the files fascinating reading. Most cases ended happily, with the missing being reunited with their families. But others didn't.

The case she was archiving now was that of Jake Nash, 13, White British, from Acton in West London. Jake had disappeared on his way home from school one afternoon in May 2003. He'd been a quiet boy with few friends; the type no one noticed until he was no longer there. Emily glanced at his photograph. He would be an adult now. If he was still alive.

It was unsettling how easy it was for people to disappear in a country of not much size at all. Emily's thoughts turned to another young boy, one who she knew would never return home. She pushed the unwanted memories from her mind, just as a young woman with short, dark hair and a mass of earrings hurried into the room.

"Don't say anything," the woman said, sitting down at the adjacent desk. "Astrid locked me in again. Can you believe it?"

Emily smiled at the sing-song melody of the woman's French accent. "That's the second time this month. Come on, Imogen. You need to come up with something new."

Imogen picked up a pencil and flicked it at Emily. "It's true! I keep telling her, 'Doll, if I'm going to stay over, please remember I'm still there on your way out.' But out she goes, locking the door behind her. I mean, am I that forgettable?"

"You should accept her offer of the spare key."

"No way, far too early." Imogen stared at Emily with deep brown eyes. "Anyway, how are you, newbie?"

"I've been here almost two months and I still get called the newbie?"

Imogen pulled things out of bags and opened folders, spreading chaos over her desk. "You didn't answer my question."

"I'm fine. In fact, I've had a very interesting morning. I've been offered a job."

"Oh? Something paid, I hope. Tell me more."

Emily hesitated. "It's nothing. Just helping someone out."

"You mean like care work?"

"Something like that."

Emily finished updating Jake Nash's file. She turned the page to the next profile: Mrs. Mary Newell, 52, African-Caribbean, mother of four, who disappeared from her home in June 2003.

"I hope it doesn't involve wiping old people's backsides," Imogen said, her face wrinkled with disgust.

Emily wasn't ready to share the details of Diane Edwards' offer with anyone. Not until she had made some sort of sense of it.

A soft knock on the door made both women look up. Carter West raised a hand. Emily's face heated up.

"How goes it in the dusty archives?" he said.

Emily fixed her gaze on the computer screen. "Fine, thank you. How are you?"

Carter was tall and toned, but not overtly muscular, with a mess of dark, wavy hair, and a blinding smile. It was his eyes Emily found most fascinating—both were shades of hazel, but where the right eye was browner, the left was a shade greener. It was subtle; something you wouldn't notice unless you were looking closely.

"I'm good," Carter said with a grin as he stepped into the room. "Just finishing up for the day."

An unsubtle clearing of the throat directed their attention to the corner of the room.

"Hello, Carter."

"Imogen, I didn't see you there."

"Funny that."

Flashing Carter a quick glance, Emily continued to enter Mary Newell's details into the database.

"I'm going to make some tea," Imogen announced, standing up from her desk. "Anyone want some?"

"Yes, please." Emily's voice was barely a whisper.

Carter shook his head.

"I'll be five minutes." Winking at Emily, Imogen sauntered out of the room.

Now there were just the two of them, Emily's fingers sped up, stabbing at the keyboard in a frenzy. She felt Carter's eyes on her.

"Good shift?" she asked.

"As good as dealing with hysterical parents can be. At least I only have them typing at me in a panic. I'm not sure I could cope with dealing with them on the phone. Sometimes I think you have the right idea, skulking back here."

Emily's lips betrayed her by smiling. "I don't skulk."

The clack of the keyboard was the only sound in the room for a short while. Carter moved closer until he was on the other side of Emily's desk.

"So, I was wondering if you had any free time next week." His eyes flicked away, then came back again. "Maybe we could finally get that coffee that keeps eluding us?"

A warm burst rose up from the pit of Emily's stomach. It was quickly tempered by a rush of anxiety. She was taking too long to answer; she could tell by the twitch at the corner of Carter's mouth, by the slight sag in his shoulders. *Say something*!

"I . . . that should be fine."

What she'd meant to say was that this week was already busy and perhaps next week would be better—which was the same excuse she'd used last time. Feeling betrayed by her subconscious, she avoided Carter's wide, toothy grin.

"Great. How about Wednesday evening?" he asked.

Her face was burning now, her heart protesting in her chest. She wasn't ready. She was only now getting to grips with herself, never mind getting entangled with someone else. She would tell him she'd changed her mind. That it was too soon.

Emily opened her mouth to say something, anything, but no words came out. Just as the quiet became an unbearable roar, her phone began to ring. Mumbling an apology, she pressed the phone to her ear.

"Where are you right now?" Jerome was out of breath, his voice taut with anxiety.

"I'm at *Lost*," she replied. "What's wrong?"

There was a pause before he answered. "Nothing. Everything's fine. Are you coming straight home?"

"You're talking to the woman with no life." Her eyes darted toward Carter. "You don't sound like everything's fine."

"Okay, good. I'll cook something," Jerome said. "And there's something I need to tell you."

Cold crept over Emily's skin. "Sounds ominous."

"I'll. . . I'll see you later."

Jerome hung up, leaving Emily to stare blankly at her computer screen. It took her a second to remember she still had company.

"Everything all right?" Fine lines appeared at the corner of Carter's eyes.

Emily nodded. Realizing she was staring at him for too long, she quickly looked away.

"Wednesday evening, then?"

She went to shake her head. Instead, she said, "Can't wait."

3

THE OLD, RICKETY lift groaned to a halt on the fourth floor of The Holmeswood. It being a fine evening, Emily had decided to walk home. Now, her calves ached. Most Londoners of a similar age were getting ready for a night on the town, but Emily wanted nothing more than to slip into a hot, foamy bath and soak away the hours.

Jerome Miller had other ideas.

"What are you doing?" she asked him, as he met her in the hall and hurriedly guided her into the living room. Seated on the sofa, she watched his tall frame move over to a cabinet and grab a bottle of Jack Daniels from inside.

"Have you forgotten I can't drink?" Emily said.

"It's not for you." Jerome ducked through the saloon doors that opened into the kitchen. When he returned with a glass and filled it with syrupy bourbon, Emily noticed his dark, reddish-brown skin was beaded with perspiration.

"What's going on?" Tiredness was creeping into Emily's voice. Everything had to be so dramatic with Jerome, on and off the stage.

He stared at the floor, then drained half the whiskey. Emily opened her mouth to speak, but Jerome held up a hand. She waited for him to empty the rest of the glass.

"Okay, here goes," Jerome said. "I've been meaning to tell you this for a few days, but we've not really seen much of each other."

"That's because you practically live at Daniel's. Wait, you're not moving in with him, are you? Because you've only been together for a couple of months now, and not to sound judgmental or anything, but slow and steady wins the race."

Jerome arched an eyebrow. "I'm not moving in with Daniel."

"Oh. Well, good. Don't get me wrong— I really like Daniel, but the circumstances you met in weren't exactly conducive to the beginnings of a romantic relationship. You should spend some time talking things over, getting to know each other."

"Thank you, Oprah." Jerome stared at his empty glass. He took a deep breath, then let it out in a trembling stream. "I *am* moving out, though."

Emily froze. She had expected this day to come. Jerome had been sleeping on her sofa for months now, and while the arrangement benefitted the two of them, the circumstances weren't exactly ideal. Jerome rarely had any privacy, and unlike Emily, he didn't have an OCD about keeping a tidy home.

Emily spied the pile of dirty clothes down by her feet and felt a sudden ache in her chest.

Jerome watched her, waiting for a response.

"Where are you moving to?" she asked him at last.

"You remember my friend, Mags?"

"The one with the tattoos?"

"Her tenant is moving out of her spare room. She asked if I wanted it. I mean, it makes sense for me to say yes, doesn't it?"

"When are you moving?"

"In two weeks."

There was an exchange between them: a pang of guilt, a flash of betrayal. Emily forced a smile. She *knew* she should feel happy for Jerome. After all, there had been a time when he'd almost had to quit London for good. And her sofa had always been intended as a temporary abode. So why did she suddenly feel so betrayed?

"Where does Mags live?"

"Well, that's the thing," said Jerome, refilling his glass. "She lives in Brixton."

"But that's—"

"South of the river. I know—the forbidden zone! But the room is cheap, and I can easily get another café job closer to home."

Emily was quiet. The word 'home' sounded strange attached to somewhere that wasn't her apartment. As for Brixton, it sounded so far away that Jerome could have announced he was moving overseas.

As if reading Emily's mind, he said, "It's easy to get to from here. You just take the Circle line to King's Cross, then the Victoria line the rest of the way. It's twenty-five minutes."

"You know I don't take the Underground."

"So you take the bus—the 63 to Elephant and Castle, then the 415 direct to Brixton. Total journey time of fifty-two minutes."

Turning away, Emily looked around the spacious living room. Perhaps it would be nice to have her home to herself once more. And she really did want to be happy for Jerome; after a run of bad luck, he was due some happiness.

"It's exciting." She reached out and squeezed his hand. "You can finally have Daniel over to stay, instead of spending every night of the week at his."

Jerome moved closer. "And we'll still see each other all the time. I mean, someone's got to keep an eye on you. Make sure you're not getting yourself into any more trouble."

"It's funny you should mention that. . ."

As Emily told Jerome about Diane Edwards' unusual proposal, she felt a rush of curiosity. There must have been a good reason for Max Edwards to have given into temptation. And how had he ended up wandering the night alone, inebriated enough to have lost his balance and fallen into the Thames?

Beside her, Jerome raised an eyebrow. "That's weird. Are you sure she's not some sort of lunatic? Because Lord knows you've had enough crazy people in your life. You and me, both."

"I'm pretty sure. She came across as . . . trapped, I suppose. As if she wants to move on, but she can't. Not until she knows the truth."

"It's pretty wild—a stranger randomly tracking you down and asking you to do something like that."

Emily shrugged. "I told her I'd think about it. I mean, it's not like I'm the police or anything, is it?"

"What *are* you thinking about it?"

"I don't know. I'd like to help her. . . And she would pay me. . ."

"Well, hello, it's not like you don't need the money right now. Especially now I'm moving out."

Emily winced. She got up and moved over to the window. In the street below, Londoners sauntered by in suits and skirts as they headed straight for the bars. Above the buildings, the evening sun burned through the smog.

Jerome leaned forward on the sofa. "I don't know, Em. What if it's dangerous?"

"Then it would be perfect for me, wouldn't it?"

She turned back to the window, hiding her glassy eyes. Out of the millions of people populating the metropolis, there was just a small handful that Emily could call friends. She and Jerome had been through so much together in the short time they'd known each other. What would it mean when he moved to the south of the city? She would see less of him. London wasn't like the village where she'd grown up. You couldn't just walk down the street and see everyone you knew in the space of ten minutes; especially when you lived on opposite sides of the river. Miles lay in between. Londoners spent so much of their time travelling—to work and back every day, or to do simple chores like shopping for food—that having to then journey across the city to see a friend for a couple of hours was tantamount to trekking across the Himalayas. When friends moved away from your neighbourhood to another part of London, you inevitably said a gradual farewell.

As if sensing Emily's melancholy, Jerome appeared beside her and slung an arm over her shoulder.

"You know, if you hadn't given me a roof over my head, I'd be back in Nowheresville, slowly losing my mind. I owe you. But I really believe this will be good for both of us. Besides, now you can finally invite whatshisname over for dinner without me having to play chaperone."

Emily's sadness was momentarily eclipsed by embarrassment. "There is no *whatshisname*. We're just friends."

"Mmm-hmm. Carter West. . . What kind of name is that, anyway?" Jerome was quiet for a moment. He pulled Emily closer. "It feels like the end of an era."

Feeling lead-like and sullen, Emily continued to watch the street below.

"That's because it is," she said.

4

SUMMER CONTINUED TO make a last stand over the weekend. On Saturday morning, Jerome sloped off to Daniel's, leaving Emily home alone with nothing planned. His news had left her filled with self-pity. She channelled her negativity into bursts of housework, then spent the rest of the day staring at the TV.

By Sunday, misery had turned to rejection, rejection to anger. *Fine. Leave. What do I care?* She had plenty of things to be getting on with, anyway—such as deciding whether to accept Diane Edwards' proposal.

By the time Monday came around, bringing fresh bills in the mail and a growing sense of despair, Emily had made up her mind. After all, what did she have to lose?

Diane Edwards was overjoyed.

"That's wonderful news, Emily!" she said over the telephone. "I can't tell you how much this means to me."

"I can't promise anything," Emily warned. "Other than to try my best."

"No one could ask for any more."

After hanging up, Emily felt better. Even if her investigation didn't end in success, at least she now had something to occupy her mind. The fee she'd earn would take care of her bills for a while, too.

She didn't have to wait long to make a start. A package arrived on Tuesday morning, which she opened with ravenous enthusiasm. Diane had sent her a stack of paperwork, Max's old work diary, and a handwritten letter.

Dear Emily,

I'm so pleased you've agreed to help me. This package contains everything I could find. Apologies for the paperwork being in such disarray. I'm not sure how useful any of it is. As mentioned in our phone call, Tim Marsden might be a good person to talk to. I know what I'm asking is a tall order, and the chance of finding out what happened to Max is slim, but as my mother always said: if you don't try, you'll never know.

Please don't hesitate to call with any questions.

Yours sincerely,

Diane Edwards.

A quick scan of the paperwork revealed a deluge of bank statements, invoices and receipts, and work-related data, most of which made Emily's eyes glaze over. Flipping through the pages of Max's appointments diary, she pulled Tim Marsden's number from a list of contacts, as well as the number for Valence Industries' processing plant in Mariner's Port.

A quick skim of the rest of the diary revealed dates and times for work-related meetings. Appointments had been scheduled for up to three weeks after Max's death. Nothing out of the ordinary presented itself.

Opening her laptop, Emily typed up the information she had already gleaned from Diane Edwards.

At the time of his death, Max Edwards, 49, had been in Valence Industries' employment for six years. On Thursday, 28 May of last year, he'd attended a fundraising gala to launch the Clean Water Project—a charitable endeavour to aid those Third World Countries where purified drinking water was scarce.

The Clean Water Project was the culmination of a partnership between Valence Industries and Earth Conservation Group—more commonly known as E.C.G.—a non-government environmental organization. Proceeds from the gala were to benefit the project, which Max had played an integral role in getting off the ground.

The gala had been held in London at the Riverside Hotel. Max had stayed overnight. He'd failed to meet his colleagues for breakfast the following morning. His body had been discovered on the bank of the Thames just three hours after Diane Edwards had filed a missing persons report.

Sucking in a nervous breath, Emily picked up her phone. Here goes, she thought. She tried Tim Marsden's mobile number first. The call went straight to voicemail and Emily hung up without leaving a message. Next, she tried Valence Industries' plant in Mariner's Port. A cheerful receptionist told her Tim Marsden would be in meetings for the rest of the day. Emily left her name and number, saying that she would try again.

What now? Ignoring the doubt whispering in her ear, she pulled up a web browser and found Valence Industries' website. The company was American, but its plants could be found all over the world. In the UK, they had the processing plant in Mariners Port, Kent, and a performance test centre in Leicestershire. The plant was where Max Edwards had worked. It was a commutable distance from Epsom, but long work days, plus two hours of journey time, meant that he and his wife would have seen little of each other during the week.

Emily scanned the rest of the site but found nothing of interest. Partly out of curiosity, partly out of boredom, she hopped over to the Earth Conservation Group's website. E.C.G. was heading several campaigns. Emily skimmed through them: climate change, fishing fleets in the Arctic, fracking, rain forest destruction, palm oil—the list went on and on.

E.C.G. also had a blog. Emily scrolled through the article previews. Feeling inspired, she clicked on the blog archives and began reading through entries from May of last year. It didn't take long to find what she was looking for.

The headline read: *Gala Raises Thousands As Clean Water Project Launches.* It wasn't a long article, just a few paragraphs detailing the night's proceedings and the burgeoning relationship between E.C.G. and Valence Industries, stating that the companies were 'leading the way to a cleaner, greener chemicals industry.'

With help from E.C.G., Valence was not only looking at ways to reduce their energy outputs, but they were also involving themselves in humanitarian efforts, such as the Clean Water Project. Max Edwards was mentioned as project lead for Valence. There was a photograph. Max was tall and broad-shouldered, handsome in a silver-fox kind of way, with eyes that were weary and knowing. In the picture, he was dressed in a tuxedo and shaking hands with a woman. The caption beneath the photograph read: *Valence Industries' Max Edwards and E.C.G.'s Anya Copeland have been working in partnership on the Clean Water Project for eighteen months.* Emily jotted the woman's name into her notebook.

Her eyes settled on the ominous pile of Max's paperwork. She would need more coffee before she could even think of wading through it.

As she waited for the kettle to boil, her gaze wandered through the kitchen, past the saloon doors, and into the living room. The only sound was the hiss of heating water. Everything else was quiet and still. Emily thought about Jerome. She had spent the best part of four days alone. It was not his fault, she knew that. So why did she feel so upset with him? The more she thought about Jerome leaving, the more the apartment seemed to close in on her. A great heaviness weighed down her shoulders. She was craving people. Contact. Not to be alone.

*

"Sit yourself down. Go on! I'll get the tea going."

Emily did as she was told, pushing a pile of books to one side and flopping down on Harriet Golding's sofa. The elderly woman's living room had always resembled a dishevelled library, but today it appeared that books had given birth to books, multiplying until there was barely room to move. Emily stared at the towers of novels, journals, newspapers, and magazines that covered the floor and every other available surface.

"Don't say a word," Harriet said, waving a papery hand. She was thin and frail-looking, like one prod of a finger would shatter her into pieces. "It'll be gone by tomorrow, mark my words. Either that or *he* will."

Emily nodded. She'd heard those words several times before.

"Anyway, let's keep our voices down. His lordship is still asleep. Lazy bugger!"

While Harriet hobbled into the kitchen to make tea, Emily continued to survey the chaos. Andrew Golding was an odd man, she thought. An odd man who had reached middle-age without ever having left the family nest.

"Here we are." Harriet emerged from the kitchen, the tea tray rattling dangerously in her hands.

Emily jumped to her feet. "Let me help."

"You sit down, I'm fine."

"Don't be so stubborn." Emily said, taking the tray from her and setting it down on the coffee table. "There's no shame in letting others help out."

Harriet huffed and puffed her way into her armchair, then grumbled while Emily poured the tea.

"I'll do the rest. You mind your own," she said, spooning a small mountain of sugar into her cup. She took a noisy sip, then set the cup down with a clatter. "Haven't seen you for a while. Keeping busy, are you?"

"I've been doing extra shifts at *Lost*. They need more volunteers."

"I don't know why you bother with all that volunteering business," Harriet said. "Well, you don't get paid for it, do you? Bit of a liberty, if you ask me."

"They're a charity. They don't make a profit."

"Still, how are people supposed to live? On bread and water, I suppose. Shouldn't you be looking for a real job?"

"I *am* looking. I just haven't decided what I want to do."

"Anything that puts money in your pocket, I should imagine. In my day, there was none of this deciding you want to be this or want to be that. You took what work you could find and you were grateful for it."

Colour blossomed on Emily's cheeks. "Well, the world's not like that now. There's more opportunity to do what makes you happy."

She briefly wondered whether to tell Harriet that she did have a job; albeit a temporary one. Then reminding herself of Harriet's scathing resentment for anything that shirked tradition or seemed out of the ordinary, she hastily decided against it.

"Hippy claptrap," Harriet sneered. "Anyway, what are you doing working for free when there are bills to pay? I know you've had a bit of money to live off, and Jerome pays his keep, but unless you find a rich man to marry, you'd better start thinking about earning a proper crust."

Her words of wisdom delivered, Harriet reached for her cup of tea. She froze halfway, then her hand moved to her ribs.

Emily's irritation immediately vanished. "What is it? Are you hurt?"

"It's nothing. Old lady aches and pains."

A few seconds passed before Harriet reached for the cup again. Emily watched her closely, noting the tightening of her lips and the tremors in her hands. But she knew better than to voice her concern. Instead, she told Harriet Jerome's news.

"Eh? What's that? Moving out? Well! Where's he going?"

"Brixton."

"Why ever would he want to move all the way down there?"

"It's not that far."

Harriet raised her eyebrows. "Are you trying to convince me or yourself? Still, I shall expect you'll miss him. He's been good company for you, and he's helped you out of a scrape or two, hasn't he?"

Emily nodded.

"Is he still hanging around with that foreign fella?"

"If you mean Daniel, then yes. The two of them can't seem to get enough of each other."

Harriet muttered into her tea and shook her head. "And what about you? Isn't it time you found yourself a nice fella? Especially now you'll be all alone. Who's going to take care of you?"

"I think I might just be able to survive on my own, thanks."

"Oh no, it's not right—a woman your age on her own. You're not getting any younger."

"I'm twenty-seven!"

"Still, a pretty girl like you ought to be married by now."

Emily rolled her eyes. This was exactly why she hadn't mention Carter West. Harriet would have her married and procreating before she'd even had a first date. Which was tomorrow evening, Emily realized with some alarm.

Harriet gave a dismissive shake of her head. "No fella, no job, no prospects. It's a good job you've got me or you'd have nothing at all!"

Emily's heart sank into her stomach. "It certainly is."

5

THE RIVER THAMES was wide and murky, its fast-flowing water a dark shade of brown. There was still a commonly-held belief that the river was heavily polluted. And indeed, there had been a time in the annals of the Thames' history when Victorians had used the river as a dumping ground for human waste. In the summer of 1858, London had experienced a long bout of unusually hot weather. The stench that had risen from the Thames during this time had been nauseating enough to shut down Parliament—leading to the creation of a proper sewerage system.

In recent years, the Thames had undergone huge changes in terms of cleanliness and biodiversity. Now, the only cause for its worrying hue was the natural silt of its riverbed.

As Emily walked along the Southbank, the great body of water rushing past on her left, memories of her teaching days filled her mind. Her cohort of young students hadn't been interested in learning about the biodiversity of the Thames. It was the story of *The Great Stink of 1858* that had kept them horrified and amused in equal measures.

The holiday season was reaching its end, and although the country's children had returned to school a week ago, there were still plenty of tourists for a late Wednesday morning. Some ambled along the Southbank, stopping for photographs in front of the Thames, while others took in the sights as they were ferried up and down in tour boats.

Keeping close to the railings, Emily picked her way through the crowds. On the opposite bank, Westminster Palace, which housed Parliament and the world-famous Big Ben, stood bold and archaic against blue sky. Up ahead, the London Eye loomed over the water. Throngs of tourists gathered at the entry point on the ground. Emily banked right, taking a wide berth via Jubilee Gardens. She emerged from the small, green space and returned to the river, passing beneath the sandwich of Hungerford Bridge and the Golden Jubilee Bridges.

Waterloo Bridge was next, followed minutes later by Blackfriars. Emily paused, perspiration beading her brow. Just ahead, the Millennium Bridge stretched across the Thames. The Tate Modern gallery was on the right, its tall central tower a ghost of the building's power station origins.

The crowds converged as choices were made to either head inside the gallery or cross the bridge to St. Paul's Cathedral. Trying to temper her rising stress levels, Emily pushed through the bodies, until she stood to the left of the bridge. She clutched the railings and peered down. The Thames was a tidal river, which meant its banks became uncovered every day. It was here, right at this spot, that Max

Edwards had been washed up and found by tourists.

Staring at the multitude of people around her, she imagined the shock of finding his bloated corpse, lying face down amid the flotsam and jetsam.

Max had disappeared somewhere between 10 p.m. Thursday and 8 a.m. Friday, but he hadn't been discovered until Saturday morning. His body would have floated along until it reached shallow ground, where it would have been left behind by the receding tide.

Emily glanced down the length of the river. Something didn't make sense. The distance between the Riverside Hotel and where he'd been found was just a couple of miles. Had it really taken an entire day for Max's body to travel such a short distance? Or had he still been alive somewhere, drinking himself into oblivion, while his wife and colleagues grew frantic with worry?

Emily stared into the muddy river, wondering if it held the answer. Drawing in a deep breath, she dove back into the crowds and made her way to her next destination.

6

TIM MARSDEN WAS in his early thirties, tall, tanned, and clean-shaven, with dark hair swept into a neat parting. He greeted Emily with a handshake that was somewhere between gentle and firm. As they sat down, she noted his tailored suit and caught a whiff of his expensive-smelling cologne. Emily had been fully expecting a Science nerd in thick-lensed glasses.

"Thank you for seeing me," she said. "I know you have a meeting to get to, so I'll keep it brief."

Tim smiled, exposing whitened teeth. "You're welcome. I'm not often in the Big Smoke, so you got lucky."

Tim had suggested meeting in London's West End because it was close to his next destination. After escaping the crowds of the Southbank, Emily wasn't looking forward to fighting her way through even larger hordes, who were on their way to visit theatres, monuments, and museums, or to empty their wallets in the high street stores of Oxford Circus. But she had survived.

The bar Tim had chosen was all chrome and glass and neon blue lighting; much better suited to drinking two-for-one cocktails at happy hour than to having a serious discussion about his dead colleague. But here they were.

It was 1:30 p.m. The bar was filled with office workers enjoying a sneaky lunch hour drink with their niçoise salads and toasted paninis, while discussing office politics and who was sleeping with whom. It was a world Emily felt unfamiliar with, and one she had no desire to get to know. It wasn't that she disapproved of the corporate landscape. It just wasn't *her.*

"I have to say I was surprised by your call," Tim said. A waiter brought over their drinks—an orange juice for Emily, and a Pinot Gris for Tim. "Especially when you told me why you were phoning."

"As I explained, Mrs. Edwards thought you'd be an appropriate person to talk—you were one of the last people to see Max alive."

"To be honest, I don't know what else I can tell you that I haven't already told Diane. How is she, by the way? I'm ashamed to admit I haven't been in touch since the funeral."

"So you knew Mrs. Edwards? You and Max were friends?" Emily realized it might be a good idea to jot down some notes. She fished out her notebook and pen, then flipped to a clean page. "Do you mind?"

Tim shook his head. "To answer your question, I was Max's assistant manager. We worked side by side on most projects, so of course we became friendly. Close, even.

"Did you socialize outside of work?"

"Not really. As friendly as Max and I were, he liked to keep work and business very separate. There were various work-related gatherings over the years, of course, and he'd occasionally bring Diane along. But you know how it is when you work closely with someone for a long time—you get to know their friends and family without ever having met them."

Emily nodded as she wrote down: *Friendly but did not socialize outside of work.* She stared at the words, hesitating before she asked her next question.

"Mr. Marsden, did you know that Max was an alcoholic?"

Tim sipped his wine, then as if realizing the inappropriate timing, smiled and set down his glass. "Yes, I did. It was something he told me very early on. But as far as I knew, he hadn't touched a drop for years."

"Why did he tell you?" She watched Tim's forehead crinkle with a frown. "If it was early on, I'm assuming you were still getting to know each other as colleagues—there must have been a reason for him to tell you something so personal."

"We were away at a conference, staying over at some hotel," Tim said. "Every evening the team would hit the hotel bar. Max made up an excuse the first couple of nights, but when I eventually twisted his arm into joining us, he stuck to orange juice. As my wife always tells me, I have as much subtlety as a brick through a window. I made a joke to Max about being an alcoholic. He told me I wasn't so far from the truth. I was mortified."

His gaze dropped to the table. Emily scribbled into her pad.

"Max's alcoholism—was it public knowledge?"

"Oh God, no. It's not the kind of thing you go shouting about at work, is it? Especially when you're in a position of authority. You know how people are—most would ignore the part where he hadn't touched a drop in years. People like labels, don't they?"

"Yes, they do," Emily agreed. She peered at her notes, which now filled most of a page but had yet to yield anything of real value. "What about the night of the Clean Water gala? What was he drinking then?"

"It looked like orange juice. But who knows."

She leaned in a little. "Mr. Marsden, I know you've already spoken to Diane, but it would help me if you could go over the events of that night."

Tim's eyes roamed the bar before returning to settle on Emily. He drank more wine, this time emptying half of the glass.

"We'd been working with E.C.G.—the Earth Conservation Group—for a number of months, getting the Clean Water Project off the ground. It was something Max was very passionate about. Despite what some people might say, we *are* genuinely trying to have less impact on the environment. We wouldn't have created an entire Sustainable Development department if we didn't have some sort of real concern. The Clean Water Project is a perfect example of that."

"All the same, the project would have also boosted Valence Industries' reputation."

"Naturally—just as any other public activity would. But that doesn't take away from the fact that it's still a worthy cause. One in ten people across the world live without clean water. Most live in isolated areas where women and children walk miles every single day to fill a jug. Most of the time, that water is teeming with bacteria. People get sick. Children die. Surely that's something needing change regardless of whether or not Valence earns a better reputation?"

The idea of a multi-billion-dollar company benefitting from providing better living conditions for the more unfortunate sat uneasily on Emily's conscience, but she had to agree.

"Please, go on."

"The launch for Clean Water was a fundraiser event. Like any other charitable cause, longevity requires sizeable donations. So, we invited various corporate CEOs, local MPs, a few minor celebrities, with the idea of wining and dining them, then pitching the project as a vital cause for concern. Max led the presentation, which was followed by a charity auction. The night was a great success. We raised thousands and got the project into the newspapers." He paused, staring solemnly into his now empty wine glass. "Although that success was obviously mired by what happened next."

Emily loosened her grip on her pen. "That night—when did you last see Max?"

"He didn't stay until the end, which surprised me. He'd spent months organizing the event and he left early." Tim shrugged a shoulder. "Max said he was tired, that it had been a long day. He stayed long enough to mingle, to talk the talk with the necessary people, but the wine was flowing and everyone was drinking. Maybe it made him feel uncomfortable."

"And what time was that?"

"Perhaps around ten. Things came to an end at eleven."

"And Max was definitely sober?"

"As a judge. Or so it seemed. I can't say the same for me, however. The rest of the night is blurry at best."

"And in the morning?"

"I knocked on his door around eight. When he didn't answer, I assumed he'd already headed down to breakfast. He hadn't. It was strange. Max was always annoyingly on time. So, I tried calling his phone, but it went straight to voicemail. I thought maybe he'd gone for a walk or something." Tim paused, took a large breath. "When he still hadn't shown after breakfast, I knew something was wrong. I called the concierge. She let us into his room. The bed was all made up, like he hadn't slept in it. His clothes were still on hangers. I half expected him to come walking out of the bathroom, like he'd been in the shower or something. As you know, that wasn't the case."

Emily scribbled into her pad. "And what did you do then?"

"I called into the office to see if they'd heard from Max. They called Diane. Then I tried E.C.G. No one had heard from him. I didn't know what else to do, so I returned to the plant." He lowered his gaze to the table. "There was nothing else I *could* do."

Emily's mind raced. Tim had helped her to frame the evening, but there was still a huge hole in the timeline of events leading up to Max's death. Across the table, Tim's initial cheer was now as drained as his empty wine glass.

"It's so strange, isn't it?" he said. "One minute he was here, the next. . . It doesn't make any sense to me."

"What do you think happened to him?" Emily watched his eyes grow round and dewy as he mulled over the question.

"Maybe the stress of the launch got to him, or maybe he'd been lying to us all. I don't know. If he *had* been drinking in secret, he did a bloody good job of covering it up. And there was no sign he'd been getting drunk in his hotel room, either. I guess he must have sneaked off to the nearest bar and gone from there."

Emily leaned back in the chair, her mind playing out numerous scenarios, which all ended with Max Edwards lying face down on a muddy bank.

Tim glanced at his watch.

"One more question, if you don't mind," Emily said. Tim waved a hand for her to proceed. "Is there anyone else you think would be worth talking to? Someone who was there that night, perhaps."

Tim rubbed his chin as he thought about it. "You could always try Anya Copeland. She was E.C.G.'s lead on Clean Water at the time. I can't tell you where she is now, though. She quit a few weeks after Max's death. She and Max, they were . . . close."

Emily raised an eyebrow. Sue recalled the name from the E.C.G. blog. Anya Copeland had been the woman pictured shaking hands with Max.

"Talk to Charlie Jones at E.C.G.," Tim said, glancing across the room. "She took over as lead when Anya quit."

Emily jotted down the name. "And you took over from Max?"

Tim hesitated, straightening the cuffs of his jacket. "Stepping into Max's shoes wasn't an easy decision to make. But I believe it's what he would have wanted. I may not be as radical as Max about environmental issues, but I *am* passionate all the same. I believe Valence Industries is doing great things with the Clean Water Project. I just wish Max was still around to see the fruits of his labour."

Marsden reached out a hand and Emily shook it. "I hope Diane gets the answers she's looking for. I'm sorry I couldn't be more help." He stared at Emily, his grave expression giving way to curiosity. "So, what's it like being a private investigator? Is it all guns and car chases?"

Emily's face began to burn. There was no way she could tell him the truth. Instead, she glanced away and said, "It pays the bills."

Out in the street, they shook hands again. Tim Marsden flagged down a black cab and Emily watched it join the queue of traffic.

Still feeling flustered, she pushed her way through the crowds to the edge of the pavement. As she headed to the bus stop, she replayed her conversation with Tim Marsden in her mind. Anya Copeland's name floated to the top of her thoughts. *They were close.* Insinuation had dripped from each word. Emily cursed herself for not asking more. Perhaps this Charlie Jones would have something to say on the subject.

But before Emily could go ahead and arrange to meet with her, there was a more pressing matter to attend to. Coffee with Carter West.

7

"SO, WHAT MADE you want to volunteer at *Lost*?"

They were sitting opposite each other in a booth at Bramfords Diner; a fifties style American café tucked away down a cobbled side street in Shoreditch. It was the first place that had sprung to mind when Carter had asked where Emily liked to go for coffee. In truth, she had only visited the diner a handful of times several months ago to meet a young receptionist named Rosa, who had helped Emily uncover the horrific goings-on at the Ever After Care Foundation. Sat here now, fingers drumming against the side of her coffee mug, Emily wished she'd chosen a different café—there were too many unpleasant memories hiding behind the colourfully-tattooed staff and retro fittings. For a moment, she was lost in them. Then she remembered Carter had asked her a question.

"I had time on my hands." It was the truth, she supposed. "How about you?"

"The same, I guess. They started out by putting me on the phone lines, but in spite of my soothing tones, I ended up getting more panicked than the callers. Which is why I ended up on social media duties."

Carter did have a soothing voice, Emily thought. It was deep and rich, with a melodic edge. She took a sip of coffee, noting that he'd also answered the question in a roundabout fashion.

"What's it like in the all-mysterious archives?" he asked her.

And now he was deflecting.

Emily shrugged. "It's strange. All those faces staring up at you from the past like ghosts. And they're being filed away, a lot of them still missing, more than likely never to be seen again."

Carter smiled, his eyes sparkling. "Sounds morbid."

Why is he smiling? Emily thought. Was that a bad sign? Had she said something stupid?

Awkward silence filled the space between them. Emily glanced around the room, catching the eye of a pink-haired waitress.

"So what do you do outside of LOST? Where do you work?" Carter swept locks of curly hair from his brow and placed his hands symmetrically on the table. They were large, strong hands, Emily noted, with neatly trimmed fingernails.

How did she answer the question without sounding completely hopeless? "I'm between jobs right now. Well, that's not completely true. I'm doing some work, but it's just a one-off thing. So, it's not between jobs exactly, more like between careers. Deciding what to do next."

Her skin prickled with heat. She sipped more coffee and sank into the booth, hoping that a hole would open beneath her and put her out of her misery. She hadn't intended to mention her current work. Panic had teased the words from her lips. Now Carter would ask about it, and she would have to lie.

Carter smiled. "So many people I know are going through career changes right now. It's great we live in an age where we can choose to do something that makes us happy, don't you think?"

Emily agreed.

"What was your old career?"

Overcome by sweaty panic, she hesitated. Should she tell him the truth? What if he then made a connection? Perhaps he already knew about her and this was a test.

"I used to teach." She held her breath and waited for it to come—the look of recognition, the expression that said, *I know who you are,* followed by a swift departure. None of that happened. Instead, Carter nodded emphatically.

"What made you leave?"

Her face was on fire. This was worse. Now she would have to tell him herself. Or she could lie. Why hadn't she lied in the first place?

"I suppose . . . it was time for a change." It was a sort of truth.

"Teaching sounds tough," Carter said. "Too much paperwork and not enough class time from what I hear. What do you think you'll do next?"

The tension in Emily's shoulders unravelled a fraction. *Good.* The conversation was moving away from that deep, dark confession.

"I'm still trying to work that out," she said. "I know I like helping people."

"Maybe *Lost* is a way into charity work. Paid work, I mean."

Emily studied him. Did he really know nothing of her exploits? The recent court case? The murders at Meadow Pines? Both had been high profile cases that the tabloids had devoured.

"Perhaps." She cleared her throat and relaxed a fraction more; enough to wonder how Carter would react if she were to tell him the nature of her present employment.

"How about you?" she asked instead. "What do you do outside of *Lost*?"

Carter sat up. "Oh, I build furniture. I know, it's not flashy and exciting, but I get a lot of satisfaction out of it. Plus, I get to be my own boss."

"You must be very skilled with your hands," Emily said, then, immediately turned scarlet. "I mean... I didn't... I meant you must be very skilled to make furniture by hand."

Carter laughed. "I suppose so, yes."

More silence. Emily's heart pounded in her chest. This was all wrong. She wanted to leave.

Carter looked up at her, ready to try again. "So, you're not from London? I detect a hint of an accent. Is it West Country?"

Emily's mouth was dry. The caffeine was not helping her nerves. All these getting-to-know-you questions kept leading back to the same place. She would have to tell Carter about her past. About Phillip Gerard. Even if she didn't tell him today and there was somehow a next time, the truth would eventually come spilling out. What was the point in trying to pretend it wasn't going to happen?

Carter stared at her, waiting for an answer.

She nodded stiffly, then pushed her coffee away.

"So, does that mean Somerset? Devon?"

"Cornwall." Emily found herself glaring at him, needing the questions to stop because she seemed unable to prevent herself from answering them.

"Oh, I love Cornwall! We used to go there as kids. We'd stay in Penzance or St. Ives, and we'd go to the beach and pretend we were abroad. Which part are you from?"

Blood pulsed in her ears. She felt like she was tearing open her flesh for Carter to look inside. What would he think when he saw darkness?

She still hadn't answered the question. Carter was staring at her uncertainly. This was all wrong. It was too soon. Who did she think she was?

"And your family?" Carter asked. "Are they still in Cornwall?"

Emily stood up. "I have to go."

Avoiding his gaze, she gathered up her jacket and her bag.

Carter's mouth hung open. "Emily, what is it? Have I said something wrong?"

She slid out from the booth, almost knocking over her coffee. "No, it's not you. I'm sorry."

His brow lined with hurt and confusion, Carter watched her go. "But Emily—"

"I'm sorry," she repeated.

Leaving Carter red-faced and flustered, Emily hurried out of the diner and into the street.

8

JEROME SAT BOLT upright with a strangled cry. Sweat dripped from his body. Blood pounded in his ears. He looked around the darkened room to see familiar shapes and shadows. He was in Daniel's bedroom. Daniel was flat on his back, mouth open, lost somewhere in deep sleep.

It was 5.07 on a still dark Thursday morning. Slipping out from under the sheets, Jerome padded to the bathroom. He drank deep drafts of water from the tap, then splashed more on his face.

The nightmare still echoed in his head. He was back in Meadow Pines, locked in an upstairs bedroom. Corpses were piled up on the floor—bodies that had been stabbed or hung or had their heads bashed in with hammers. And they were coming to life; their limbs creaking from *rigor mortis* as they untangled from each other, their feet unsteady on the floor. Teeth gnashed and fingers clawed as the dead forced him to the open window, where the rain lashed down outside, and the drop to the ground was impossibly high. It was the same nightmare that had been haunting him every night for weeks.

Drying his face with a towel, Jerome perched himself on the edge of the bath and waited for the palpitations in his chest to fade. Usually it took anywhere between five and ten minutes. The trembling in his hands took longer.

"You're safe," he whispered to the silence of the bathroom. "You're at Daniel's. You're in the bathroom. Nothing can hurt you. You're safe."

By the time he returned to the bedroom, the sun had begun its slow ascent. Daniel was now lying on his side, snoring softly. Jerome crept past the bed, picked up a spare blanket, and draped it over himself as he sank into the armchair. He waited another ten minutes, listening to Daniel's quiet purrs. When enough light was sneaking in at the edge of the curtain, he picked up the playscript at his feet—Shakespeare's *Othello*—and started going over his lines. He was probably too tall to play Othello, his frame too slim, his skin not dark enough for the archetypal, muscled black man the producers were no doubt looking to cast. But such details were not going to deter him. It was the first audition he'd won since Meadow Pines, and it was for the lead—a role he was rarely given the opportunity to play.

By the time Daniel's alarm began beeping, Jerome had showered, dressed, and breakfasted. He brought coffee to Daniel, kissed him on the forehead, then slung his overnight bag over a shoulder.

"You're leaving?" Daniel's voice was still groggy, his Italian accent heavy with sleep.

"I have my audition."

"But that's not until eleven. I thought you were going to stay here and rehearse."

Jerome picked up his script and rolled it into a tight tube. "I thought I might go for a walk first."

"For three hours?"

His pulse was racing again. His mouth running dry. An image flashed in his brain: a body slumped in a tool shed, blood splashed across the walls like angel wings.

Creases appeared on Daniel's forehead. He put down his coffee. "What's wrong?"

"I'm fine. I didn't sleep well, that's all."

"You didn't sleep well the other night either. What's going on with you?"

Daniel reached out a hand, but Jerome took a step away from the bed.

"Have you. . ." he began, then paused to open the curtains. Light rushed in. Jerome stood still, mouth twitching, sentences trying and failing to come out. He wanted to tell Daniel about the nightmare. About how every time he closed his eyes he saw blood and death. About how exhilarated he'd felt leaping from the bedroom window and running through the forest at night in a desperate bid to save Emily's life. But he couldn't tell Daniel any of these things.

Instead, he muttered, "I should probably go."

Daniel pushed back the sheets and climbed out of bed. "Talk to me. What is it?"

"I'm fine."

But he wasn't fine. He was cold and sweaty, and he suddenly wanted nothing more than to be left alone.

Daniel moved to put his arms around him.

"It's probably the audition," Jerome said, turning to leave.

"It's more than that. You've been—"

Jerome silenced him with a kiss. "Stop worrying and start praying I get a call back."

Before Daniel could interrogate him further, he hurried from the room.

"Good luck!" Daniel called after him in a concerned voice.

Jerome raced through the house and out to the road, where he marched through Bermondsey streets, walking until the panic subsided, until the awful pictures in his head had faded into darkness.

9

AN UNEASY CHILL ran up Emily's spine as she entered Brick lane. Not so long ago, she'd been holed up here in a cramped hotel room, hiding from the eyes of Doctor Chelmsford. Now, as she walked the long, narrow street, famous for its Indian curry houses and vintage clothing stores, she pushed away memories of a much darker time. But then Carter West found his way into her thoughts. The date had been an utter disaster. Fortunately, Carter hadn't been in touch since.

The Earth Conservation Group was situated just off Brick Lane, on the first floor of a small office block. It was just after 6 p.m. and employees were heading home for the day. Emily introduced herself to the receptionist, a young man in his early twenties, who eyed her impatiently before picking up the phone.

Charlie Jones appeared a minute later. She was a tall woman, with wavy, dark hair and savage grey eyes. Her smile did nothing to melt the fierceness.

"Thanks for waiting." She shook Emily's hand, nodded goodbye to the receptionist, then ushered Emily into a small office at the back, where posters detailing various E.C.G. campaigns—including the Clean Water Project—covered the walls.

"You find us okay?" Charlie waved Emily toward her desk.

The office was cramped, the desk littered with paperwork. Street sounds floated in through the open window.

Emily nodded. "Thank you for seeing me at short notice. I know it's an unusual situation."

"It's fine. But you can understand why I thought you were a journalist calling." Charlie paused to tidy her desk. "So, Max's wife hired you to look into his death?"

"That's right."

"Can I ask why?"

How much could Emily tell her? Perhaps an exchange of information would put Charlie at ease.

"Because until the night of his death, Max had been a recovered alcoholic for almost ten years. She wants to know what made him drink again."

Charlie linked her fingers and rested her hands on her stomach. "I didn't know Max was an alcoholic. Not until after he. . ."

"Perhaps you could tell me a bit about his work for the Clean Water Project," Emily said. "How long had he and Anya Copeland worked together?"

"For about eighteen months. Valence Industries approached us to help them become more involved in environmental issues. They suggested we partner up on a project. Of course, it was a complete greenwash, but whatever their reasons, we were happy to see such an environmentally hazardous industry demonstrating some accountability."

Emily shook her head. "Greenwash?"

"Businesses using environmental issues to make themselves look caring and responsible. Works wonders for their image. And that's exactly how we felt about Valence. But when they came to us with Clean Water and the funding to get it going, it seemed like the perfect opportunity. Of course, we thought it would be a case of them taking a back seat while we took care of the hard work—believe me, that happens a *lot.* But to our surprise, Max Edwards shows up one morning, ready to get his hands dirty."

Emily nodded. "Max had been involved in environmental groups for years. It was a passion."

"So we learned. He had all sorts of ideas to develop the project. Anya had been over the moon. She honestly thought we were getting another number-crunching suit. But Max was different."

"They had a good working relationship?" Emily's pen hovered over her notebook.

Parting her lips, Charlie hesitated. "Yes. They got on like a house on fire."

"They were good friends?"

"You could say that..."

Charlie plucked a pencil from the desk and began rolling it back and forth between finger and thumb. There was something there, hidden between her words. The same insinuation that Tim Marsden had expressed.

"You worked on the Clean Water Project, too?" Emily asked.

"I took care of a lot of the administration, as well as overseeing recruitment drives for skilled volunteers."

"So you worked alongside Max?"

"Not directly. We'd talk sometimes, but most of my contact with him was through team meetings. I could tell he was passionate about green matters, though. About a lot of things. . ."

A hint of frustration crept into Emily's thoughts. Charlie was dancing around now; clearly, she had something to say.

"The night of the Clean Water charity gala—the last time Max was seen alive—were you there?"

The pencil came to a halt between Charlie's finger and thumb. "Yes, I was."

Emily leaned forward. "Can you remember anything from that night? Anything out of the ordinary?"

"About Max?"

Emily nodded.

"Apart from disappearing before the night was over, no."

"Do you recall what he was drinking?"

"I wouldn't have taken any notice. Why would I?" Charlie hesitated again. Her gaze moved from Emily to the desk to the door.

"Miss Jones, as I mentioned in our phone call, I'm not the police and I'm not here to get anyone into trouble." A little of Emily's frustration sneaked into her voice. "I'm just trying to help Diane Edwards understand what happened to her husband. Is there something I should know? About Max and Anya, perhaps. . ."

Charlie shook her head, then let out a frustrated sigh.

"I'm not one for gossip. Especially when the subject of that gossip is a friend," she said. "But you know what office politics are like. Everyone has an opinion about everyone else, and once the rumour mill starts grinding, it's hard to shut it down. There was talk. About Anya and Max. About how much time they spent together in this office with the door closed. About the way they looked at each other when they thought no one was watching. We all knew Max was a married man, and Anya was a single parent who'd been on her own for a long time. You can imagine the conversations at the water cooler."

"Max and Anya were having an affair?" Emily ran a hand over her chin as she contemplated this small revelation.

"I didn't believe it, not at first," Charlie said. "Anya and I were friends. She barely talked about Max inside or outside of work."

"What changed your mind?"

"Actually, it was the night of the gala." A deep crease appeared in the centre of Charlie's forehead. "As I said, I didn't see anything out of the ordinary where Max was concerned, but about twenty minutes after he'd said goodnight, Anya told me she had to go home. The babysitter had called saying Josh was sick. That's Anya's son. Of course, I didn't think anything of it. I told her to go, I'd take care of things."

A flash of betrayal lit up her eyes.

"Not long after, I decided to step outside for some fresh air. I'm not a big drinker, but I'd had a few glasses of wine. As I went to leave, I saw Anya in the lobby. She was coming out of the lift, and she was crying. But before I could catch up with her, she ran out. At first, I was confused. Why had she lied to me? Then it all fell into place—the rumours were true. Anya had been upstairs with Max, in his room."

As Emily absorbed Charlie's words, she began to wonder how Diane might react to the news of her husband's affair. Of course, there was still no definitive proof the affair had taken place, but Charlie's story was certainly a persuasive piece of evidence.

"Did you confront Anya when you next saw her?"

Charlie stared at her desk. "I was too upset. We were supposed to be friends—not best friends, but still—she'd lied to me. I was angry, and she must have realized that I knew because the next morning, she barely spoke a word. To anyone. In fact, her behaviour that whole morning was off. Like she didn't know where she was or what she was doing." Charlie let out a heavy sigh. "Then we got the call that Max was missing. The next day he was dead. Anya didn't show up to work again. We received her resignation in the mail."

Emily jotted notes on her pad. The timing of Anya's resignation could not be ignored.

Charlie continued. "I tried calling in those first two weeks. She didn't reply to any of my messages. I was worried. Of course, rumour control saw her resignation as the behaviour of a woman grieving the death of her married lover. I didn't know what to think. Then her mobile phone number suddenly wasn't working. Her landline had been disconnected, too. I went over there, to see what was going on. The house was empty." Charlie paused, worry paling her skin. "One of her neighbours told me a removals van showed up the week before. I haven't heard from Anya since."

"Why would she move?" Emily thought aloud. If Anya really had been having an affair with Max, it would explain the depth of her grief. But to quit her job and relocate seemed like an extreme reaction. "What about her family? Have you been in touch with them?"

Charlie, who looked lost in unhappy thoughts, shook her head. "If Anya wants to forget everyone and start over somewhere new, then let her."

A hint of doubt crept into Emily's mind. But doubt of what? She leaned in closer. "What do you think happened that night at the hotel? Why was Anya crying?"

Charlie shook her head. "I couldn't say. Maybe things came to an end between them."

It was highly possible, Emily thought, chewing her lower lip. Perhaps Max had ended ten years of sobriety because he'd just had his heart broken. It made perfect, tragic sense.

But that hint of doubt continued to taunt her long after she'd said goodbye to Charlie Jones and started toward home. There was only one way she could find out if the theory held any weight. She would have to find Anya Copeland.

10

"SOUNDS CUT AND dry to me." Jerome swallowed a mouthful of beer and wiped his lips with the back of his hand.

They were sitting at the dining table, empty plates pushed to one side. Outside, the night sky was a smudge of charcoal and olive-green. The road below was quiet, interrupted by the occasional wail of sirens. Emily stared at her notes. Everything she had uncovered so far pointed to an illicit affair that had ended in the most tragic of ways. And yet that niggle of doubt continued to bloom, unfurling its petals to reveal a black hole. She glanced at Jerome, who'd picked up his phone and was busy texting.

"I'm not so sure," she said.

"How come?"

"I accept that Max and Anya could have been having an affair. And I can understand her quitting her job. But to pack up and move out? It's a bit extreme, isn't it?"

"I don't know. People do crazy things all the time. Especially when they're grieving."

Emily chewed on her lip, trying to put her thoughts in order. "But still. . ."

She got up and cleared the plates away, then returned to the table with her laptop. Done texting, Jerome leaned back and swigged his beer.

"You know, maybe it is what it is. They had an affair, it ended badly. The guy drank himself stupid and jumped in the Thames."

"You think he jumped?"

"People have done worse things when they're drunk."

"Define worse than killing yourself."

"Oh, I never divulge my drunken tales of shame. If you weren't there, it didn't happen."

Emily had considered the possibility that Max Edwards had committed suicide, but until now, hadn't given the idea much credence. She turned her attention to the computer and typed 'Anya Copeland' into the search engine. The results revealed a couple of links to E.C.G.'s blog, but little else of relevance.

"What about family? E.C.G. must have her next of kin on file."

"Not anymore. She hasn't worked there in over a year."

Jerome took control of the laptop. "Well, everyone on the planet is on Facebook, right? Even *you're* on Facebook."

"What's that supposed to mean?"

Logging in, he stopped to check his notifications, then typed Anya Copeland's name into the search bar. "This should be easy—there are just a few results. Which one is she?"

Emily examined the profile summaries. Two Anya Copelands lived in the USA, while a third was a teenager from Scotland.

"None of them." Picking up her phone, she opened the browser and scrolled through her bookmarks. "This is an article about the Clean Water gala. That's Anya in the picture with Max Edwards."

Jerome examined the photograph with a raised eyebrow. "Oh yeah, they're definitely hot for each other. But you're right—none of these profiles belong to her."

"Maybe her security settings are set to maximum, so she doesn't show up in search results."

"Who even does that?"

"Someone who doesn't want to be found." Emily took back the laptop and spent the next few minutes searching the rest of the major social media sites. Failing to find any trace of Anya Copeland, she tried searching online telephone directories. It was as if Anya hadn't just relocated but vanished from the face of the earth.

"Weird," Jerome said.

"It's not just weird," Emily replied. "It's frustrating. Anya Copeland is my only real lead. How am I supposed to find her?"

"More importantly, how are you going to tell Diane Edwards that her dead, alcoholic husband was boning someone half her age?"

"I'm not telling her anything, not until I have a concrete explanation."

"You know what else needs an explanation?"

Emily held up a hand. "I don't want to talk about it. I went on a date. It didn't end so well. I shouldn't have agreed to go in the first place. End of story. Anyway, life is far too chaotic for that sort of thing right now."

Jerome emptied his beer bottle and added it to the collection on the table. "Life *is* chaos, Emily. There's no point in thinking everything's love and flowers when people are busy shooting each other in the face."

He got up and went to the fridge for another beer. When he returned, his eyes were dark and angry. Emily stared at the empty bottles on the table, then back at Jerome.

"Wasn't it your audition today?" she asked, realizing she'd forgotten until now. "How did it go?"

"Yeah, fine. Great, in fact. They want me back for round two."

"That's brilliant!"

"Yeah."

The smile faded from Emily's lips. On stage, Jerome was a fine actor. In real life, however, he was hopeless at masking his emotions.

"What's the matter?"

"Nothing. Everything's fine. Besides, we were talking about you. Do you like this guy or not?"

"Actually, I thought we were talking about Max Edwards."

Jerome took an angry swig of beer.

"We're not teenagers, Jerome," Emily said. "It's not just a question of who likes who. It's more complicated than that."

"It's as complicated as you want to make it. Look at me and Daniel. We enjoy the time we spend together, we have feelings for each other, but we're not rushing to Ikea to buy furniture just yet. You need to stop turning everything into a drama. Just relax. You're acting like a relationship is this huge, overwhelming thing that's going to come crashing down on you like a tsunami."

Emily glared at him. Tiredness was making her body sluggish and heavy. "My focus right now is Max Edwards. If you want to help me with something, help me find Anya Copeland." She was about ready to give up for the evening. Perhaps she would have a hot shower to clear her mind, then grab an early night. But as she stared at Jerome's glowering face, an idea came to her. "As a social worker, Daniel must have a lot of contact with schools, right?"

"Yeah, he works with a few schools in the borough."

"So, he could gain access to class registers. . ."

"I have no idea. What are you up to?"

"Anya's son, Josh, is about five years old—he would have just started school. . ."

Jerome put down his beer and stared at Emily. "No. You're not getting Daniel involved in this."

"I wouldn't be getting him involved. I would be asking for his help. There's a difference."

"Absolutely not. It's one thing having me running around forests in the middle of the night, dodging psycho-killers, but I'm not having Daniel anywhere near that kind of danger."

"This isn't dangerous. It's nothing like Meadow Pines."

"Anyway, I bet he doesn't even have access to that kind of information. And where would he start? There must be hundreds of schools in London. You don't even know if that woman and her kid are still in the city."

"But still—"

"And have you thought about the ethics of what you're asking him to do? He'd be breaking all kinds of child protection acts."

Narrowing her eyes, Emily turned away and stared at the table. "Can't Daniel speak for himself?"

"No. He can't." Jerome took another large gulp of beer. "I'm sorry Em, but you'll have to find a different way. Or maybe you should just go back to Diane Edwards, tell her what you've learned, and call it quits. After all, it's not like you're some ace detective or anything."

Emily clenched her jaw, sending pain up to her cheekbones. She loosened it, then shook her head. "What's wrong with you tonight?"

"I haven't had enough beer, that's what's wrong." Jerome drained the rest of the bottle and shot her a challenging glare.

Emily was confused. Where had Jerome's sudden hostility come from? But if he was unwilling to talk, she wasn't going to push.

"I'm tired," she said. "I'm going to bed."

As she got up from the table, she placed a hand on Jerome's shoulder. His muscles tensed beneath her fingers.

"I mean it, Em," he muttered. "Don't go asking Daniel."

Leaving Jerome staring angrily at the table, Emily made her way to the bedroom. Max Edwards' paperwork sat in piles on the bed, still waiting for a detailed analysis. Dumping it on the floor, she lay down and stared up at the ceiling. She wondered what had just happened with Jerome. She'd seen him in bad moods, but this was different.

Her mood sank lower until she knew she would have trouble sleeping tonight. Reaching toward the bedside table, she hit the play button on her CD player. Kirsten Dewar's soothing voice floated over the room, her words whispering into Emily's ears like a lullaby: "Imagine you are in a calm place. Somewhere you feel safe. A forest, or a beach. Take a moment to feel the warm sun on your face, a gentle breeze against your skin. . ."

She had heard the therapist's words a hundred times, but their power had not diminished. Soon, she was no longer in her bedroom, or the city with its millions of people pressing down on her. She was lying in a forest glade, surrounded by bluebells and snowdrops, a spotlight of warm sunshine pushing back the shadows. Kirsten's words echoed over the treetops like birdsong, like the wind.

Soon, Emily was asleep. Darkness stole through the forest, devouring trees, until only a thin sheathe of light protected her. Then darkness devoured the light, too.

11

FRIDAY MORNING BROUGHT a blue sky dotted with clouds. Jerome had already left to work the breakfast shift at the café. Emily was glad—last night's conversation had left her feeling waspish and confused. Jerome had no right to tell her who she could or couldn't turn to for help. Daniel was an adult, fully capable of making his own choices.

And what was wrong with Jerome anyway? He'd been in a foul mood all night, spouting doom and gloom. It wasn't like him at all.

Taking her usual position at the centre window, Emily sipped coffee and stared at the street below. Cars and buses, crawling bumper to bumper, choked the air with exhaust fumes. Pedestrians filled the pavements, pushing and shoving their way to work. Across the road, customers sat in the window of *Il Cuore*, the Italian café Jerome had worked in when the two of them had first met. Emily rarely went in there now.

She would find Anya Copeland herself. How difficult could it be? Besides, she had other avenues yet to explore that might shed new light on Max Edwards. His paperwork was one, and the Riverside Hotel was another.

Retrieving the hotel's phone number from Max's diary, Emily placed a call to the manager—Mr. Manik Singh—who agreed to a brief meeting at 5p.m.

Now feeling more motivated, Emily sat down with Max Edwards' stack of paperwork and began the laborious tasks of sifting and sorting. After an hour, she had made several categorized piles, including one for household bills, which revealed nothing out of the ordinary, and one for bank statements. Max's accounts appeared to be in order, and his role as Sustainable Development manager for Valence Industries came with an enviable monthly salary.

The other piles were concerned with his work, including annual sustainability reports for the last few years that detailed a gradual reduction in Valence's GHG emissions, water usage, and hazardous waste, as well as a gradual increase in energy efficiency.

The rest of the papers were of little interest, but one thing was clear: Max Edwards had been dedicated to his job, and during his time with Valence, had played an integral role in transforming the company into a much greener one.

Emily let out a dissatisfied sigh and scrunched her shoulders up to her ears. Max's paperwork had proved of little value. And why would it? The more she thought about it, the more she began to believe in the affair theory. Perhaps meeting Manik Singh might change her mind.

*

Although the Riverside Hotel's contemporary glass exterior was indistinguishable from the office buildings lining this stretch of Grosvenor Road, its interior was a remarkably grand affair. The lobby was wide and high-ceilinged, with black and gold pillars and luxurious furnishings. The floor was buzzing with people. Business types milled about in groups or sat alone taking calls. Hotel staff dressed in matching black and gold uniforms went about their duties in a deliberate, aloof manner.

Emily approached the desk and introduced herself. Mr. Singh appeared a minute later. He was a short British Indian man in his late forties, with a shiny bald pate and a welcoming smile.

"Ms. Swanson, I presume." He offered her his hand and a welcoming smile. "A pleasure to meet you."

In his office, he ushered Emily toward a set of white leather armchairs. The view from the window was unremarkable—a street scene of cars and pedestrians.

"So how can I help you today?" Mr. Singh folded his hands neatly on his lap before answering his own question. "Oh, that's right, you wanted to talk about the Clean Water gala from last year."

"More specifically about the death of Max Edwards," Emily said.

The manager's face drooped into a frown. "Awful business. He didn't die here, you know. Not at the hotel. He was found in the river. And the gala was a great success. My staff worked very hard that evening."

Emily nodded. "Do you mind if I take a few notes?"

Mr. Singh eyed her notebook. "I suppose not. But I don't know what I can tell you about that night, or about that man."

"I'm trying to help Mrs. Edwards establish a timeline of events leading up to her husband's death. We know he was at the gala all evening, then went up to his room at around 10 p.m. When Max didn't show up for breakfast next morning, his colleagues alerted the concierge, who entered his room to find the bed unslept in and his belongings still there."

"Which were all handed into the police," Mr. Singh quickly added. "We were very helpful to them, as I hope we can be to you now."

Emily leaned forward. "I was wondering if I could view the CCTV footage from that night. It might help if I knew what time Mr. Edwards left the hotel. Even if I could just see the footage from the lobby."

"I'm afraid I can't help you with that, Ms. Swanson. You see, regardless of the laws surrounding data protection, the footage no longer exists."

"Why? What happened to it?"

"All of our CCTV footage is held for thirty days before being erased. It's standard practice. If you'd come to me ten months ago, I may have been able to help you. I held onto the footage from that evening for the police, but they never asked to see it, and so it was deleted."

Emily slumped in the chair. She'd been counting on the footage to reveal exactly when Max Edwards had left the hotel. Now it was gone; erased from time.

It made sense why the police hadn't viewed the tapes. To them, Max was an open and shut case, so any time and resources spent on viewing the footage would have been a waste of precious funding.

"I don't suppose you saw the tapes yourself?" Emily asked.

"No, I did not." Mr. Singh glanced at the wall clock. "I apologize, Ms. Swanson, but overseeing the running of this hotel is more than a full-time job. Is there anything else I can help you with today?"

There had to be something here. Max Edwards couldn't have disappeared into thin air.

"What about the staff who were working that night? Perhaps someone saw Mr. Edwards after the gala had ended."

"Well, there are the night porters. . ."

"Could we find out who was on duty?"

"It was over a year ago, Ms. Swanson. Porters come and go."

"But it would be possible to find out? After all, a guest disappearing only to be found dead is unlikely to be forgotten in a rush."

"Unfortunately, I expect you're right. . ." Mr. Singh rubbed his chin as he considered Emily's request. "Very well. I shall make some enquiries. If I find anything of significance, I shall let you know. You have a card?"

Emily shook her head, realized how unprofessional she looked, then quickly wrote her number down on a piece of notepaper. Her embarrassment was still in full bloom as she left the hotel and headed back home.

12

RUSH HOUR WAS in full-swing across the city. Millions of people filled platforms and pavements, and squeezed in and out of trains, buses, and cars. As Emily pushed open the door to The Holmeswood, she felt grateful for the sudden quiet. Once inside her apartment, she kicked off her shoes and headed for the bathroom. She stopped. Laughter rang out from the living room. She heard Jerome's voice, followed by Daniel's. And then she heard another voice—one that instantly made her hands clench into fists.

"Emily!" Jerome sat at the dining table, wine glass in hand, his chair turned to the guests on the sofa. "Look who's here!"

Emily's gaze shifted from Daniel, who smiled and said hello, to the dark-haired young woman sat next to him.

"Emily Swanson! How the hell are you? Jesus, don't look so pleased to see me!" Helen Carlson raised her glass. Her lips spread into a smile that didn't quite reach her eyes.

Max Edwards' paperwork was no longer sitting in neat piles on the table. It was now by Helen's feet, with his diary resting on top. Emily's eyes grew round and wide.

"What a great surprise, isn't it?" Jerome said, slurring his words.

"It's certainly a *surprise*." Emily remained standing, feeling like an uninvited party guest. She glared at Helen. "Why are you here?"

Helen laughed, splashing wine over the edge of her glass. "I see your welcoming charm hasn't changed a bit. After everything we've been through together, I thought you'd be pleased to see me. And to think I nearly died as well!"

She threw her head back and laughed again.

"But you didn't." Emily's gaze returned to Jerome.

"Isn't it funny?" he said. "I was talking to Daniel about your case, and he said, 'Why don't you call Helen?' Which was a great idea, wasn't it? Because Helen's just moved to the city and she's writing for the *London Truth*."

"Never heard of it." Emily's angry eyes swung from Jerome to Daniel, who'd found something interesting at the bottom of his glass.

"Actually, it's a new current affairs fortnightly, featuring exposés, investigative journalism, that type of thing," Helen said, swinging her wine glass.

"I've looked everywhere for Anya Copeland," Jerome said. "Social media, phone directories, business directories... But it's like she doesn't exist."

"Which is why I'm here." Helen set her glass down on the floor, close to her foot. Emily watched it with mounting anxiety.

"Helen's going to help," Jerome explained.

"Yes, I can put two and two together, thank you." Emily turned to Helen. "But I'm sure I'll manage fine on my own. Sorry that

Jerome's wasted your time."

She stooped down and swept Max Edwards' paperwork into her arms, then turned to the living room door.

Helen stopped her. "Come on, Emily. Don't you think you're being a little ridiculous? What's the problem? You didn't like my story? I thought it was very respectful. I mean, I *could* have written about all of that business with Phillip Gerard, but I didn't."

"And I'm supposed to be grateful?"

Anger churned Emily's insides as she glowered at Helen. The last time she'd seen the journalist, she was being stretchered to a waiting helicopter, her skull fractured by a blow from a hammer. Of course, Emily had been relieved to hear Helen had survived the attack, but she had been less pleased about her subsequent stories in the newspapers.

"I thought I made you look heroic," Helen said, sounding wounded.

"'Withdrawn introvert, Emily Swanson, overcame her own battles with mental health and crippling anxiety to reveal the killer's identity,'" Emily quoted. It was one of several extracts from Helen's article that were now burned into her mind.

The journalist shrugged a shoulder. "What can I say? I report the facts."

"Well, here's a fact for you: I don't need your help."

Emily marched to the door. She was furious—with Jerome for involving Helen without any discussion; with Daniel for suggesting they contact Helen in the first place; with Helen for being Helen. And although she hated to admit it, she was angry with herself.

"Come on, Emily!" Helen's voice sang out behind her. "Stop behaving like a spoiled brat. You know I have access to resources that could help you, so let me help you!"

Emily turned around. "Why would you want to help me?"

"Emily Swanson, I'm offended." Helen pressed her hand against her chest. "Are you accusing me of having an ulterior motive?"

"You're a journalist, aren't you?"

"Touché. Okay, fine. When Jerome called me today and told me about your case, it caught my interest. And I suppose I owe you for sort of saving my life."

"For giving your career a boost more like."

Helen stared at her shrewdly. "I'll help you find this Anya Copeland woman. I owe you that much. But if there *is* a story there, I want an exclusive."

The two women locked eyes. Emily tightened her grip on the paperwork. "I see that hammer to the head did nothing to soften you. Thanks, but I'll be just fine on my own."

Before Helen or anyone else could argue with her, she darted toward her bedroom. It was a childish decision, she knew. Childish, stubborn, and stupid. But she hadn't agreed to help Diane Edwards to gain further public attention, and she was sure Diane wouldn't want her name in the news either.

Dumping the paperwork on the floor, Emily threw herself onto the bed. What had Jerome been thinking? No doubt the three of them were in there laughing at her right now.

Well, let them laugh!

A soft knock on the door made her sit up. Before she could answer, Jerome appeared.

"Can I come in?" He swayed in the doorway, brow pulled down over his eyes.

Emily shrugged. "Do what you like."

Jerome entered, coming to a halt at the foot of the bed. Neither of them spoke for a full minute. Then he said, "So, I guess it wasn't a good idea calling Helen."

"No. It was not." Emily pushed herself up against the headboard.

"I don't see what the problem is. Okay, so you didn't like what she wrote about you, but she has connections. She can help you find Anya Copeland."

"You don't think I can find her by myself?"

"You asked me to help you find Anya," Jerome said, his eyes narrowing. "Well, this is me helping. I know you're not a fan of Helen but think of the resources you'd have at your disposal."

"I don't care about that, Jerome. You should have asked me first. I don't need Helen Carlson getting in my way."

Jerome moved closer. Emily could smell the alcohol seeping from his pores.

"You're being ridiculous," he said. "If Helen can help you find Anya Copeland, you'd be stupid not to put up with her for a couple of days. I'd do it."

"I don't trust her."

Jerome's frown grew deeper. "Your problem is you don't trust anyone."

"What is *that* supposed to mean?" Emily winced, feeling the sting of his words. When he didn't answer, she said, "What is going on with you? You've been acting strangely ever since you told me you were moving out. Where's all this anger coming from?"

"I'm fine," Jerome snapped. "Maybe you should worry about yourself. You should be busy figuring out what you're actually going to do with your life instead of running around thinking you're Nancy Drew."

Emily stared at him. "You sound just like Harriet."

"Well, maybe Harriet has a point. All this playing detective without stopping to think you might be putting the people around you at risk. Or maybe you do think about it, but you just don't care."

His voice was raised now. Emily folded her arms and stared at the bed, trying to contain her anger.

"Of course I care. What's going on? If I've done something to upset you, then you need to tell me."

He looked away, channelling his anger into the carpet. There was a long, painful silence. Then he said in a low voice, "You know what? Take Helen's help, or don't. Do what you like. Either way, I don't care."

Emily watched Jerome back out of the room and close the door. Tears stung her eyes. What the hell had just happened?

She sat on the bed, feeling guilty and shocked. A minute later, she heard footsteps and murmurs out in the hallway, followed by the front door opening and closing. Silence smothered the apartment. Emily waited a minute more, then made her way to the bathroom. She took out a sleeping pill from the bathroom cabinet, spent a minute trying to convince herself not to take it, then swallowed it down with water.

As she lay in bed, waiting for the chemicals to take hold, she stared into the shadows of the ceiling. Was she really putting the people around her at risk without a moment's thought? Her eyelids grew heavy. Her thoughts were extinguished like candle flames, until only one remained, flickering in the dark: perhaps Jerome was right.

13

SATURDAY PASSED QUIETLY. Jerome stayed away, leaving Emily to skulk around the apartment, sinking further into a dark mood. On Sunday morning, she woke feeling groggy and disoriented; the aftereffects of taking another sleeping pill. Bored and restless, she thought about crossing the hall to visit Harriet, but her already fragile ego forced her to change her mind.

Instead, she left The Holmeswood and walked through quiet streets, until she came upon St. John's Garden. Perching on a bench, she looked around the tiny island of trees and fauna surrounded by rows of Georgian houses.

Time passed slowly. Pavements began to fill with people, the roads with traffic. The pressure in Emily's chest refused to ease.

She needed somewhere bigger, quieter—a place where she could turn her back on the city and forget where she was, even if it was just for an hour.

It took three buses to get there, but eventually Emily arrived at Hampstead Heath. The sky was a deep azure, spoiled only by a smattering of cloud. People milled about, some with excited dogs straining on leashes, others with towels slung over their shoulders as they headed to the bathing ponds. As Emily headed deeper into the Heath, green slopes of long grass rose up on her left. The path turned and she stepped off it, heading through a field of wild flowers where groups of people picnicked on blankets. By the time she'd reached the trees on the other side, the back of her neck was hot and sweaty.

Entering the wood, she found the trunk of a fallen tree and sat down. The shade was cool against her skin. Above her head, birds sang out from the rusting canopy. Time seemed to slow down with each of Emily's breaths. Gradually, her mind cleared of troublesome thoughts. Her lungs contracted and expanded in slow, fluid rhythms.

You can do this. Forget Jerome for now. You need to focus on finding Anya Copeland.

There had to be other ways of tracking her down that didn't involve Helen Carlson. As Emily sat in the cool forest shade, the minutes floating away, an idea came to her. It was such an obvious idea that she berated herself for not thinking of it earlier. But her excitement was short-lived. For this idea to work, she was going to need help from Carter West.

*

Monday morning brought more sunshine. As the bus turned onto London Bridge, Emily gazed over the murky water of the Thames. On her left was HMS. Belfast, the once active Royal Navy cruiser that was now a permanently docked floating museum. Tower Bridge lay beyond, its iconic towers prominent against the cobalt sky. To her right, the Tate Modern's chimney stack stood out like a flag pin on a map: here lay the body of Max Edwards.

Arriving at *Lost*, Emily took a moment to straighten her outfit and go over her apology. Entering the call centre, she looked for Carter. He was not here.

Her hopes sagged as she made her way to the archives. Collecting a new folder, she sat down at her desk. It was then she noticed him.

"Good morning." Carter waved from Imogen's desk.

Words collided in Emily's throat.

"Imogen couldn't make it today," he said. "Something about being locked in her apartment. I was just finishing up, so the boss asked me to take her shift."

Emily continued to stare. Unlike the helplines, a shortage of volunteers in the archives wasn't going to cause any damage. She wondered if Carter had deliberately volunteered to take the shift. Emily felt flattered, which was better than the awkwardness currently prickling her skin. Then her mind filled with memories of their disastrous date.

The database now open and ready for input, Emily opened the archive folder to the first page and began typing in the details of thirty-six-year-old Aidan Williams, who had disappeared from his home, leaving behind a wife and two young children.

Carter cleared his throat. Emily looked across to see his curiously-coloured eyes were sad and puppy-like.

"Listen, about the other evening," he began. "I'm sorry if I upset you. I talk too much when I'm nervous. Perhaps I was asking too many questions, but I didn't mean to offend you."

The muscles in Emily's shoulders softened a little. There was nothing to forgive, really. After all, Carter had only been asking the questions that were always asked on first dates. It was just that most people tended not to be hiding a dark and anguish-filled past. How was Carter to know Emily wasn't most people?

"Dating makes me nervous, too," she said. "I was rude to leave like that."

Across the room, Carter relaxed a little. His smile, warm and familiar, returned.

"My sister always said I suffered from a case of verbal diarrhoea. I guess she was right."

Their eyes met. For a moment, she thought he was going to ask her out again. Part of her hoped that he would. The rest of her ran from the idea.

Emily stared down at the open folder on her desk, into the blank eyes of Aidan Williams, who'd had a long history of depression and anxiety, who'd attempted suicide twice before.

Think of something to say.

"I'm sure, in this case, she'd say you were being too hard on yourself," Emily smiled.

"More like she would have told me I'm an idiot." There was hesitance in his voice, as if he was momentarily lost somewhere inside a memory. "She would have also told me to try again."

Carter stared across the room with hopeful eyes, just as Emily realized he was talking about his sister in the past tense. Perhaps she was not the only one with a painful past.

"What do you think?"

She'd zoned out for a second. "Hmm?"

"About coffee take two?"

"Oh. I want to..." She did. Maybe. "But I can't this week. I have a lot going on."

"The new job?"

Emily hesitated. "Yes. It seems to be taking over my life."

Did she tell him? Why was she keeping it a secret? Was helping someone in pain come to terms with their past really so shameful? Because it *was* shame that was preventing her from telling Carter. Shame and embarrassment. Because she didn't want to use the words 'private investigation' for him to laugh in her face.

"Another time then, perhaps," Carter said.

Emily watched him working at the computer for a few seconds, his disappointed eyes fixed at the screen. She tapped her fingers on the desk. *Ask him.*

"Listen, I know it's probably inappropriate, but I was wondering if you could help me with something."

Carter looked up.

"I'm trying to find someone. Someone who for all intents and purposes has disappeared."

"A friend?"

"Not exactly. I've tried everything I can to find her, but with no luck. I was wondering, seeing as how you're the social media guru around here, if we could maybe post a shout out for her. . . Perhaps someone will know where she is."

She held his gaze with a hopeful smile.

Carter leaned forward over the desk. His lips curled into a smile. "That's a very mysterious request. This person who's not exactly a friend, has she been reported missing?"

The truth of the matter, Emily realized, was that she hadn't even thought to check. Face heating up, she entered Anya's name into the system and checked the results.

"No, she hasn't. At least, not to us."

Carter stared at her for a long time. "It's not exactly protocol if she hasn't been reported."

"I know."

"What's this all about, Emily?"

Just tell him.

"The new job. . . I'm helping someone to find out what happened to her husband. This woman—Anya—she might be the only person who knows the answer."

"Her husband?" Carter's stare was making her uncomfortable. "What exactly is this new job?"

"Please, Carter. I know it's a strange request, but I really need to find this woman." She pleaded with her eyes, but she could tell he was wavering. "I promise to tell you all about it over coffee take two."

Carter stared at her for a second more, then returned to the computer. Emily did the same, entering the last of Aidan Williams' details. After her behaviour at Bramfords Diner, Carter's reluctance was understandable, she supposed. But knowing that didn't stop disappointment sweeping through her.

Heaving her shoulders, Emily turned to the next profile. When she next glanced up, she saw Carter staring at her with a mischievous smile on his lips.

"What's this woman's full name?" he said.

Emily's disappointment vanished in an instant.

14

BY THE TIME Emily reached the Wellbeing Centre for her five o'clock appointment, she was hot and sticky and wishing she had dressed in something looser than jeans and a T-shirt. Kirsten Dewar was sitting in an armchair, looking cool and collected in a cotton top and pencil skirt. She sat with her legs neatly crossed, notepad balanced on her knee. She smiled pleasantly as she waited for Emily to empty half a glass of water.

"It's days like this I miss the countryside," Emily said, wiping her mouth with the back of her hand.

Kirsten gave a slight nod. "How are you this week?"

"Oh, fine." Emily sat back on the leather couch and cast a cursory glance around the sparsely furnished room. A fan sat on the desk in the corner, shifting back and forth, the cool air falling short.

Kirsten glanced down at her notes. "Last session, we talked about the future, about what you might like to do with your life. Any thoughts or reflections?"

"Actually, it's funny you should mention that," Emily said, "because I sort of have a job."

Kirsten scribbled onto her pad. "Tell me more."

Taking a deep breath, Emily told Kirsten about Diane Edwards' proposal, and her subsequent investigation into the death of Max Edwards. When she'd finished talking, she sat back and studied the therapist's face.

Kirsten's pen scratched against paper. She looked up with a slight frown. "How did Diane Edwards find you?"

"She read about me in the newspaper."

There was a pause before Kirsten spoke again. Fresh beads of perspiration formed on Emily's skin.

"This is a very unusual situation, Emily. Why did Diane come to you and not to someone of an official capacity? The police, for instance."

"The police already closed the case: 'Death by misadventure.' Then Diane read about Meadow Pines and about the court case last month. She said she saw something in me."

"What did she see?"

"An understanding of what it's like to lose everything, to be left with unresolved questions."

"And you know how that feels?"

"Yes, I do. Except the difference between Diane and myself is that I've found my answers."

"Do you think you can help her?"

"I think I can try."

Kirsten nodded. The scratch of pen against paper irritated Emily's ears. "I know how it looks," she said. "That helping Diane is really about helping myself. And perhaps that's true. But perhaps it's also about what you and I discussed last session. I've been thinking a lot about my future, about what I want to do. All my life, I've been helping people—teaching, my mother, volunteering at *Lost*, the Ever After Care Foundation, St. Dymphna's, Meadow Pines—what if helping people is what I'm supposed to do? And if by helping people I help myself to become stronger, to become happier, then surely that's a good thing."

Kirsten put down her pen. "I think helping people is a wonderful thing to do, and I think all of the people you've helped would agree. However, willingly putting yourself into a potentially dangerous situation concerns me, Emily. You have, after all, almost been killed twice in less than twelve months."

"Police officers risk their lives every day. Fire and rescue. Medics on the frontline in warzones. Think of all those lives that would be lost if they didn't put themselves out there."

Kirsten was quiet. She picked up her pen and wrote down a few notes, then looked up at Emily again. "You're right. Women and men all over the world put their lives on the line every day. However, those men and women are all highly trained and highly qualified. They follow tried and tested procedures, and although that does not eliminate danger entirely, it certainly reduces their risk of dying."

Emily stared at her. The room had become unbearably hot. "So, are you saying I shouldn't even try to help Diane? That I should play things quiet and safe? My whole life was quiet and safe. Then my mother died and so did Phillip Gerard. Quiet and safe can't protect me anymore."

"What I'm saying, Emily," Kirsten said, her warm smile reaching her eyes, "is it seems you may have already chosen your path. Perhaps what you should now consider, is how you go about making that path less dangerous to travel."

Emily leaned forward on the sofa. "You mean join the police force, something like that?"

"I'm not a careers advisor, but perhaps conducting research will give you some answers. In the meantime, can I advise you to tread very carefully where Diane Edwards is concerned?"

Emily nodded. "Of course. But there's nothing to be concerned about. It looks like her husband had been having an affair. The affair ended. He drowned his sorrows, then accidentally drowned himself. Affairs of the heart are never easy, are they?"

Looking up from her notes, Kirsten Dewar raised an eyebrow. "Oh? Something to tell me?"

Carter West appeared in Emily's head.

"Never mind," she said.

15

IT WAS JUST past eight when Emily returned home. A familiar voice startled her as she unlocked her apartment door.

"Hello dear, you just missed Jerome."

Harriet stood in her doorway, gripping the jamb. Although she was pale and tired-looking, her eyes glinted with mischief.

Emily sighed. "Did I?"

"Oh yes. He was in a terrible mood. Barely said hello. You two haven't had a fight, have you? Is that why he's moving out?"

"I have no idea what's wrong with Jerome. I haven't seen him since Friday."

"Is that so? I wonder what's the matter."

Emily excused herself before Harriet could pry any further. The truth was that Jerome hadn't texted or called since their fight. And now he was sneaking in and out to pick up fresh clothes for the week. She was still angry with him, but she was also convinced that something was wrong. Jerome was not in the habit of getting drunk and lashing out. And he had never avoided her like he was doing now.

Slipping out of her clothes and into a bathrobe, Emily wondered again if she had done something to upset him. She ran a bath. Feeling miserable, she sat down on the bed and waited for the water to cool. She couldn't let this go on. Jerome was her closest friend and she was not prepared to lose him. She would call him and ask to meet. And if he refused, she would see if Daniel could shed any light. But she would do it tomorrow. Right now, she was going to soak away her troubles in the bathtub.

As soon as she'd made the decision, her phone buzzed. Emily snatched it up. But it wasn't Jerome calling as she'd hoped.

It was a text message sent from an unknown number: *Have you talked to Evan Holt yet?*

Puzzled, she stared at the words. She didn't know an Evan Holt. So why did the name sound vaguely familiar? She tapped out a reply: *Think you have the wrong number.*

A second message came soon after: *Check the diary.*

Emily's heart skipped a beat. Scooping up Max Edwards' diary from the floor, she carefully flicked through the pages. First, she checked the list of contacts, then moved from appointment to appointment, until she came to the Clean Water Project's launch night. There, pencilled in on the morning after Max's disappearance, was: *Evan Holt. 10 a.m.*

Fingers trembling with excitement, Emily picked up her phone again and typed: *Who is Evan Holt?*

Seconds passed. She tapped out another message: *Who is this?*

Emily waited but there were no more replies. Intrigued now, she dialled Tim Marsden's mobile number.

"I'd prefer it if you didn't call on my personal number," he said, his voice tinged with annoyance.

Emily apologized and asked about Evan Holt.

"Never heard of him," Tim said. "Is this to do with Max?"

"According to Max's diary, he had a 10 a.m. appointment with Evan Holt on the morning after the launch."

The line went quiet. Then Tim said, "Max never mentioned any appointment. We were supposed to be driving back to the plant that morning. Evan Holt, you said? If he was anything to do with Valence or Clean Water, I'm sure I would have heard of him."

Retrieving her notebook, Emily wrote down: *Evan Holt???*

"I wonder who he could be," she said.

"I have no idea. Well, if that's —"

"One more quick question, if you don't mind, Mr. Marsden."

A sigh, then, "Go on."

"I spoke to Charlie Jones. Did you know there was a rumour that Max and Anya Copeland were having an affair?"

Tim Marsden blew a stream of air through his nose. "You shouldn't believe everything you hear, Ms. Swanson. Goodnight."

He hung up, leaving Emily alone with several more questions. What had he meant? That Max and Anya weren't having an affair, after all? Emily's head felt overcrowded with thoughts and voices. It seemed the deeper she delved into the death of Max Edwards, the more questions she was unearthing.

Which meant it was time to find some answers.

Forgetting about her bath, she grabbed her laptop, opened a web browser, and entered 'Evan Holt' into the search bar. A second later, she was staring at a long list of search results. There were Facebook and LinkedIn profiles, Twitter accounts; the list went on.

She tried narrowing down the search by typing: 'Evan Holt Valence Industries'. The results came up empty. Next, she tried 'Evan Holt Clean Water Project', but with no success. She would have to tackle each search result, each profile and account. And even if she did find the right Evan Holt, how would she know? If only those text messages had been less mysterious.

Determined not to spend hours trawling through the results, Emily returned to the search bar. Max Edwards was a sustainable development manager. He was a passionate environmentalist. Both facets of his life were entwined. Fingers moving like lightning across the keyboard, Emily typed: 'Evan Holt environment'.

She quickly scanned through the results. Her stomach flipped. A third of the way down the page was a link to a news story.

The headline read: *Live Here, Die Young—the Truth About Environmental Racism, by Evan Holt.*

16

THE LIONS INN was a traditional British pub, resplendent with sticky red carpet, shabby furnishings, and poor lighting. A few lone afternoon drinkers sat at the bar nursing pints of beer. One of them stared at Emily as she hurried past.

She hadn't slept well, but she had resisted taking more sleeping pills. Her mind had gone into overdrive, flitting between thoughts of Jerome and her conversation with Kirsten Dewar, but mostly centred on her phone call with investigative journalist Evan Holt. It had taken a while to locate his contact details, but what he'd had to say had made it worth the trouble. Now, as she approached the man sitting at the back of the pub, she wondered if trouble was exactly what she was about to get herself into.

"Evan Holt?"

The man was late-forties, with a paunch and thinning hair, and skin that hadn't seen much daylight. An empty glass sat on the table in front of him, next to a freshly-poured beer. He shook Emily's hand and offered to buy her a drink, which she politely refused.

"Thanks for seeing me," she said, taking out her notebook and pen. She flipped to a clean page, wrote Evan Holt's name at the top, and underlined it twice. Evan watched her with mild amusement.

"You're welcome. Actually, I'm glad you called," he said. "It's good to know someone else shares the same concerns about what happened to Max Edwards."

"I'm not sure that we do just yet. You were a little cryptic on the phone."

Evan picked up his beer and stared at Emily, making her feel uneasy. "What I have to tell you is best not discussed over the phone."

"Oh?"

"You never know who's listening in."

Emily gave a half nod; paranoia was an understandable side effect of investigative journalism. Returning Evan's gaze, she waited for him to elaborate. When he didn't, she started asking questions.

"So Max had a story he thought you would be interested in?"

Evan nodded. "We were supposed to meet to discuss it. He never showed. At first, I put it down to a hoax—it happens a lot."

"But Max wasn't a hoax."

"No. He wasn't." Evan took a large gulp of beer. "He called one day, said he'd been following my articles about environmental racism, that they'd struck a chord with him, especially because of his own background in activism."

"I'm sorry—environmental racism?"

"Basically, first world countries making hundreds of millions by exploiting poorer, developing countries through the sale of toxic products that are harmful to the people and their land. I know, I made the same shocked face when I first learned about it, but believe me, there are companies out there who don't give two shits about the lives they're damaging, just so long as they make a profit.

"I'm talking whole towns, families— destroyed in the name of fattening the bellies of the rich. And as a matter of fact, it's not just developing countries who are suffering. Just look at what happened in the US with the town of Flint. A whole community of mostly impoverished African Americans left to drink poisoned water despite repeated complaints *and* a 2011 report stating the water source was toxic. Now tell me, would that happen in a town of rich white people? I don't think so."

Emily scribbled into her notebook. She was troubled by what she was hearing, and by exactly how environmental racism was connected to Max.

"What did he tell you?" she said, looking up.

"That he had evidence to prove the company he worked for were up to no good."

"Valence Industries?"

Evan nodded.

"Evidence of what, exactly?"

"Have you heard of TEL?"

Emily shook her head. "Sounds familiar, but..."

"TEL—or Tetraethyl lead—was a chemical added to fuel that helped slow down the burning process, thereby allowing drivers more distance for their money. Everyone thought leaded fuel was great, until they realized just how harmful TEL had made it. The US and most of the world banned the sale of leaded fuel throughout the 1970s, 80s, and 90s. Our so-called Great Britain was the last developing country to get rid of it in 1999."

"What was so dangerous about TEL?" Emily asked, her curiosity piqued now. Surely any chemical additive was harmful to the environment.

"Okay, bear with me—because this next bit's going to sound a little crazy." Evan paused to take a sip of beer. His eyes flashed: *wait till you hear this.* "There was concern about the impact TEL was having—not just on the environment, but on people. Namely, children. Researchers found that TEL attacks the nervous system. Its effects are permanent and irreversible. In children, normal exposure can lead to delays in development—both physically and cognitively—as well as cause detrimental effects on behaviour. Extreme exposure can lead to deafness, blindness, seizures, coma, even death."

Emily had put her pen down and grown quite still.

"Studies into the effects of TEL in the US showed a direct link between the effects of lead exposure on the nervous system of children and a rise in violent crime. May I?" Pushing his glass to one side, he took Emily's notebook and pen and turned to a clean page.

"The largest source of post-war lead was leaded fuel. As it became widely used, lead emissions from cars rose steadily between the 40s and 70s—in fact, it almost quadrupled. But then, as unleaded fuel was introduced and began to replace leaded fuel, emissions plummeted. So, if you chart the rise of atmospheric lead caused by the rise and fall of leaded fuel consumption, you get this." Evan drew a large, upside down U on the page, and labelled it: *Atmospheric Lead Levels.*

He smiled to himself. "Here comes the crazy bit. If you chart violent crime rates in the United States, you'll see a dramatic rise between the 1960s and the 1980s, but then a drop—and it's a steady drop—that begins in the 1990s." He drew an identical upside-down

U shape and labelled it: *Violent Crime.*

"Uncanny, isn't it?" Evan tapped the pen against the notebook. "Identical patterns but set twenty years apart."

Emily stared at both diagrams. Her jaw dropped as she made the connection. "Twenty years for children affected by TEL to grow into adults."

"You could think I was making this all up, but go take a look online and you can find the research easily enough. Like, for example, the study in Cincinnati that found young offenders are four times more likely to have high levels of lead in their bones than the general population." Evan retrieved his beer and took a sip. "My point is, nearly all these studies were conducted by independent bodies, in different cities and states, and then in different countries, including right here in the UK. Almost every one of those reports had the exact same findings."

Horrified, Emily stared silently at Evan's diagrams.

"No one should be surprised by this," he said. "We've known for decades that lead is highly toxic. Even in the 1940s, behavioural changes were documented in children who chewed the leaded paint from the railings of their cots. They went on to display high levels of aggression and violence, and to suffer all kinds of developmental delays. And yet, here we are eighty years later, still talking about the harmful effects of lead."

Emily felt a chill slip beneath her T-shirt. "And why *are* we talking about it? If TEL was banned in the UK in 1999, what does it have to do with Max Edwards, with Valence Industries?"

What she'd just heard sounded like something out of a science fiction story. Chemically-induced violence? From everything Emily had learned about Valence Industries, the company had been working hard to reduce its impact on the environment, not increase it.

"It has everything to do with Valence Industries," said Evan. He leaned forward, eyebrow arched, a knowing smile on his lips.

Emily couldn't hide her shock. "What are you saying? That Valence still produces TEL?"

"That's why Max contacted me. He'd discovered that Valence Industries is the *only* chemicals company in the world to still produce TEL. And they're selling it to a handful of developing countries where leaded fuel has yet to be banned."

Leaning back in her chair, Emily stared at the journalist. Thoughts careered and collided in her head. "But I thought you said TEL was banned from sale in the UK."

"It is. But there are no current laws prohibiting its exportation. I've looked into it—what Valence is doing is perfectly legal. The moral and ethical implications, however, are completely fucked. That's why it's been trying to cover up the whole nasty business."

Emily couldn't believe it. "But all the environmental work it does. All the work Max Edwards was doing—the Clean Water Project, the sustainability. . ."

"Green wash," Evan shrugged.

There was that phrase again—the same phrase Charlie Jones had used at E.C.G.

Emily's head was spinning. Before meeting with Evan, she'd been certain Max Edwards' death had been the result of a doomed affair. But now her theory didn't seem to carry any weight at all.

"You sure you don't want that drink?" Evan said.

Emily shook her head. "Max told you all this?"

"Some of it. Like I said, when he didn't show, I put it down to a hoax. But he got me curious. When I learned he was dead, I started looking into things. It wasn't hard to find out which countries are still selling leaded fuel. Unsurprisingly, they're all in chaos, headed by governments who don't give a damn about their people. Once I'd pinpointed the countries, it was easy enough to work backward and find out who was providing the fuel."

"It doesn't make sense." Emily was starting to feel overwhelmed by all that she had learned. "So, you're saying Valence was using Max as a smokescreen? Hire someone with a passion for the environment to help create a positive green image for the company, and then hide behind him while they make a fortune by selling TEL."

"That's exactly what I'm saying."

"He must have been furious when he found out," Emily said.

"He'd sounded pretty pissed off on the phone."

"But that still doesn't explain his death."

"Maybe the anger got to him and he hit the bottle. Or maybe he didn't touch a drop. . ."

Emily wrapped her arms around her ribcage and eyed the men at the bar. "What do you mean? The coroner's report said—"

"I know what the coroner's report said," Evan replied. "I'm not disputing the cause of death. I'm disputing *how* he died."

Emily stared at Evan, the realization of what he was suggestion hitting her fast and hard. "Surely you don't think that Valence. . . But you said yourself, it was easy to track the TEL back to Valence Industries."

"Easy for me because Max told me what to look for."

"But they wouldn't have. . ." She looked around the bar again, making sure no one could hear her. ". . .killed him. Like you said, Valence isn't breaking any laws. Someone was bound to find out what they're doing sooner or later."

"I'm sure Max Edwards isn't the first person to meet a sticky end at the hands of a greedy corporation, and he certainly won't be the last. Not by a longshot." Evan leaned forward. "Here's what I think. I think there's more to the story. I think Max found out about TEL, and then dug deeper and found something worse."

Emily was quiet, processing everything. "What do you think it could be?"

Evan shrugged his shoulders again. "I don't know. But every lead I've chased so far has turned up empty. Whatever Max found out, I highly doubt he was working on his own. He was an environmentalist with a political past, which means he would have known people who could have helped him get deep inside Valence. Who knows, maybe he even had inside help."

Pulse racing, Emily sat up. "Anya Copeland. She led the Clean Water Project for Earth Conservation Group. She worked closely with Max. There'd been rumours they were having an affair. The night he disappeared, she was seen coming down from his hotel room. Two weeks after his death, she quit her job and disappeared. Moved home, changed her number, vanished into thin air."

Evan arched his eyebrows. "Interesting. Any luck finding her?"

"Not yet." Anya's elusiveness was made worse by the fact Emily had limited resources with which to find her. But now more than ever, it was imperative that she did find her—everything that Emily had thought she'd discovered about Max Edwards' death had just been obliterated by one, short conversation.

She felt quietly embarrassed. Perhaps she'd made a mistake turning down Helen Carlson's help. But it no longer mattered because now she had Evan Holt—a highly experienced investigative journalist who'd taught her more about Max Edwards and Valence

Industries in the last twenty minutes than she'd learned in an entire week of working alone.

But how had she come to learn about Evan Holt?

"Maybe I can put some feelers out," Evan said, staring into his now empty glass. "Do you have Anya's last known address?"

Who had sent her that text message? Only a handful of people knew Emily was investigating the death of Max Edwards. Even fewer knew she was in possession of his diary.

"Emily?"

She froze.

The night she had returned home to find Helen Carlson in her living room, Max's paperwork and diary had been moved from the table and had been sitting on the floor. Right beside Helen Carlson's feet. A fire sparked in the pit of Emily's stomach.

"Emily, are you all right?"

Her skin was prickling with anger. Regardless of Emily's refusal of help, Helen had found a way into the investigation. And now Emily was indebted to her.

"I'll get Anya's address," she said, pushing her anger down.

"Good." Evan nodded as he leaned forward. "Because we're going to put our heads together and figure out exactly what it is that Max Edwards found. But Emily—be careful who you share this information with. We don't want Valence Industries finding out we're onto them."

Emily stared at him. "Don't worry. I'm not so amateurish that I'll go shouting it in the streets."

"Point taken. Sorry, it's not often I work in collaboration. And I know you're pretty new to this, so. . ."

Emily's mouth fell open. "You've been looking into me?"

Evan flashed her a sheepish grin. "If I'm going to work with someone, I need to know I can trust them."

It was understandable, she supposed, but she couldn't help feeling like an organism under the lens of a microscope.

"I'm going to follow up a few leads overseas, see if I can find anything more," Evan said.

"And I'll get Anya's old address." A thought struck Emily as she stared at her notebook. "Have you spoken to anyone at Valence Industries apart from Max?"

"No. It would be good for the story if we could get closer, though. Their UK CEO, Jonathan Hunt, has had a lot to say publicly about all the good the company's been doing for the environment. I'd love to get a direct quote from him, just so I could then serve his balls up on a plate. Men like him deserve all the humiliation they can get."

"What about an interview with him?" Emily asked.

"My ugly mug is all too familiar in the world of investigative journalism. One sniff from Hunt's PR people and I'm not getting anywhere near. It would be interesting to talk to him, though."

It would, Emily thought. An interview played in the right way could even shed some light on Max Edwards' death. But if Evan Holt couldn't get close... Her heart sank into her stomach as she realized who *would* be able to get close. There had to be another way.

"I've been in touch with Tim Marsden, Max Edwards' former right-hand man," she said. "He might be persuaded to agree to an interview with you."

"No one's going to listen to the words of an assistant. It needs to be Hunt. He's the one in charge of UK operations. He'll know exactly what Valence Industries is up to."

Damn it! Emily bit down on her lower lip, then heaved out a heavy breath. "I know someone who can help. Another journalist."

Evan looked up. "The one from Meadow Pines?"

The man really had been doing his homework. "Yes. Helen Carlson. She's writing for London Truth now."

"Can she be trusted?"

"I'll let you find that out for yourself."

Emily had no idea if Helen could be trusted with such delicate information. But she had to hope her journalistic integrity and passion for a story would work in everyone's favour.

"Fine. Put her in touch with me," Evan said. "In the meantime, let's see what else we can dig up. And Emily? Please remember to keep a low profile."

Emily's eyes burned into him.

"Sorry," he said.

17

HELEN PULLED UP in front of The Holmeswood at 10 a.m. on Friday morning, and beckoned Emily to the blue Renault. The road was still crammed with traffic and it took almost five minutes before Helen could reinsert the vehicle into the flow.

"Christ, I hate London drivers. Everyone's a selfish bastard."

The strain of driving in the city was already showing on Helen's face. She blasted the horn as a car slid into the space in front.

Emily sank down in the passenger seat and peered out of the window. Streams of unsmiling faces filed past.

"Any joy with the Copeland woman?" Helen asked.

Emily shrugged a shoulder. "Still working on it."

"What about getting Daniel involved? Maybe we could find Anya by finding her kid."

"I already thought of that but Jerome is refusing to let me talk to Daniel about it."

"Well, that's deeply unhelpful. I didn't realize Jerome had such a tight hold on his boyfriend's reins."

"He's trying to protect him, that's all."

They took a left at the crossroads, narrowly escaping the changing traffic lights.

"Can't you speak to Jerome, get him to *unprotect* him?"

"Jerome and I aren't exactly on speaking terms right now."

It was true. Jerome hadn't replied to Emily's text message asking to meet and talk things over. He'd also ignored her phone calls and voicemails.

Perhaps this is it, she thought, as she watched the pedestrians moving up and down. *Perhaps Jerome is finally done with our friendship.* The thought was too painful to have inside her head.

"Still?" Helen snorted. "Well, you better not be blaming me."

"Not everything is about you, Helen."

"So, what *is* the problem, then? Actually, on second thoughts, I don't care. And I think it's about time I have a go at finding Anya. Show you how the professionals do it."

Emily sank lower in the seat, feeling uncomfortable in the trouser suit she was wearing. It was bad enough she'd be spending the next few hours with Helen, but to know Helen would have full control over the interview with Jonathan Hunt was making her bad mood that much worse.

Up ahead, the lights turned from red to amber. Helen honked the horn. "Hurry the hell up, assholes!" The traffic got moving again. She glanced over at Emily, who had all but disappeared beneath the window. "Look, whatever your damage is, you better have dealt with it by the time we get to the plant. I need you all smiles. I know that's a tall order for you, but for God's sake try." She returned her gaze to the road. "And for the record, I'm not happy about having to take you along."

Emily pulled herself up and brushed down her jacket. "The only reason you're getting your hands on this story is because of me. I have every right to come along. Besides, Evan wants me to be there."

"The only reason *you* have this story in the first place is because I gave you Evan Holt. So, I have every right to be here, too. And anyway, if you'd agreed to let me help you in the first place, I wouldn't have had to be so damn sneaky. As soon as I saw Evan Holt's name in the diary I knew this was going to be something big. Evan is a very well-respected investigative journalist. If it wasn't for me, you'd still be running around claiming broken hearts and clandestine affairs."

Emily returned her gaze to the passenger window. "You know, you could have just come out and told me about Evan Holt."

"And where's the fun in that? Besides, you'd pissed me off."

"What if I hadn't worked out it was you that sent the message?"

Helen smiled as the traffic finally broke up. She pressed her foot down on the accelerator. "Come on, Emily. You're stupid, but you're not *that* stupid."

It took almost an hour to break free from the city. Helen surprised Emily by leaving her to her thoughts. She used the time to text Carter: *Any luck with Anya Copeland?* He replied a few minutes later: *Nothing. Sorry. Any other ideas?*

Emily could think of none. But since her meeting at the Lions Inn, she had tracked down Anya's previous address and had passed it on to Evan. Hopefully, he would have better luck finding her. Or perhaps Helen would.

Now, as they headed southeast along the A2, urban chaos falling behind them, Helen cleared her throat.

"Here's how today's going to happen. The feature for which I'm interviewing Jonathan Hunt concerns Valence Industries' efforts to reduce its impact on the environment, as well as its more philanthropic endeavours such as the Clean Water Project. As far as he's concerned, we're writing for Star News Chronicle. There's no way Hunt would entertain the idea of an interview with London Truth."

"What if his people check?"

"I have a friend on the Chronicle who owes me a favour—we're covered. All you need to do is flash a smile, take some notes, try not to fuck things up."

"Aren't you going to record the interview?" Emily asked, ignoring Helen's attempts to rile her.

"Yes, but you're my intern and you need to be doing more than just twiddling your thumbs. I don't want any distractions. What I do want is Jonathan Hunt eating out of my hands."

Emily studied her face. "I hope you're not planning anything. Evan said in no way are we to mention TEL."

"I know what he said. Take a pill, why don't you." Helen shot Emily a teasing smile. "Just relax, okay? I've got it covered."

Emily's eyes narrowed. "What if I think of some questions?"

"You keep them to yourself. You're the intern. Your job is to watch and learn—in silence." Helen cast a quick glance over Emily's attire. "By the way, you look like you're dressed for a day trip to the morgue. At least undo that top button for Christ's sake."

Emily glared at the journalist. Begrudgingly, she did what she was told. Helen inspected her once more.

"No makeup?"

"I don't wear it."

"Well, today you're not you—you're my intern. And she at least wears eyeliner. There's some in my bag."

"Do I use my real name?"

"I thought about that. Seeing how you've been snooping around, it might not be a good idea. So for today, your name is Meryl Silkwood."

Forests and fields zipped past the windows as the A2 merged with the M2. Traffic had thinned out considerably, prompting Helen to hit the accelerator.

They headed northeast, past Higham and on to Cliffe Woods. The road narrowed, slicing through villages of whitewashed houses with red slate roofs. Soon, they were driving along a winding private road. Wide stretches of gloomy-looking marshland rolled out in all directions.

Emily fidgeted in the passenger seat, shooting anxious glances at Helen. It was a gamble having her involved. The journalist had already proven at Meadow Pines that her ambition was greater than her compassion. That kind of reckless determination was either going to pay off in a good way—getting the required quote from Jonathan Hunt—or it was going to alert Valence Industries to the fact the company was being investigated. But it was a risk Evan Holt was willing to take, even when Emily had warned him about Helen's ruthless ambition.

As Valence Industries loomed on the horizon, a silver fortress of steel towers, turrets and pipes, Emily hoped bringing Helen on board was the right choice.

"Here, put this on."

Helen handed her a Star News Chronicle ID badge. Her temporary moniker, Meryl Silkwood, was printed to the right of her photograph. The word 'Intern' was printed in large red letters at the top. Emily clipped it to her shirt, just as the car approached a security barrier.

"Helen Carlson, Star News Chronicle. I have an appointment with Jonathan Hunt." Helen flashed her ID and a toothy smile as the security guard peered down from his cabin. His steely eyes narrowed as he examined the badge, then the car's passengers.

"One moment."

As he called up to the plant, Emily and Helen shared a look that was equal parts excitement and nerves. The guard hung up the phone. The security barrier began to lift and the guard waved them through.

They drove the rest of the way in silence. Valence Industries loomed up ahead like a futuristic city. It was such a strange, alien construct, like nothing Emily had seen before.

Helen drove into a parking bay and switched off the car engine. "Nervous?" she asked, handing Emily a stick of eyeliner.

Emily pulled down the visor and began applying the makeup. "Are you?"

"Nerves are healthy. They keep you on your toes. Besides, being overconfident leads to mistakes."

One eye quickly made up, Emily went to work on the other. When she was done, she leaned back a little and peered at her reflection. Meryl Silkwood stared back.

"Okay," Helen said, nodding in approval. "Let's go make a fool out of Jonathan Hunt."

18

RECEPTION WAS THROUGH a set of double doors and past a second security guard, who searched their bags and checked their badges. The receptionist, a dark-haired woman with a polite if slightly aloof smile, signed them in and asked them to take a seat. By the time Jonathan Hunt arrived ten minutes later, Emily's anxiety had worked its way into her limbs, making them shift from one uncomfortable position to the next, and prompting Helen to put a firm hand on her shoulder.

Jonathan Hunt was in his mid-fifties, tall, with a shock of peppery hair slicked to one side. His expensive suit had been well-tailored, tucking in at the right places to disguise his paunch. As he approached, his stern face broke into a measured smile. There was nothing genuine about it, Emily noted; it was just part of the show.

"Mr. Hunt," Helen said, an equally disingenuous smile spreading across her lips as she shook his hand. "Helen Carlson. Star News

Chronicle. Thank you so much for agreeing to speak with me."

"Oh, the pleasure's mine, Miss Carlson." His voice was solid, confident, like a man well-rehearsed in dealing with the press. Until he eyed Emily. "And who's this?"

Confusion momentarily rippled across his face, and Emily realized he'd had no idea Helen would be bringing company. It was a bold move on Helen's part, she thought; one that could end the interview before it had even started. Again, she silently wondered if involving her had been the wisest choice.

"This is Meryl, our intern," Helen said. "My apologies, Mr. Hunt. I should have phoned ahead and asked if I could bring her along, but in my excitement, she completely slipped my mind."

Jonathan Hunt's eyes were fixed on Emily's own. The temptation to look away was overwhelming, but she returned his stare and smiled.

"She'll just be sitting quietly, taking notes. Or if it's too much trouble, I'm sure Meryl won't mind waiting in the car."

The CEO's gaze shifted back to Helen.

"There's no need for that. We all have to start our careers somewhere." He leaned in and inspected Emily's ID badge. "Isn't that right, Miss Silkwood?"

"Of course." Emily nodded, then mentally recounted her new name over and over, as Jonathan Hunt led them past the reception desk and through a labyrinth of corridors. Outside his office, they were greeted by his personal assistant; an attractive young woman who smiled as they approached.

"Tanya, I'm in a meeting now for the next forty minutes. Take any messages. And would you mind bringing some coffee?"

"Of course, Mr. Hunt." The PA eyed the women as they were ushered into his office.

Hunt gestured to a sofa and armchairs. It was a large room with a view of the marshland. In the far distance, the Thames estuary wound its way toward the North Sea.

Now seated, Emily pulled out her notebook and pen, while Helen removed a digital voice recorder from her bag and placed it on the coffee table.

"A recording *and* notes. Is this an interrogation?" Mr. Hunt said, a teasing smile on his lips.

"It's a good opportunity for Meryl to practice her Teeline shorthand. The recording is for me—I would hate to misquote you." Helen's finger hovered over the record button. "May I?"

"Certainly. I do hate being misquoted—you know how journalists can be . . . present company excluded, I'm sure." Hunt clasped his hands together. "Shall we dive right in? I'm afraid time is against us."

"Of course."

Coffee arrived. The young PA placed the tray wordlessly on the table, then retreated to her desk outside. Attempting to quell the feverish beating inside her chest, Emily fixed her gaze on the carpet.

Helen went to work. Her first set of questions covered the evolution of Valence Industries, tracking its growth from a small plant in Illinois to its current status as dominant global empire. Next, she delved into the company's reasons for implementing a sustainable development department.

Jonathan Hunt listened carefully, with his head cocked at an angle and his eyes fixed on Helen. Every answer he gave was carefully delivered, as if he were reading from a teleprompter.

"We were aware of the negative impact the chemicals industry can have on the environment," he said. "But it was not until we conducted thorough research into the subject that we realized just how destructive that impact was. Yes, advances are being made every day in the field of chemistry toward more environmentally-friendly processes and materials, but the question I ask is: are we doing enough? I, for one, do not wish to bear the responsibility of my grandchildren growing up in a world where crops cannot grow, or water is poisoned, or the very air they breathe is toxic. Which is why I set up the sustainability department."

He paused, eyes shifting from Helen to Emily, a fixed, self-congratulatory smile on his lips. Emily returned his smile as she jotted down notes. If Valence Industries was responsible for selling TEL in developing countries, then Hunt was either in the dark about it, or he was a convincing liar.

Helen nodded. "So, you'd say the environment is something you've always been passionate about?"

The CEO gazed at Emily for a second longer, then turned his attention to the journalist.

"Let's say it was a gradual process. I'll admit I had a lot to learn at first. My daughter will be pleased to hear she was instrumental in opening my eyes to all manners of environmental issues. It was through her that I learned just how much industrial pollution is contributing to the very real threat of climate change." He paused, eyeing his captive audience. "I want Valence Industries to be a pioneer of change within the chemicals industry. To lead by example. The sustainability department was just the beginning. But it was a good place to start.

"Within the first three years of the department's inception, we reduced our greenhouse gas and energy emissions by almost twenty percent, and we introduced water and waste reduction programmes with very promising results. You see, I believe that to tackle a global problem, you must first begin at home. Only then can you extend a helping hand to the Third World."

Helen smiled. "All those reductions must save money as well."

"It's an agreeable by-product, shall we say? But the money we save is used to further our research into more sustainable and safer processing methods of our products. And of course, we also invest heavily into other environmental causes."

"Such as the Clean Water Project?"

"Among them, yes."

Helen leaned over, making a play of checking Emily's notes. "Perhaps you'd like to tell us a bit more about the Clean Water Project—how you became involved; who set it up; how successful it's been."

Emily listened as Hunt spent the next five minutes reiterating much of what she'd already learned about the Clean Water Project. Unsurprisingly, there was no mention of Max Edwards. Emily chewed her lower lip, desperate to fire some of her own questions at the CEO. As Hunt spoke, his eyes wandered back to Emily, then moved down to her hands. She had stopped taking notes. Distracting him with a smile, she picked up her pen and began scribbling on the page. By the time Hunt had finished talking, his gaze was like a pendulum, swinging back and forth between Helen and her intriguingly quiet intern.

"I'm impressed," Helen said. "It's refreshing to hear a global company like Valence Industries can act so conscientiously. You and your sustainability team should be commended." Helen leaned forward an inch, her smile fading. "But there's one issue that confuses me, Mr. Hunt. I'm sure it's some sort of misunderstanding. . ."

Emily's heart thumped in her chest as she shot a glance at Helen. What was she about to say?

Jonathan Hunt leaned back in his chair, his charismatic charm momentarily withdrawing enough to catch a glimpse of something hostile beneath.

"Oh? And what's that?"

Emily swivelled her eyes back to Helen. *Don't,* she thought. *Don't you dare.*

But it was too late.

"It's just that we've heard rumblings of Valence Industries' involvement in the processing and exportation of TEL, I believe it's called. Tetraethyl Lead? Am I pronouncing that right?"

Jonathan Hunt was unmoving, like a snake eyeing its prey. Emily swallowed and dropped her gaze to her notes. Inside, anger burned its way through her body. The one question Helen was not supposed to ask had just been dumped in Hunt's lap like a pile of shit. But now the question was out, she couldn't help but wonder how he would answer.

The silence in the room grew thick and cloying, like the air before a thunderstorm. Hunt's expression remained unchanging; a half smile frozen on his lips.

"I thought we were here today to discuss our positive impact on the environment," he said at last.

It was all over. But no one had told Helen that.

"We are, Mr. Hunt. But don't you think it's an issue that should be addressed? The export of TEL to developing countries does seem to conflict with everything we've discussed today. After all, TEL has been banned in almost every corner of the world, and with very good reason."

Hunt's left eye twitched once, then was still. "Suddenly I have the distinct feeling there may be an ulterior motive for this interview."

"I can assure you there are no ulterior motives," Helen said. "I'm sure it's probably some sort of miscommunication. After all, it makes no sense that Valence Industries would be involved in something so unethical—no matter how legal—when your passion for the environment and the health of our children is so abundantly clear."

Helen flashed a smile. Unaware she was holding her breath, Emily's eyes swivelled between interviewer and interviewee.

"Quite." Jonathan Hunt smiled coolly. He nodded at the wall clock. "Unfortunately, that's all I have time for today. If you have any further *appropriate* questions, please email them to my PA."

Standing, the CEO buttoned his jacket, then shook hands with his visitors.

Helen flashed him one last smile. "Thank you for your time, Mr. Hunt. It's much appreciated."

"I'll look forward to reading your article with great interest." He walked them out to the PA's desk. "Tanya, would you mind showing our guests out?"

Shooting Emily one last glance, he retreated to his office and closed the door.

*

"Did you see him squirm? The slimy, lying shit!"

Valence Industries shrank in the distance as the blue Renault made its way along the private road, back toward civilization. Emily had managed to contain her anger while they'd been escorted from the plant. But now it erupted like a volcano.

"What the hell have you done?" she hissed. "One question, Helen! That's all you had to stay away from. But no. You had to let your overinflated ego ruin it all!"

"Relax, would you? We have him on tape practically orgasming over how committed he is to saving the planet. Did you hear his exact words? He didn't want his grandkids breathing in toxic air! Do you know how amazing that quote's going to be right next to a picture of kids sucking on exhaust pipes? Shame on him!"

"You already had your quote, so why go and mention TEL?" Emily bit down on her lip. She was furious. But more than that, she was scared. "You're reckless, Helen. And bloody arrogant!"

Helen slowed the car. They were approaching the security barrier. "Everything will be fine. Now turn that frown upside down and smile."

The security guard watched them through the cabin window. Emily looked straight ahead. On the other side of the barrier, a car was approaching; a silver, sporty number that looked like it cost more than Emily's annual rent.

"You better hope everything will be fine," Emily said, with a forced smile. "But I can guarantee that Evan will *not* be happy."

The security barrier was lifting. Helen rolled the car forward.

"Leave that teddy bear to me. I agree it was a risky move, but it was one I was prepared to make. Sometimes the risky questions get you the best answers."

"Well, not in this case." Emily glanced into the wing mirror and saw the chemical plant in the distance. Valence Industries was making a fortune selling their poison to the vulnerable, and they were creating that poison right here, right behind her. "I hope for everyone's sake you haven't just complicated matters."

"It's fine. We have the quote. End of story."

Emily shook her head. The muscles in her shoulders were knotted and tight. She was about to tell Helen how it very probably wasn't the end, when she glanced across at the other car.

"Shit!"

"What is it?"

Emily immediately turned her head. "That's Tim Marsden!"

"Are you sure?"

"Of course, I'm sure!"

"Did he see you?" Helen pressed down on the accelerator, sailing through security and past the silver car.

Spinning around, Emily stared through the back window. "I don't know. Maybe."

"Well, let's not panic just yet. Let's go meet Evan and figure out our next move."

But as they zipped along country roads and back on to the A2, Emily could do nothing but panic. She knew only too well what happened when corrupt men in power discovered you were watching them. It was bad enough Helen had potentially informed Valence Industries it was under investigation, but what about Tim Marsden?

Emily was now convinced he had seen her. That their eyes had met. But would he tell Jonathan Hunt? It was entirely possible—when she'd met Marsden last week, his loyalty to the company had been resolute.

Pressing her head against the window, Emily closed her eyes. As London's cityscape appeared in the distance, glinting in the emerging sun like Emerald City, she counted her breaths in and out, and wondered if they'd just made a terrible mistake.

19

EVAN HOLT LIVED on the thirteenth floor of a local authority-owned tower block; the kind that all over London were being sold to property developers, who would paint the walls magnolia, throw down laminate flooring, and advertise the property as: 'modern apartments to rent with panoramic city views'. But Evan lived in a less than desirable part of Elephant and Castle, where most people feared to tread at night, and so the chance of his tower block being snatched up for redevelopment was minimal.

In some ways, Evan's apartment reminded Emily of Harriet Golding's home. Stacks of newspapers and magazines covered most available surfaces, making sizeable rooms feel cramped and claustrophobic. But unlike Harriet, Evan seemed unused to receiving visitors. Emily watched as he picked up journals to make room on the sofa, then spent the next few moments turning in slow circles, attempting to find the journals a new home. Once they were sitting down, Emily and Helen reported back on their visit to Valence Industries. Helen played select extracts from the recording of her interview with Jonathan Hunt. Then she surprised Emily by admitting she had asked Hunt about TEL.

"It was impulsive," she explained. "Sometimes you need to ask the risky questions, right?"

Evan's pensive expression remained the same. If he was angry, he wasn't letting on. "Well, it's out there now, I suppose. The question is, will Hunt do anything about it?"

"There's something else," Emily said. "Tim Marsden saw me as we were driving out."

"He *may* have seen you," Helen corrected.

"But if he did, it's possible he would have mentioned it to Jonathan Hunt. It won't take more than a few seconds to work out Meryl Silkwood doesn't exist."

Evan surprised Emily by laughing. "Meryl Silkwood? What kind of alias is that?"

Helen picked up a magazine and pretended to examine its cover. "I wouldn't worry about it," she said. "As soon as I mentioned TEL, alarm bells would have gone off. It won't take long for Hunt's people to dig around and find out who I really write for. Then they'll think they're being investigated by London Truth. So let them."

"That puts you at risk," Emily said.

"What are they going to do? They must know the truth about TEL will come out eventually. I'm sure they have a whole PR campaign already prepped in the event of exposure."

Evan removed a pile of newspapers from a wooden stool and perched on its edge. "Helen's right. I'm sure they're fully prepared and briefed. They'll expect their reputation to take a hit. The environmental groups they're working with such as E.C.G. will want to distance themselves immediately, and that's going to cause problems for the projects they've been collaborating on. But Valence know they'll survive this, and they'll continue selling TEL until the law says they can't."

Emily was outraged at such a notion. But she wasn't alone.

"Come on, they wouldn't dare!" Helen cried. "The press will drag them through the mud. There'll be a public outcry demanding a change in exportation laws. Eco-activists will be all over them."

"And you think that will stop them?" Evan smiled as he clasped his hands across his stomach. "Companies like Valence Industries rule the world. They're wealthy and they're powerful. They know they can sell poison like TEL and get away with it, too. If they have a problem, they flash some money and they make it go away. Tell the world about TEL and yes, you'll hurt them. But the pain will be a bee sting. Soon, it will fade. Some other scandal will grab the public's attention, and then it'll be business as usual. The only thing that's going to stop Valence Industries from producing and selling TEL is if the law changes. Or if we find something incriminating."

"Like the death of Max Edwards," Emily said.

Evan shook his head. "Bigger than that. I'm sorry, Emily, but the accidental death of a known alcoholic isn't going to cut it. Regardless of what we may or may not believe about Max Edwards' death, there isn't a shred of evidence to prove he was murdered." He was on his feet again, pacing the room. "But what we do know is that Max found something. And whatever it is, he believed it was powerful enough to ruin them."

Her face pulled into a scowl, Helen leaned forward on the sofa. "What if we don't find that evidence? What if Valence try to stop us running the story? I say we make a move on it now, while we can. Maybe the story won't take them down, but it will punch a hole in them—maybe even wide enough for the eco groups to do the rest. And who says a public outcry won't force a change in exportation laws? It's too great a chance to pass by."

"But if we hold on for just a while longer, we could find out more," Evan said. "We still have leads to chase. Max must have had help to get his evidence, so let's find out who helped him. We look into his history as an environmentalist, specifically at his involvement with the more, shall we say, passionate groups. Plus, there's still Anya Copeland. And I'm waiting on some intel from overseas that could prove useful."

Helen's eyes narrowed. "What intel?"

"I have a guy looking into Valence's market competitors. I want to know why no unleaded alternative has tried to take its crown."

"Maybe it's because they're sitting around waiting for something to happen instead of striking while they can."

"Maybe if you had a little more experience under your belt, you'd see that waiting is sometimes your best weapon."

As the journalists continued to argue, Emily slowly detached herself from the conversation. What exactly did Max Edwards mean to them?

For Evan, he was just an information source that could help him expose yet another corrupt company, while cementing his reputation as an investigative force to be reckoned with. For Helen, Max Edwards meant another step up the career ladder. More than a step. A story as shocking as the wilful poisoning of millions of children would win interest from the major media players—as would working alongside renowned investigative journalist Evan Holt.

But Max Edwards was surely more than just a helping hand. He was a man, a husband, a son, a friend—a passionate believer in right and wrong. And yes, he'd been flawed and he'd been troubled. And yes, his alcoholism had damaged Diane just as much as it had damaged him. But Max Edwards was whole and human. It hurt Emily to think he'd been reduced to nothing more than a stepping stone.

This was not why Diane had hired her. Not to further Helen's career. Not to help Evan prove yet again just how toxic the world really was. And yet it seemed the only way to discover what had really happened to Max Edwards was for Emily to play her part in doing both these things.

The journalists had ceased arguing and now stood on opposite sides of the room. Amid the silence, Emily cleared her throat.

"I'm going home," she said, scowling at them both. "I'll visit Max's wife tomorrow and ask her about his activist friends. I need to give her an update, anyway."

Feeling exhausted and her head still reeling from the day's events, she turned to leave.

"I'm away for the next few days," Evan said. When Helen glared at him, he added, "It's for another story. I'll be back next week."

"What do you think, Emily?" Helen stared at her from across the room. "Should we wait or should we run the story?"

Emily avoided the journalists' competing gazes. "I agree with Evan. We don't know what we're dealing with yet, especially now Jonathan Hunt and co. know they're being investigated. Who knows what kind of repercussions there could be."

Folding her arms, Helen sank back on the sofa. "There are always repercussions, no matter what road you take," Evan said, looking away. "It comes with the territory."

With his words still echoing in her ears, Emily left the flat and hurried to the lift. As she reached the graffiti-covered lobby, her phone started ringing. But it was not Jerome as she'd hoped.

"Miss Swanson? It's Manik Singh calling. I have information that may prove to be of use. One of the night porters claims to have seen Mr. Edwards leave the hotel during the night. He wasn't alone."

Emily's anxiety was swept away by a wave of excitement. "Really? Who was with him?"

"Perhaps if you come to the hotel you could speak to the night porter yourself? He'll be on duty at nine."

"I'll be there as soon as I can," Emily replied. Her tiredness now evaporated, she hung up and hurried across the lobby, out into the darkening street.

20

ANDY BARTLETT WAS a tall and pimply nineteen-year-old, whose body jerked and twitched beneath his ill-fitting uniform as he answered Emily's questions. At first, Emily thought it was nerves, then she noticed the empty bottle of cola stashed behind the reception desk. Mr. Singh had already left for the night. The lobby was empty. Piano music and subdued chatter floated out from the bar.

"So this man," she said to Andy, who seemed to be having a hard time making eye contact. "What time did he show up?"

"About three, three-thirty. He was hanging around the lobby, said he was waiting for a friend to come down. I thought it was a bit weird 'cause it was so late. But then that guy came down—Mr. Edwards—and I was like, okay then, maybe he's a drug dealer, 'cause they were whispering and then Mr. Edwards pulled out an envelope. But he didn't give it to the guy. He gave it to me. Asked if it could be sent out with the morning post. I said, yeah, whatever. He tipped me a fiver, then the two of them left."

"And Max—Mr. Edwards—he didn't come back?"

"Not that I saw, and I was on till seven."

"What about the envelope he gave you? What happened to it?"

"I put it with the rest of the mail, so I suppose it went out in the morning with everything else."

"You don't remember who it was addressed to?"

Andy shrugged a shoulder up and down.

"What about the man that was with Mr. Edwards. Did you hear his name? What did he look like?"

Andy's gaze moved up to the lobby ceiling, high above his head. "Can't remember a name. He was old, maybe forty-something. Blond hair in a ponytail. And he had a beard as well, I think."

The description didn't fit anyone Emily had met so far. "And how did they seem with each other? Were they friendly?"

Andy replied with another shoulder shrug.

"Did Mr. Edwards leave of his own free will?"

The porter stifled a laugh. "The bloke didn't have a gun on his back if that's what you mean. They knew each other; you could tell."

Questions running through her mind, Emily glanced over the lobby. Who was this man that Max had disappeared with? What had the envelope contained, and who had been its recipient? She turned back to Andy, who'd picked up his phone and was busy texting.

"There's nothing else you can remember about that night? Nothing that stands out?"

"Nope," the porter replied, his eyes glued to the phone screen.

Irritated, Emily snatched the phone from his hand and placed it on the desk. Andy's expression flicked from shocked to annoyed to scolded schoolboy.

"I doubt I would have remembered anything at all if the guy hadn't died," he said, shrugging.

"And you didn't tell any of this to the police? To anyone else?"

Andy shook his head and stared longingly at his phone. "No one asked."

Emily had no more questions. She asked for the porter's phone number, which he reluctantly gave her, then told him she would be in touch.

"So, you're like a private detective or something?" he asked, meeting her gaze for the first time.

"Something like that." Emily said goodnight, crossed the lobby toward the exit, then stopped. "One more thing. Did Mr. Edwards seem like he'd been drinking?"

Andy glanced up from his phone. "You mean was he drunk? Don't think so—he seemed pretty sober to me."

Emily's mind raced as she left the hotel and hurried along the dark street. Max Edwards had left the Riverside Hotel at three in the morning with a man he knew—and he'd been sober. The more Emily was finding out about Max Edwards, the less credible the coroner's conclusion of 'death by misadventure' was becoming.

21

THE 11:17 A.M. train to Epsom Downs was half empty, giving Emily a row of seats to herself and the space to stretch out her weary limbs. When she'd finally gone to bed, sleep had evaded her. There had been too many thoughts swimming in the mirk of her mind, all knotting together until she'd started to get a headache.

Now, as she travelled toward Diane Edwards' home in Surrey, those thoughts were no less clear. And it wasn't just Max Edwards clogging her brain; Jerome was in there, too. She had sent him another text message, had tried calling him again, but his response had been stony silence.

Then there was her conversation with her therapist, Kirsten Dewar. Perhaps when this was all over, she would take Kirsten's advice. After all, conducting a little research wasn't the same as making a commitment, and having options was better than holding onto an uncertain, blank future.

When Emily arrived at the house just after 1 p.m., Diane greeted her with a polite smile and showed her into the kitchen, where a pot of tea and a plate of sandwiches waited on the table.

"I didn't know what you eat, so I kept it simple," Diane said.

Emily wasn't hungry at all, but for the sake of politeness she nibbled on a cheese sandwich.

"I'm very curious about what you've found so far," Diane said, watching her eat. "But I'm sure you'll share your findings once you're ready."

"I will. I don't want to tell you anything without the proof to back it up," Emily said.

Diane's face soured. "Sounds like you've discovered something that will be painful to hear."

"I just want to be certain of all the facts," Emily explained. "The last thing I want to do is give you misinformation."

"Of course."

Diane fell silent, staring emptily into her teacup. It couldn't be easy for her, Emily thought—delving into the past, reliving every negative feeling.

"I need to ask you a few more questions about Max. Did he talk much about his work?"

"I know the Clean Water Project was his focus for that last year or so," Diane said. "He told me snippets here and there about how it was progressing, the countries where it would be implemented, that kind of thing."

"And did Max ever talk about his colleagues? The people he worked with on the project. . ."

"He mentioned names from time to time. Of course, there was Tim Marsden, who I'd met on occasion. There were others, but if

I'm honest, most of the time I was half listening."

Emily hesitated. "What about Anya Copeland?"

The twinge in Diane's left eye was small but telling. "I. . . Yes, I think he mentioned her. Why?"

Her eyes were filling with hurt, growing wet and shiny.

"It's nothing to worry about for now," Emily said. The panic on Diane's face remained. "There's a man, perhaps a friend of Max's—forties, blond hair in a ponytail. Does that sound like anyone you've met before?"

Diane shook her head then stared out at the lawn, deep lines creasing her forehead. Emily continued with her questions. "Was Max still in contact with friends from his activist days? People he went on protests with, eco group members. . ."

The women stared at each other, searching their expressions for clues. Diane heaved her shoulders, expelling a heavy breath.

"What is this about, Emily? I know you don't want to misinform me, but now I'm worried. Was Max in some kind of trouble?"

Emily looked away, wondering if she should share what she'd learned with Diane. After all, nothing would ever hurt more than the news of her husband's death, which had clearly broken the woman into a hundred pieces. But causing needless suffering—especially without a shred of evidence—was not Emily's way of doing business.

"To be honest, I'm not sure," she said. "But what I do know is there are still some questions that remain unanswered, and I was hoping you might be able to help with one of them."

She asked Diane about the blond man again. "Does he sound familiar? One of Max's friends, perhaps."

Diane pressed her hands together and stared out the window. "If truth be told, Max didn't have a lot of friends. He lost most of them during his drinking days. It doesn't sound like any of Max's friends I know of, but that doesn't mean anything."

"What about friends in environmental groups? You said he was quite the activist in his younger days."

Diane was lost in thought for a few seconds. Her eyes lit up with an idea. Beckoning Emily toward the hall, she showed her into a small, windowless office, with just enough space to fit a desk and a one-drawer filing cabinet.

"Max spent the last year of our marriage hidden away in here," Diane said. She hovered in the doorway as if the boundary that had been set by her husband continued to exist. She pointed to a shelf above the desk. "Those are photograph albums from his younger days. He quite liked taking pictures. Wasn't very good at it, though. I haven't looked through them in a while, but there are pictures from back in the day. Be careful with them, won't you?"

"Of course." Emily cast her eyes over the rest of the office, imagining Max Edwards hunched over the desk, plotting to take down corrupt corporations. "Did Max have a computer at home?"

"Yes, but it was stolen in the break in, along with everything else."

Emily stared at her. "You were robbed?"

"You hear about thieves casing houses, don't you? Watching and waiting to see when people come and go." Diane heaved her shoulders as a sad sigh escaped her lips. "Those animals waited until I was on the way to church to bury my husband."

Emily stared at the empty surface of the desk. A coincidence? She wasn't entirely convinced. Regardless, the robbery would have been a kick in the gut for a woman who'd already suffered so much.

"They turned the house upside down," Diane continued. "The police were very kind and very thorough, but they never did catch them. These days, they rarely do." She continued to hover for a few seconds more, then said, "I'll be in the kitchen if you need me."

She closed the door behind her, leaving Emily in the centre of the cramped room. The walls closed in around her. Opening the door again, she took the photograph albums down from the shelf and began working her way through the pages. It seemed pointless wading through the pictures without Diane, but she persevered.

Many of the photographs were taken in the late 80s and early 90s. Several depicted various environmental and human rights protests across the country and beyond. Here was Max, wearing a CND T-shirt, carrying a placard that demanded the collapse of the Berlin Wall. And here was Max, halfway up a tree in protest against the construction of the Newbury bypass. In these early photographs, his eyes crackled with fiery conviction.

Now Emily could see why he'd been driven to expose the wrongdoings of Valence Industries. The company had betrayed his beliefs. It had used him as an unwitting distraction while it had indulged in the very activities he'd spent much of his life fighting against. And Valence was still doing it; only now with Tim Marsden in his place.

Emily continued to flip through the albums, scanning through the photographs and pinpointing faces that showed up repeatedly over the years, including those belonging to a number of blond-haired men.

She found Diane sitting at the kitchen table, busy writing a list. Outside, clouds smothered the sky and spots of rain speckled the windows.

"I've been trying to think of names," Diane said. "People that Max used to hang around with in those days. But it's been so long and my memories are rusty."

"Perhaps this will help."

Emily placed the albums in front of Diane, who regarded them through wary eyes. The next few minutes were spent with Emily pointing at various men and Diane attempting to recall their names. By the time Emily had turned the final page, they had identified four people who matched the description the night porter had given. Diane hadn't seen any of them for years and didn't know where they could be found.

Emily went to close the album, but Diane held up a hand. She continued to stare at the photographs on the page, at her husband's happy, defiant face.

"That girl," she said, without looking up. "Anya Copeland. She and Max worked together?"

"That's right." Emily could see the muscles in Diane's face growing taut. She waited for her to ask more, but her silence was a clear indicator of her suspicions. Had there been other indiscretions during their marriage? Emily decided it was not her business to ask. But she did have one more question.

"After Max passed away, did you receive anything from him in the mail? A package?"

Diane squeezed her eyes shut and shook her head. "No, I didn't. Emily, what's this all about?"

Emily put a hand on her arm. "I'll explain everything soon. I just need a little more time."

"Then lucky for you," Diane said, staring up at her, "that time is all I have."

22

LATE AFTERNOON RAIN was coming down in heavy drifts as Emily left Diane and made her way to the bus stop. Diane had not permitted her to take photographs from the album, so Emily had taken copies using her phone camera. She thought about sending the pictures to the night porter, Andy Bartlett, then decided twenty-year-old images weren't going to help refresh the young man's memory.

As Emily hurried along the pavement, she saw just two other people braving the bad weather: a young mother on the opposite side of the street, who was getting soaked as she rolled a pram in front of her, and a man walking behind Emily, who was dressed in a navy-blue raincoat, his face obscured by an umbrella.

As the bus pulled up and Emily boarded, she briefly thought about asking for Helen's help to locate the men on Diane's list, then decided to leave her as a last resort—all Helen had achieved so far was prove she couldn't be trusted. Emily had been wrong to involve her in the investigation. Now she would have to live with any repercussions.

Heading to the back of the bus, Emily sat down in a window seat. The driver pulled away, then jolted to a halt. The doors opened again and the man in the navy-blue raincoat stepped on board. Water dripped from his shaved head. Emily watched him thank the driver, before returning her gaze to the window. Her mind wandered back to her conversation with Kirsten Dewar. Once life had returned to normal, she would have a serious think about her future. Until then, her focus had to stay glued on Max Edwards. Everything else—her apartment, her career, her finances, Carter, even Jerome—would be tackled when she was ready.

Two hours later, when Emily stepped out of Farringdon rail station, the rain was still coming down hard. Hopping on the crowded bus that would take her back to The Holmeswood, she wedged herself in between the other standing passengers. Water dripped from raincoats and folded umbrellas. A young couple stood centimetres in front of Emily's face, their lips locked in a passionate kiss. She looked away. Then caught her breath.

In between the bodies, she saw a flash of blue raincoat and the back of a shaved head. Was it the same man she had seen outside of Diane Edwards' home? The same man who'd then jumped on the bus seconds after her? She stared at the back of his head. What were the chances that he would be taking the exact same journey?

Her heart thumping, Emily pushed her way toward the back of the bus, until she had positioned herself behind two tall men.

The bus ground to a halt and the doors opened. People got out. More climbed in, pushing the passengers closer together. Emily stared through the gaps. She could no longer see the man in the blue raincoat. Was she being paranoid? After all, how many men wearing blue raincoats were milling about the city right now? Hundreds, if not thousands.

When she exited the bus a few minutes later, her shoulders heaved with relief. A handful of other passengers had stepped off with her, but there were no men in blue coats. As the bus waited to reinsert itself in the traffic, Emily turned to walk the last stretch of the journey home.

She froze. Someone was watching her. She could feel their eyes boring into her skin.

Turning to look back at the bus, she saw a man's face peering at her through one of the lower deck windows. It was just for a second. Then he was gone. But a second had been long enough to send slivers of ice sliding down the back of Emily's neck.

23

EMILY SPENT THE rest of the evening at home with the door locked and all the lights switched on. The rain grew heavier until it sounded like it would smash through the windows. Emily watched the street below, looking for conspicuous figures. She stared across the street at the steamy glass front of *Il Cuore*, then retreated to the kitchen. Throwing together a quick pasta dinner, she ate at the table while she searched online for the names and faces of Max's old friends.

Now that she was warm and dry and had a full belly, she wondered if the man in blue really had been following her. Perhaps she had imagined that face at the window. After all, paranoia could make you see things that weren't there. And it wouldn't be the first time she'd succumbed to paranoia. Then again, she reminded herself, it wouldn't be the first time she'd caught the attention of the wrong people, either.

Outside, the rain eased off. Emily returned her attention to the four names Diane had given her: Ben Adams, Callum O'Brien, Jason Dobbs, and Lucas Meyer. She approached each one systematically, scouring social media websites to gradually produce four groups of identically named people. She then went through each group, eliminating the men who didn't match the blond man's description.

Next, she whittled the groups down by analysing Facebook and Twitter profiles for mentions of environmental causes or political activism. It was a long and tedious task, but eventually she had eliminated Ben Adams and Callum O'Brien. Next up was Jason Dobbs. Emily changed tactics, Googling the name along with the keyword: *environmentalist.* The second result down stopped Emily in her tracks. She clicked on it and an obituary notice filled the screen.

> *Jason Henry Dobbs, 47, from Crystal Palace, London, passed away on Friday, 29 May. Mr. Dobbs, who was a passionate environmentalist involved in a number of green causes, leaves behind his wife, Lucy, and his two daughters. A non-religious funeral will be held at Crystal Palace crematorium on Wednesday, 10 June at 3:45 p.m. No flowers at request of family.*

There was no photograph, but Emily knew she'd found something—Jason Dobbs had died the day after the Clean Water Project launch. The same day Max Edwards was discovered missing.

"Max's death wasn't an accident," she whispered to the room. Whatever he'd discovered about Valence Industries had ended his life. Jason's, too.

Emily jumped up from the table and hurried out to the hall, where she double-checked the door locks. Then she moved from room to room, making sure she was quite alone.

She had to tell someone.

But Evan wouldn't be back for another few days, and she certainly didn't trust Helen with this new, revelatory information.

Returning to the living room, Emily read over the obituary notice again and wondered if there was a slim chance this was not the Jason Dobbs she was looking for; that the date of his death and his passion for the environment were pure coincidence.

Right. And there's a chance Jerome might talk to me again, too.

She would need to confirm Jason Dobbs' identity. Perhaps tracking down his wife would reveal new information. For now, she closed the laptop, switched off the living room lights, and returned to the windows. People milled up and down the street, but fewer in number now. Across the road, *Il Cuore* was shrouded in darkness, the last of its customers ejected for the night. Her skin crawling, Emily wondered about the man in the blue raincoat. She wondered if he was down there right now, watching her.

24

CRYSTAL PALACE WAS a peaceful, leafy suburb surrounding a triangle of cafes, restaurants, and antique dealers, with panoramic views of the city. Lucy Dobbs lived on a quiet lane just off Church Road, on the ground floor of a large Victorian conversion. It was a nice home, Emily thought; welcoming and comfortable.

She sat with Lucy in the living room, where a tortoiseshell cat was stretched out in front of the window, basking in the sunlight. The steep climb up Anerley Hill from the train station had burned more than a few calories, leaving Emily hot and sticky. Now she sipped iced water while she listened to Lucy speak.

"We hadn't seen Max for years," Lucy said, brushing auburn hair from blue eyes. "It was his drinking, I suppose. It became more important to him than his friends. So, you could say it was a bit of a surprise when he showed up out of the blue last year. I thought Jason would tell him to get lost—they'd been close back in the day, and

Jase had been pretty hurt when Max dropped him for the drink. But my husband was always too soft. That day when Max showed up, he forgave him straight away. Then it was like they'd seen each other yesterday, not twelve years earlier."

"How long was that before your husband passed away?" Emily asked, noting the way Lucy flinched at the words.

"About a month. Max said he wanted Jason to help him with something. I thought he had some nerve, showing up after all that time just to ask for help. I mean, not even a phone call to ask how Jase was doing. I don't understand it."

"What did he need help with?"

"Jason said he wanted help building a website."

Emily noted the scepticism in her words. "Your husband was a designer?"

"Computer programmer, but he did some web stuff on the side." Lucy leaned back and glanced over at the framed photographs sitting on the mantelpiece. Two girls in their late teens stared back. "I thought that was weird, you know. I mean, there are thousands of web designers out there. Why go to the trouble of showing up on the doorstep of someone you haven't seen for twelve years just to ask them to do your website? I assumed it was a flimsy excuse for Max to get in touch with Jason again. You know what men are like—can't actually have emotions about anything, have to turn them into something practical. Well, that's what I believed at first."

Emily followed her gaze to the mantelpiece. "Your daughters?"

"They're both at university. Neither of them wanted to stay in London. I thought with all the universities in this big city, why go anywhere else? But they're both like their dad. Last year wasn't easy for them. For a while, I thought Ellie was going to drop out. She was closest to him. But she struggled through. She gets her stubbornness from her mum."

Emily returned her gaze to Lucy Dobbs and asked her next question. "I know this is not an easy conversation for you, but the obituary didn't say how Jason passed away."

The motherly love in Lucy's eyes was swallowed up by darkness. "They say he jumped from Hornsey Lane Bridge. Died on impact."

"I'm sorry. It must have been a terrible shock."

"There'd been a campaign going on for years to get a safety fence erected on that bridge. People seemed to like jumping off it. The fence went up five months after Jason died." Lucy glanced away, tears brimming in her eyes. "Five months. . ."

Setting her glass on the table, Emily silently compared the circumstances of both deaths. Max Edwards had died from an alcohol-induced fall into the Thames. Jason Dobbs had died by jumping off a known suicide bridge. Even if they hadn't died around the same time, the friends' deaths mirrored each other in uncanny ways.

"Did Jason ever. . ." How did she put this? "Had Jason ever displayed suicidal tendencies before?"

A sigh escaped Lucy's lips. "Jason suffered from depression. Had done since he was a kid. The doctors said it was a chemical imbalance, something he couldn't help. But he'd been taking antidepressants for years. His depression was well-managed. Yes, he had bouts here and there, that's to be expected, but he would talk to me and we'd work through it together. The girls didn't always quite understand it, but still. . . Jason had been doing really well for a long time. Until Max showed up." She said his name through clenched teeth. "All that bullshit about designing websites. Max was involved in something and he came to Jason because he needed help."

"Help with what?"

"I don't know. Jase kept saying he was helping with the damn website, even when I accused him of lying. They'd go off somewhere together or disappear into Jason's study for hours on end. It was obvious they were up to something, just like the old days. Back then, they were always plotting, always scheming ideas for this protest and that demo. There'd been one time years ago, the two of them had fallen in with a group of radicals. I didn't like it. Then I found out they'd been planning to break into a pharmaceutical facility and free all the animals kept there for testing. I lost my mind. The girls were barely toddlers. I told Jason: if you want to risk being thrown in jail then you go ahead, but you'll be doing it as a single man with restricted access to your kids. Needless to say, that little venture didn't get off the ground."

Lucy paused, shook her head. "No, they were up to something. But Jason wouldn't tell me what. He kept saying not to worry, everything's fine. Then he was dead. They both were—on the same damned day." She turned to Emily, her face fraught with desperation. "Do you know what it was? What they were doing to get themselves killed?"

Emily avoided the woman's gaze. "I'm still trying to find out."

It seemed senseless to cause Lucy further distress when there was still no definitive proof. Besides, wouldn't telling her put her at risk? Emily thought about the man in the blue coat again. No, it was safer to keep what she knew to herself for now.

"I went to the police, you know," Lucy said, as she pulled at the hem of her skirt. "As soon as I found out Max was dead too, I went straight to the police station and demanded to speak to someone. Sergeant Wallis agreed it was strange the two of them died within hours of each other. He suggested they'd had a suicide pact. He said there was no evidence to suggest otherwise, even when I insisted they'd been involved in something. I gave him Jason's computer, demanded that he take a look to see what he could find." Lucy's skin grew pale as she threw her hands in the air. "There was nothing. The whole computer had been wiped clean. And that was the end of it—the police stopped listening."

As Lucy dabbed her eyes with a tissue, Emily got up and crossed the room. First Max Edwards' computer was stolen. Now Jason Dobbs' computer had had its hard drive erased. Valence Industries was nothing if not thorough. Growing increasingly troubled, Emily turned her attention to the family photographs on the mantelpiece. One in particular caught her eye.

"Is this recent?" she asked.

Lucy came up beside her. "It's from a couple of years ago. We went camping in the Lake District."

In the photograph, Jason Dobbs stood in front of a khaki-coloured tent, dressed in shorts and a T-shirt with a wind turbine printed on the front, along with the slogan: *Blow Me!* His blond hair was pulled back in a ponytail. Days of stubble sprouted from his chin. He was smiling, white teeth on show, wrinkles at the corners of his eyes, as he flexed his biceps for the camera.

Pulling out her phone, Emily asked if she could take a copy. Suddenly lost for words, Lucy nodded. Then she reached out and grasped Emily's hand.

"That stupid bastard should have closed the door in Max's face," she said, tears spilling from her eyes. "He would still be here right now. My girls would still have a father."

Emily squeezed her hand. "When was the last time you spoke to Diane?"

"Years ago. We only knew each other through our husbands."

"Perhaps when this is all over, you should get in touch. Perhaps you could help each other."

Emily turned but Lucy tightened her grip on her hand.

"Promise me," she said, eyes locked on Emily's. "Promise me you'll find out the truth. If someone did this to Jason, I need to know. They need to be punished."

Emily stared back. She could feel Lucy's pain seeping through her fingers and into her veins. "The only promise I can make is that I'll do my best to find out the truth."

"Then I hope your best will be enough," the woman said.

*

After Emily had said goodbye, she immediately sent a text message to the Riverside Hotel night porter, Andy Bartlett, along with the picture she'd taken of Jason Dobbs.

A deep knot of anxiety twisted in her stomach. Diane Edwards and now Lucy Dobbs were relying on her to restore justice. To prove to the world that their husbands were good men. More than that, the women were depending on Emily to set them free.

Her legs feeling stiff and heavy, Emily journeyed back to the station. Every five metres or so, she looked over her shoulder or glanced at passing cars, wondering if she was being followed.

This is no way to live, she thought. But she wasn't sure if she was thinking about Diane and Lucy, or herself.

25

BY THE TIME Emily had returned to The Holmeswood, evening had fallen, casting the city in a monochrome hue. As she pressed the lift call button, her phone buzzed once in her hand. Andy Bartlett had sent a text message: *Pretty certain that's him. Do I win a cash prize? Or how about a date? Lol.*

Emily felt a rush of excitement. She quickly replied to the night porter's text message: *How about my gratitude and respect? Thank you!* As soon as she'd sent the message, her phone began to ring.

"Well, hello stranger," Helen said. "You've been awfully quiet. Where the hell have you been?"

Emily's shoulders tensed. "I've been busy. Speaking of which, have you had any luck with Anya?"

"Not yet. That woman really doesn't want to be found, does she? Anyway, what do you mean you've been busy? What are you hiding from me?"

"Nothing."

The lift arrived and the doors slid open. Emily was startled by a man exiting the lift. He nodded politely as they crossed paths. As the doors slid closed, Emily watched him cross the foyer, then she pressed the button for her floor.

"Actually, that's not entirely true," she said, figuring that Evan would be back tomorrow so it was safe to tell Helen about the death of Jason Dobbs and his mysterious meetups with Max Edwards. As she spoke, Helen listened without interrupting.

"Jason's wife said he was a computer programmer. What if he was helping Max hack into Valence's system so he could have a good look around?" The lift trembled as it came to a halt on the fourth floor. "There's something else. The night Max disappeared, the hotel porter saw him meet a man in the lobby. They left together around 3 a.m. The porter's just confirmed it was Jason Dobbs."

Emily rounded the corner and walked to her apartment.

"Someone *has* been busy," Helen said at last, her words clipped.

Emily couldn't help but find a little pleasure in her annoyance. "I thought I'd wait until I had something more concrete. But it's convincing, isn't it? Max turns up out of the blue on Jason's doorstep. A month later, they both die on the same day, one a suicide, the other a tragic accident."

"If Max hadn't been digging around Valence's dark corners, I'd call it a suicide love pact."

"You're not funny. What do you really think?"

"The plot thickens," Helen said. "This Jason guy's wife had no idea what the two of them were up to?"

Emily stopped outside her apartment and searched her bag for the keys. "No, but when she found out about Max, she went straight to the police and. . ."

Someone was behind her. Emily spun around.

"Hello, dear."

Harriet Golding was standing in her doorway across the hall. Emily wondered how much of the conversation she'd heard.

"Helen, I need to call you back."

"Okay, but I'm jumping on the train home in two minutes," Helen breathed in her ear. "If you can't get me, try again in thirty minutes."

Emily hung up. "Hello, Harriet."

"Everything all right, dear?" the elderly woman asked.

"Yes, fine. Andrew tidied up that mess yet?"

"Oh yes, he's a good boy, really." Harriet had a curious, twitchy smile on her lips. "You never told me you had a gentleman friend."

Finding her keys, Emily selected one and slid it into the lock. She wondered how Harriet had found out about Carter West—not that he *was* Emily's gentleman friend. Had Jerome been by again and said something?

"I don't know what you're talking about, Harriet," she said, cheeks flushing.

"Rubbish! I spoke to him just a few minutes ago. Didn't you see him on your way out?"

Emily froze.

"I just happened to be near my front door, minding my own business, when I heard someone coming out of your apartment," Harriet said. "Of course, I assumed it was you, and seeing how I haven't seen you all week, I thought I'd say hello."

Emily stared at her door, then back at Harriet. The hallway seemed to tip ninety degrees.

"I hope I didn't sound rude, but I had no idea you had a . . . guest. So, I asked him who he was. He said his name was Colin and he was visiting you from out of town. He was very polite. Said he was just popping to the shops so he could make you dinner tonight. How fancy! My husband never cooked me dinner, not once. And anyway, what must you think of me to keep him a secret! I mean, he may be a little too old for you, but. . ."

The man in the lift.

Emily's heart thudded. She turned the key. The door was already unlocked.

"What's the matter, dear?" Harriet said, the excitement draining from her face.

Emily gave the door a gentle push. "I don't know any Colin."

Behind her, Harriet began to stutter. "But he. . . I thought. . . He wasn't. . . Oh dear. . ."

The door came to a rest, bumping gently against the wall. Everything looked in order in the hall: the coat stand in the corner filled with jackets; the pictures on the walls; the imitation chandelier hanging from the high ceiling.

Blood rushing in her ears, Emily took a step forward.

"You shouldn't go in there, dear," Harriet said, holding on to the doorjamb. "You should call the police."

Emily cocked her head and listened. She heard the quiet hum of electricity and the faraway buzz of traffic. Somewhere down the hall, water pipes knocked and clunked.

"Was he carrying anything?" she whispered, desperately trying to recall the stranger's face.

"I don't remember. Sorry, love. Here, I'll call the police for you." But Harriet remained in the doorway, watching Emily move slowly down the hall.

The living room door was ajar. Through the gap, Emily saw shards of broken glass. She turned her head to check the other end of the hall. Then she entered the living room.

The man hadn't just broken into her home. He'd defaced it. Picture frames were torn from the walls. Cushions were slashed open, their guts spread over the room. Jerome's belongings were strewn across the floor.

Numbness consumed Emily's body as she entered the kitchen. Shards of crockery littered the surfaces. Food had been pulled from the refrigerator and dumped on the floor.

A similar scene was waiting inside her bedroom. Clothes lay on the carpet like bodies at the scene of a massacre. Bedsheets were torn. Blood rushing in her ears, Emily realized her laptop was gone, along with Max's paperwork and appointments diary.

Tim Marsden *had* seen her leaving Valence Industries, and he'd informed Jonathan Hunt, who'd quickly realized that Meryl Silkwood did not exist, that the interview had been a ruse to get him to admit to exporting TEL. And now Valence had entered her home and obliterated it, taking all the information she'd gathered about Max Edwards.

Emily felt sick and faint. Suddenly she couldn't breathe. She didn't feel safe in here.

Snatching up a handful of clothes, she stuffed them into a bag, then ran from the bedroom. Harriet was still hovering in the doorway, her face wrinkled with guilty lines.

"Did he get much?" she asked in a quiet voice.

Emily shut the front door and locked it. She couldn't stay here. She had to go. But where? Jerome was still not talking to her, and

Helen was—

Emily caught her breath. "Helen…"

"Why don't you come in and I'll make the tea while you call the police?" Harriet said with mounting concern. "Andrew's inside. He'll know what to do."

Emily wasn't listening. She pulled out her phone and dialled Helen's number. The call went straight to voicemail.

"Damn it!" She turned to Harriet. "I have to go. If anyone comes back, do not approach them."

"But, what about—"

"I mean it, Harriet. Stay inside with Andrew. Lock the door. I'll call you later."

Harriet stared at her with troubled eyes. Her mouth began to twitch. "But where are you going?"

Emily turned and hurried to the lift. Once she was inside and travelling downward, she made another call. A deep and melodic voice answered.

"Emily? I… How are you doing?"

"Daniel, I need your help."

"I'm not sure he'll want to—"

"This isn't about me and Jerome. I need Helen's address. Now, Daniel. Please!"

The lift reached the foyer. Emily raced out into the street. Long shadows stalked the pavements, devouring the last of the daylight. There were still plenty of people around. Emily weaved her way between them, glancing over her shoulder as she raced to the train station. Daniel's text message came through with Helen's address. Emily tried Helen's number again.

26

BY THE TIME Emily staggered out of Mile End station, darkness had already settled over the city. Although most of the journey had been over ground, the last stretch had taken her deep beneath the streets. Claustrophobic panic had sucked the breath from her lungs, leaving her paralyzed and stricken. Now, as she crossed the busy street and took a right onto Grove Road, she struggled to regain her balance. *You're all right,* she told herself. *You can breathe again. Relax.*

Traffic was quieter here. People milled along the pavements. Emily passed a strip of takeaways and ducked beneath a railway bridge, moving further away from the noise.

The map application on Emily's phone instructed her to take a right. She did so, passing a pub on the corner, where drinkers sat outside in the warm air, smoking cigarettes and talking about their days—normal days, where normal things had happened and no one had broken into their homes.

This road was darker. Pools of orange streetlight glowed like beacons in the shadows. Glancing behind, Emily tried to remember the last time she'd had a normal day. She came to a startling possibility that perhaps, for her, this *was* a normal day. One look back over the events of the past year could easily confirm it.

The road merged onto a long tree-lined street of Georgian terraced houses. Helen's house was on the other side, pitched in darkness. The front door was open a few centimetres; not enough to notice if you were passing by, but enough to get Emily's pulse racing even harder.

"Helen?" She pushed the door open. The streetlight did little to illuminate the darkness. "Are you in there?"

Emily was rooted to the doorstep, too afraid to enter. She hadn't called the police yet. She should have done so the moment she'd entered her ransacked apartment. Taking out her phone, her finger hovered over the keypad.

She hesitated. What if Helen was up there right now? What if she was hurt, maybe even unconscious on the living room floor? What if not going up there right now decided whether she lived or died? Helen had already escaped death once at Meadow Pines, and it had been a narrow escape. Would she be lucky enough again?

"Damn it." Emily stepped forward.

Just in front of her, the darkness moved.

A shadow hurtled forward like a blast of wind, slamming into her body with enough force to lift her off the ground. Arms flailing, Emily flew back and hit the path hard. Dazed, she rolled onto her knees, just in time to see her assailant dash into the street.

As Emily staggered to her feet, a car engine roared to life. Headlights dazzled her. Tires screeched. The car sped away.

Her breaths coming hard and heavy, Emily touched the back of her head. Spots of blood came away on her fingers. Wincing, she turned back to the house. Now she had no choice but to go up there.

"What the hell are you doing here?"

Emily spun around. Arms laden with shopping bags, Helen stood behind her, staring in confusion. Her gaze moved past Emily, to the open door.

"And why the hell are you breaking into my house?"

The world spun a little. Emily's head throbbed.

"They know about us," she said. "We need to go somewhere safe."

Helen stared at her in long, disconcerting silence, made even more terrible by the fact she always had something to say.

At long last, she spoke. "Where do we go?"

27

THE ANTISEPTIC FELT like acid against her scalp. Emily winced with each dab of the cotton swab and gripped the edge of the bathtub until her fingers hurt, too. The good news was that the wound was superficial. The initial nausea had passed and she didn't seem to be showing any obvious signs of a concussion. What she did have was a dull, throbbing headache.

Done with cleaning the wound, Jerome handed Emily a foil strip of painkillers.

"Here, take two of these," he mumbled.

They were the first words he'd spoken to her since she and Helen had shown up at Daniel's house forty minutes ago.

Emily hadn't wanted to come here, but it had also been the only place she'd wanted to be. Now here they were—Helen and Daniel drinking beers in the living room, while Jerome tended to Emily's headwound.

"Thank you." She swallowed the pills with a glass of water.

Avoiding her gaze, Jerome nodded, disposed of the cotton swab, and replaced the antiseptic in the medicine cabinet. He hovered by the door, clearly not wanting to be anywhere near Emily, and yet clearly not wanting to leave her alone.

She stole a glance at him and winced, this time not because of the head wound.

"Jerome, I. . ." She wanted to say more. She wanted to throw her arms around his neck and embrace him. Instead, she remained seated, staring at the floor tiles.

Silence filled the bathroom. Then in a quiet voice, Jerome said, "I'm sorry."

Emily looked up. "I'm sorry, too."

Words flooded from Jerome's mouth. "I was horrible. All those terrible things I said. . . I never meant any of it. And I'm sorry I've been avoiding you. I've been so ashamed. You're right—I should have asked about Helen first. But I was only trying to help. And I hate that we're not talking. I hate that I let pride get in the way of our friendship."

Their eyes briefly met, then went opposite directions. Jerome sidled over to the bathtub and sat down.

"It's more than that, though," Emily said at last. "You've been off with me ever since you told me you were moving out. Before that, even. I know you're busy with Daniel, but. . . I don't know, I get the feeling you've been avoiding me. Have I done something wrong?"

"No, it's not that."

"Then what is it?"

Jerome turned to face her. His mouth opened and closed, then he shook his head and looked away.

"Next week, you'll be gone," Emily said. "Off to the other side of the river. And then that will be it. We'll see each other less and less. You'll be busy with work, with auditions, with Daniel. I don't want it to end this way, not with you hating me."

Irritation flashed in Jerome's eyes. "You think our friendship is going to *end?* You really believe you mean so little to me?"

"No. I. . ." She couldn't look at him. "I. . . I'm scared of being alone. You and Harriet, you're the only friends I have."

She hated how she sounded. So pathetic and needy. Like a child in the playground with no friends to play with. Hadn't she proven to herself this year how strong she could be? How independent. But everyone she'd ever cared about had left her—her mother; Lewis; the people she'd thought were her friends until Phillip Gerard died. And now Jerome was moving to the other side of the city.

Maybe she was destined to live a life of solitude. But despite enjoying her own company, it didn't mean she wanted to spend the rest of her days alone.

"You have other friends," Jerome said. "What about Imogen? And don't forget Carter West."

"Work colleagues aren't the same as friends."

"Well, maybe you need to make them more than colleagues. London is a big city, Em. It's not easy to meet people when you're new here. You have to make the effort." His hand slid along the edge of the bathtub, moving closer to Emily's. "Besides, you're still missing the point. I may be moving to the other side of the river, but I'm not going anywhere. We may see each other less—that's just life—but we *will* still see each other. And you *will* meet new people. New friends. And none of them will be as great as me. But you won't be alone. Because that part of your life is over. You just need to *let* it be over."

They were quiet again. Emily wiped her eyes.

"Thanks for *mansplaining,"* she said.

Jerome moved closer. "You're welcome."

Emily reached out a hand and Jerome gently squeezed it. Waves of relief rolled through Emily's body. She knew their friendship would not come out of this entirely unscathed, but she took comfort in knowing that time and forgiveness would repair much of the damage. For the first time that evening, she looked at Jerome without feeling completely wretched. Jerome's expression did not share her relief.

"What is it?" she said. "I'm worried about you."

He drew in a long breath, then let it out in a sad billow. "You're right. The reason you haven't seen so much of me lately isn't just because of Daniel."

"Oh?" Emily froze, unsure where the conversation was heading.

"I'm not doing so good, Em. I'm not sleeping. I can't eat. I lied to you the other day. My audition didn't go well. In fact, it sucked. I knew those lines inside and out, but I froze. Nothing would come out. I just kept staring at them and they kept staring at me. It was humiliating."

"What is it? What's going on with you?"

Jerome let out another shuddering breath. "It's Meadow Pines. I thought I was okay about everything. I thought I'd put all the blood and the bodies behind me. But I'm not like you, Em. I don't have the stomach for it. Every time I close my eyes, that's all I see. Blood and bodies. And you—you almost died."

"But I didn't because you saved me." Emily gripped his hand tighter. "Why haven't you said anything? You're always telling me not to bottle things up. Have you told Daniel how you're feeling?"

"Daniel would think I was crazy."

"He was there too, Jerome."

"But he didn't see the things I saw."

"Then talk to me." Something Jerome had said a moment ago registered in her mind. "Are you saying part of the reason I haven't seen you lately is because I remind you of Meadow Pines?"

Jerome looked away. "I don't understand how you do it. How you can deal with murderers and psychopaths, or risk your life trying to save people you don't even know. I don't understand how you can survive all that and then *still* come back for more." He turned to face her. "I've been avoiding you because I felt our friendship was dangerous. Because I felt *you* were dangerous to be around."

Emily was stunned. And then she wasn't because it made perfect sense. Ever since Jerome had known her, he'd been embroiled in all kinds of life-threatening atrocities. Their friendship had been borne from danger and nurtured by trauma. Was it really so shocking they would suffer because of it? That Jerome would suffer?

"I don't know why I do the things I do," Emily said, dropping her gaze. "Perhaps it's atonement for what happened with Phillip. Perhaps it's because I just can't help myself. Sometimes I wonder if it's because I like it. But it does affect me, Jerome. The only difference between you and me is that I have medication and therapy to help cushion it all."

"That's not the only difference," said Jerome. "You *want* to help all those people."

"Don't you?"

He was quiet for a long time, his eyes shifting back and forth.

"When those doctors and their men had me cornered at Ever After, it was you who took the photos to the police," Emily said. "If you hadn't done that I'd be dead, along with all those other patients you helped save. At Meadow Pines, you could have gone with Daniel to get help, but you chose to stay. And you risked your own life to save mine. To save Helen's. Don't you see, Jerome? You may not think you want to help, that I'm dangerous to be around—and maybe I am—but the point is, *you* keep coming back for more. And if it's not to help, then why is it?"

For a long time, Jerome stared at the wall. A tear slipped from his right eye and splashed on the tiles.

"Every day, I feel scared," he said. "Scared that I'll never make it as an actor, that I'll still be waiting tables when I'm seventy. Scared to hold Daniel's hand in the street because some shining example of society deems it acceptable to scream abuse at us, or worse. Scared that you're going to get yourself killed. Scared to go to bloody sleep. Where does it end?"

Emily moved up beside him and threw her arm around his shoulders. "I have no idea. But if you find out, feel free to share. In the meantime, I suggest we use our friends as emotional crutches, and attempt to muddle on through."

An impatient knocking broke through the quiet.

"Oh, just kiss already," Helen called through the door. "Some of us need to pee!"

Emily rolled her eyes. "Of course, some *friends* shouldn't be allowed within a hundred metres of your emotions."

Jerome smiled and rested his head on her shoulder.

*

Shadows twitched and shuddered as an old black and white gangster film played noiselessly on the television. It was just after 2 a.m. Daniel had said goodnight an hour ago, leaving Emily, Jerome, and Helen curled up on the sofa. None of them wanted to sleep. Helen hadn't even wanted to stay, but Jerome had insisted, just in case the men returned.

Emily's head ached and her body was heavy with exhaustion, but her mind was wide awake, busy replaying the events of the past week. So much had happened that she'd barely had time to process it all. And what about her vandalized apartment? Her insurance would cover most of the damage, but how long would the money take to come through? It wasn't just the money, though. Her home had been violated. Her sanctuary stolen. Right now, she didn't feel like returning to The Holmeswood ever again.

Helen's voice interrupted her thoughts. "You know, the fact that they went to the trouble of finding out where we both live tells me something."

"That they wanted to intimidate you?" Jerome said. "Because, you know, job done."

Helen sat up, prompting Emily to do the same. "It tells me we've intimidated *them*. Whatever Max Edwards found, it has to be big."

Emily frowned. "You mean besides TEL?"

"More than that. Think about it—breaking into both our homes is like waving their hands in the air and admitting they're guilty. But the question is, guilty of what? We know what they're up to with TEL, and they know that despite being within the law, a media scandal is going to hurt. But they also know it won't come anywhere close to destroying them."

Emily raised an eyebrow. "You've changed your tune. Just the other day you were arguing with Evan until you were blue in the face that the TEL scandal was enough to take them down."

"Yes, well, call that a knee-jerk reaction. Let's keep focused, shall we? So, Valence's top dogs know that a media furore is inevitable and there's nothing they can do to stop it. At the same time, they also know it's not going to ruin them. Agreed?"

Emily nodded.

Jerome blinked tiredly at the television screen. The detective was trapped inside a warehouse, getting shot at by men in suits and trilbies.

"So, why go to the trouble of trashing our homes?" Helen said.

Jerome stifled a yawn. "I already told you—because they want to scare you. If they deter you from running the story, it buys them time to rake in the money."

"Or..." Helen said. "Max's evidence is still out there somewhere and Valence Industries has no idea where."

A memory triggered in Emily's mind. "The envelope! Max must have known Valence was onto him, so he sent the evidence to someone for safekeeping. The question is, who did he send it to?"

"He must have been working with someone else. A third person," Helen said.

"It has to be Anya Copeland. But then why hasn't she done anything with the evidence?"

"Maybe they killed her, too."

"I don't think so. They'd already have whatever it is back in their hands, so why break into our homes?" Emily leaned forward and tucked a hand under her chin. "But they must be wondering how we're getting our information."

Helen stared at her. "I doubt they know about Evan, so they're probably thinking Anya Copeland is our source."

"Which means we need to find her fast."

On the TV, the gun fight was reaching a crescendo. Bodies littered the floor. The detective fired his final bullet, just as more bad guys showed up.

"Evan is due back tomorrow," Helen said. "Maybe he'll have a lead on where Anya's hiding."

Leaning back, Emily pulled her knees up to her chest. "Evan's name is in Max's diary. Valence will work out who he is."

"He'll be safe for a while. Even if they recognize his name, they still have to find him."

"Okay, so we'll warn him tomorrow. I'm sure he'll have plenty of places where he can lay low for a while."

Helen agreed. Jerome announced he was going to bed. He squeezed Emily's hand and she squeezed back.

An hour later, Emily lay awake on an inflatable mattress while Helen lay asleep on the sofa. It hurt her head to lie on her back, so she curled up on her side, listening for movement outside the windows, and worrying about what the morning would bring. She hoped Evan would return tomorrow with something useful, because she had reached a dead end. Agreeing to help Diane Edwards had seemed like such a simple task, but here she was, injured, afraid, and in hiding. And yet there was part of her that crackled like electricity. Perhaps Jerome was right to be scared for her. Perhaps she really did like the danger.

28

THE FRONT DOOR was still locked, which hopefully meant that Emily's intruder had not returned. Entering the apartment with Jerome and Helen close behind, she moved from room to room, making sure there were no more unwelcome guests waiting to pounce. As Jerome surveyed the destruction, his expression grew graver—more so when he saw his belongings scattered across the living room.

Helen whistled. "Wow! I got off lightly in comparison."

In the morning light, the damage looked much worse. Emily had yet to call the police, which meant they would ask why she had waited until now to report the break in. The truth was that last night she'd been too busy getting knocked off her feet and making amends with Jerome. And she still had no proof that Valence Industries was responsible.

But if she was going to make a claim on her insurance policy, the police had to be involved. Emily reluctantly called the local station. After a brief interview, she was told an officer would be sent out later that day. In the meantime, she should expect a forensics team within the next four hours. Nothing should be touched.

"Four hours? Screw that, I've got better things to do with my time," Helen said, when Emily suggested she should also call.

"What about insurance?" Jerome asked.

"What insurance? Besides, we know who did it, so what other reason is there to involve the police?"

Emily thought Helen was behaving nonchalantly for someone whose home had just been broken into; though perhaps her apathy was a mask to hide her true feelings—if she *had* any true feelings.

Helen glance around at the mess. "I'd love to stay and help, but I have to go to work."

"Will you be safe?" Emily asked. "What if they're watching us right now?"

Helen waved her away. "What are they going to do? Jump on me in broad daylight? I'll be fine. If you hear from Evan first, call me."

When she was gone, Jerome looked at the destruction and shook his head. "I'll stay with you if you like, until the police come."

Emily nodded. There was still an awkward shadow hanging over them, but it was beginning to fade. "That's kind, but you don't have to."

"Actually, I do. I've run out of clean underwear."

Emily called *Lost* to tell them why she wouldn't be in today. Then after twenty minutes of hanging around, she and Jerome invited themselves across the hall for tea. Harriet scolded Emily for not having called last night as she'd promised, then proceeded to interrogate her about the break in. When she was done with Emily, she moved onto Jerome, demanding to know the intricate details of his imminent departure.

The forensic team showed up two hours later and went to work, taking photographs and dusting for fingerprints. When they were gone, Emily and Jerome went to work themselves, restoring order to the apartment. By the time Constable Taylor arrived to take Emily's statement ninety minutes later, they'd filled three refuse sacks, and the only room they'd yet to tackle was Emily's bedroom.

The police officer took Emily's statement. When he asked why she'd taken so long to report the crime, she shrugged a shoulder and mumbled something about being in shock.

Constable Taylor voiced his concern that nothing had been stolen from the apartment. "Do you know anyone who might have a personal grudge against you?"

Emily glanced at Jerome, then shook her head and told the police officer about the man in the lift.

When Constable Taylor was finished with his questions, he told Emily the Burglary Unit would be in touch, then headed across the hall to speak to Harriet. It was now 4 p.m.

"You neglected to mention how you got that bump on your head," Jerome said, his hands dug deep into his pockets. "Or that certain items *were* taken."

Emily returned his gaze. "Minor details."

After filling a duffel bag with clean clothes, Jerome picked up his jacket and hooked it over his shoulder. "I have to go to work. Will you be okay?"

"I'll be fine," Emily said, ignoring the flutter of panic in her chest. "Maybe."

"You know you can stay at Daniel's again tonight. I'll be back by ten."

Emily's mind raced back to last night and her heart began to thump wildly in her chest. Perhaps she didn't feel so safe here after all.

"Do you think he'd mind?"

"As if he has a choice." Jerome gave her a brief hug, then handed her a key. "See you later."

When she was alone, Emily stood in the centre of the living room and looked around. The sofa had tears in it. The dining table was missing two chairs. Except for a print of a lake in a cracked frame, the walls were now bare.

That man had been able to enter her home without forcing the lock. Which meant he could return at any time.

A chill ran down the back of Emily's neck. Pocketing Jerome's key, she left the living room, bolted the front door, and moved to the bedroom to continue cleaning.

The memory box she kept at the back of the wardrobe was lying on its side, its contents spilled on the carpet. Until now, Emily had kept her emotions under control. But seeing the bottle of her mother's favourite perfume, the charm bracelet she'd given Emily on her sixteenth birthday, and all those old photographs, made tears course down her face. As she gathered up the precious items and carefully placed them back inside the box, she noticed the bracelet her mother had given her was missing a charm—a lucky horseshoe.

Sadness turned to anger as Emily scoured the room. The charm was gone. Jonathan Hunt would answer for this, she vowed, along with every other heinous crime he and Valence Industries had committed.

As Emily stood, quietly seething, her phone began to ring. She checked the caller ID to see it was Carter. No doubt news of the burglary had spread through the volunteers at *Lost.* In no mood to talk, Emily let the phone ring out. Seconds later, a chime announced that Carter had left a voicemail. But Emily was in no mood to listen to it, either. Instead, she finished picking up her clothes and replacing her torn bedsheets. When the phone started ringing for a second time, she snatched it up to switch it off.

But it wasn't Carter calling again. It was Evan Holt, and his voice crackled with excitement.

"Emily? I'm on my way back from the airport. Listen, why don't you grab Helen and meet me at my place at eight? I have news."

"You're not the only one," Emily said, her voice grave. "They know about us, Evan. They broke into my apartment. Helen's, too. They took my laptop and Max's diary."

Evan was quiet for a moment. "Were you there? Are you okay?"

"We're fine, but I'm worried. Your name was in that diary—what if they figure out who you are?"

"Let's not worry about that now. Besides, with what I've just found, they're not going to have time to stop me."

"Your contact got back to you?"

"Not on the phone. My place at eight tonight. And Emily?"

"Yes?"

"Try not to worry. I have a feeling this will all be over soon."

Emily could hear the smile in his voice, attempting to soothe her worries. She hoped it was justified.

They said goodbye. Emily debated if she should call Helen. On one hand, she was a liability—if she had kept tight-lipped about TEL, then Emily's apartment would still be intact and Valence Industries would have no idea it was being investigated. But on the other hand, leaving Helen in the dark would make her vulnerable.

And who had brought Helen on board in the first place, knowing full well she was a potential risk? Emily stared at her reflection in the wardrobe mirror. Then turning away, she dialled Helen's number.

29

THE BLUE RENAULT pulled into the multi-storey car park just before 8 p.m. On Emily's insistence, Helen parked on the ground floor. The level was half empty and poorly-lit, but the car would be immediately accessible if they needed it.

"You could have parked outside of Evan's. It's closer," Emily said. The sound of the passenger door shutting was like a sonic boom, making her jump out of her skin.

Helen laughed. "Are you kidding me? The last time I did that, I was lucky some little shit didn't slash my tires."

Evan lived two streets away. They headed toward his home at a brisk pace, both checking over their shoulders. It wasn't completely dark yet, but the streetlamps had come on, creating comforting, tiny islands of light. There were just a handful of people around, moving quickly along the pavements with their heads down and their bags clutched to their sides.

Emily and Helen took a right on to the next street and were greeted by tower blocks and derelict buildings. Some parts of the city were deliberately forgotten about, Emily thought, unnerved by the deprivation. And so were the people who lived within them. But her understanding did not stop her from feeling afraid.

Turning the corner, they saw a group of hoodie-wearing teenage boys loitering outside Evan's building in a cloud of marijuana smoke.

"See what I mean?" Helen whispered, gripping Emily's arm.

One of the boys catcalled behind them as they reached the building and ducked inside. The stench of stale urine burned their nostrils as they entered the lift.

Helen was unusually quiet. Perhaps even she was feeling afraid, Emily thought. She wondered what information Evan was about to share with them. He'd sounded confident on the phone, going as far to say that the investigation would be over soon. Emily hoped so. Her paranoia was becoming overwhelming. Every person on the street had become a potential danger, every creak in her apartment a sign that her intruder had returned. This was not what she had expected when she'd agreed to help Diane Edwards, but here she was yet again, staring danger in the face.

The lift reached the thirteenth floor and the doors slid open. Evan's apartment was directly opposite. Emily crossed the hall and knocked on the door. As she waited for him to answer, she shot a nervous glance at Helen. When Evan didn't answer on the second knock, Helen shook her head.

"Maybe he went out," she said, producing her phone and dialling Evan's number.

Pressing her ear to the door, Emily heard a tinny ringtone playing from somewhere inside the apartment. As they waited for

Evan to pick up, Emily held her breath while Helen tightened her grip on the phone. The phone rang off. They stared at each other with wide, dilated eyes.

Without another thought, Emily tried the door handle. The door swung open.

"Evan?" She stared into the gloom, hearing only silence. "It's Emily and Helen. The door was open. . . We're coming in."

With Helen trailing behind, Emily stepped into the apartment and headed toward the living room. Something crunched under her foot. She glanced down to see a trail of broken glass glinting on the carpet. The rest of the room was intact. But there were tell-tale signs. An armchair had been recently moved, the grooves in the carpet still visible from where it had previously sat. A large framed print on the wall hung at a lopsided angle.

Emily chose her footing with quiet care, moving through the living room and into the cramped kitchen. It was clean, undisturbed, except for a shot glass sitting in the sink. She moved on to Evan's bedroom, which was dark and stuffy, then tried his office. It was a tiny room, made smaller by the notes, press cuttings, photographs, and maps that were plastered to the walls. His desk was a cluttered mess. Reference books and journals filled shelves and lay in piles on the floor. Emily was momentarily entranced by the room; it was like looking inside Evan's brain. Then Helen tugged on her arm.

There was only the bathroom left to check. The door was closed. Emily moved to open it, but Helen pulled her back.

"Don't touch anything," she whispered.

Pulling her sleeve over her hand, Emily pressed down on the door handle. The door was surprisingly heavy, and she had to lean into it with her shoulder. As she caught sight of the reflection in the bathroom mirror, she saw why.

Evan Holt's naked body was hanging from the back of the door, the cord of a dressing gown tied around the towel hook and wrapped tightly around his neck.

Emily staggered into the bathroom, her legs like marshmallow, her eyes wide with disbelief.

Helen stumbled in after her, almost falling into the bathtub as she caught sight of Evan's body. "Jesus Christ!"

He was dead, his face flushed a purplish hue, his bloodshot eyes staring lifelessly across the bathroom. Pornographic magazines lay open on the floor. Emily gaped at them, feeling a strange rush of embarrassment. But it only lasted for a few seconds. Then horror invaded every cell of her being.

She had a sudden urge to move away from him, but she was paralyzed. *They* had done this to him. The realization made her head spin, made her want to climb into the bathtub and rock quietly into catatonia. Valence Industries had killed Evan Holt. But she could never prove it—because just like Max Edwards and Jason Dobbs, Evan's death had been staged to look like he'd caused it himself. Only this time, Valence had added a touch of sleaze. Killing Evan Holt was not enough, it seemed—they wanted to destroy his reputation as well.

Helen was by Emily's side, gently tugging her arm. "We need to leave. Now."

But Emily couldn't move. This was all her fault. She should have been more careful with the diary.

"Emily, come on! We have to go!"

Taking one last look at Evan's tortured face, Emily allowed herself to be pulled from the room. But as they passed Evan's office, she dragged her heels. There was no computer, she noted, and there were rectangular gaps on the walls where parts of Evan's research had been removed.

"Come on, Emily!"

Helen pulled her arm, this time with force.

They hurried out of Evan Holt's apartment, closing the door behind them. Emily pressed the call button, but somebody was already in the lift, moving upward. Flashing a terrified glance at Helen, Emily felt dread crawling up her spine. She watched the floor numbers light up on the panel, bringing whoever was inside closer to them. *Ten. Eleven. Twelve. Thirteen.* The lift bell chimed. The doors slid open, but Emily and Helen were already running down the hall.

Throwing open the fire escape door, Helen pounded down the steps, with Emily close on her heels. By the time they'd reached the fifth floor, they were breathless and sweating. Somewhere above them, they heard the boom of a fire door slamming, then echoed footsteps coming down the stairs. The women picked up speed, reaching the ground floor and peering into the foyer. Satisfied it was empty, they ran from the building and out to the road.

The gang of boys was still gathered outside and getting high. Emily and Helen hurtled past them, running through the streets until they reached the multi-storey car park. It took a moment for Helen to still her trembling hands enough to unlock the car then insert the key into the ignition.

"We have to call the police," Emily said, feeling strangely numb as she watched the car park entrance. "We can't just leave him there."

"Just hold on a second!" Helen shifted the gearstick into reverse, backed out of the parking bay, and spun the car around.

Hands clamped to the wheel, she slammed her foot on the accelerator.

The car shot out of the car park, hurtling its passengers down the street at breakneck speed, until they were far from the tower block and what lay inside.

30

NEITHER OF THEM spoke until they'd cleared Elephant and Castle and joined the traffic of Borough High Street. Emily sat in the passenger seat, rigid and numb as she stared out the window. The true horror of what they'd just witnessed was only now sinking its claws into her.

"I'll call the police and say I'm a concerned tenant," Helen said. "I'll tell them Evan's place is being broken into."

Emily stared at her. "It's too late. We have to tell the police what we've found out about Valence. About what they've done to Evan and the others."

"We don't have a shred of proof. For all intents and purposes, Evan died choking himself while choking the chicken. You really think the police are going to take on a company as big as Valence Industries on the word of a hack journalist and a crazy woman? Because that's how they'll see us."

She was right, of course. Valence Industries was clever about how it disposed of potential threats. And any evidence Evan had acquired was now back in the company's hands.

Emily clutched her chest as anger burned her insides. Valence was going to go free. It would continue to poison millions of children, who would grow up into angry, violent, damaged adults. Jonathan Hunt and his fellow conspirators would walk free from the murders of Max Edwards, Jason Dobbs, and now Evan Holt. Emily felt suddenly powerless. How long would it be before Valence Industries caught up with her and Helen?

"Where are we going?" She checked the wing mirror, but the string of cars behind made it difficult to tell if they were being followed.

Helen shook her head. "I don't know. But this isn't over, Emily. We can't just let it go, even if we wanted to."

Emily wondered if she did want to. Did she want to return to her life where she was running out of money, where bills needed to be paid, where she had no idea what she was doing?

As if on cue, Emily's phone buzzed, announcing a text message from Carter.

Valence Industries had backed them into a corner. The only weapon Emily had against the company was knowledge—but without proof, it was a weapon with a dull blade.

"What do you suggest we do?" she asked as the car rolled onto London Bridge. Below, the dark water of the Thames reflected myriads of city lights.

"We start again," Helen said. "We know they're selling TEL and where. So, we follow the trail just like Evan did, until we find out exactly what they're hiding."

"And we do that from the safety of where, exactly? They know who we are. They know where we live. They're not going to let this go."

Emily was troubled by her own cynicism. She stared at her phone screen. Just last week, she was making a fool of herself over coffee with Carter. Now she was giving serious thought to jumping on a train with a one-way ticket to the remotest corner of the country, where she could not be found.

With nothing more to say for now, Emily opened Carter's text message. Under the right circumstances, she thought she might like to spend more time getting to know him. He was kind and caring, and he had tried to help her without demanding immediate answers. It was a shame the right circumstances were unlikely to ever materialize.

For now, she read his text message: *Are you okay? You need to check your voicemail!*

Helen had retreated into silence, her gaze pinned on the road in front, streetlights reflecting in her eyes like flames. Emily pressed the phone to her ear and listened to the voicemail Carter had left earlier that evening. Her hand shot out and gripped Helen's arm.

"Are you trying to get us killed?" Helen yelled, shaking her off. "Because, hello, doing a fine job of that without crashing the car."

Emily hung up and immediately called Carter back.

"Can I come over?" she asked when he picked up. "Can I come over right now?" Grabbing notebook and pen from her bag, she scribbled down Carter's address. "I'll be there as soon as I can. And Carter? Thank you!"

She hung up. Helen glanced at her.

"Who was that? What's the matter with you?"

Despite the horrors of the last hour, despite the hopelessness she'd felt, Emily found herself smiling in the dark.

"We might not have to start from the beginning, after all," she breathed. "I think we just found Anya Copeland."

31

CARTER LIVED ALONE in a quiet, leafy neighbourhood in West Hampstead, in a two-bedroom ground floor flat with a rear garden he didn't have to share with the upstairs neighbours. Emily and Helen had pulled up outside just after 10 p.m. Helen had been relegated to waiting in the car. She had complained bitterly at first, but Emily had explained that Carter knew nothing about Valence Industries, and only the barest of bones about her being hired by Diane Edwards. It was safer for him this way, she'd explained. Besides, Carter was already curious, and Helen's presence would only lead to further questions.

"I thought we'd had no luck with the shout out," Emily said. She was sitting next to Carter at the breakfast bar in the kitchen, huddled over his laptop.

Carter nodded. "We didn't. So, I spoke to my manager and talked her into stepping things up."

"You talked to Kelly? And she agreed?"

"She was a little suspicious at first because it wasn't an officially reported case. But when she heard all about how Anya has a history of running away and how one whiff of the cops will send her bolting with her young child, she folded like a wilting flower. I've been posting Anya's picture on our Facebook page and Twitter feed three times a day for the last few days. And *voila*! An upstanding member of the public got in touch to say she thinks she's seen her."

Carter looked immensely pleased with himself. His expression soon turned to one of concern. "Is everything all right? You look, I don't know . . . stressed?"

"It's been a long day." Emily momentarily drifted back to Evan Holt's bathroom. She pushed grisly images from her head. "So, I'm impressed. Where is she?"

Carter stared at her with doubt in his curiously coloured eyes, then pointed at the laptop screen. "Southfields, near Wimbledon. The woman who got in touch is pretty convinced Anya Copeland is the lady she sees with her son in the park weekdays after school. The same lady whose son attacked her daughter one afternoon when he couldn't wait for his turn on the swings. Took a chunk clean out of her, apparently. Anyway, she sent us this."

He clicked the mouse and a photograph appeared on the screen. It had been taken from a slight distance and showed a grassy play area teeming with smiling children, who were clambering like ants over swings, slides, and see-saws. But the children were not the focus of the image.

Two lonely figures stood at the edge of the play area: a mother and her young son; one holding onto the other as they watched the merriment.

"It's not the best image, but. . ." Carter dragged a slider at the bottom of the screen and enlarged the picture. "What do you think? Is that her?"

Emily took out her phone and found the picture of Anya and Max taken at the Clean Water gala. She carefully compared one image to the other. The hair was different—longer, wavier—and she'd lost weight—but Emily was certain the woman in the park was indeed Anya Copeland.

For the first time in days, she felt a spark of hope.

"That's her." Smiling, she turned to Carter. Her hand flew to his shoulder. "Thank you. You don't know how much this means to me."

Carter grinned. "Glad to have atoned for my sins."

Their knees bumped together. Emily returned her gaze to the picture on the laptop screen. Josh; that was the son's name. Even though he'd been snapped from a distance, Emily could still read his body language: tense shoulders; arms stiff by his sides; hands balled into fists. Josh Copeland was not a happy child.

"What's the name of the park? There must be schools nearby."

"Just a second. . ." Their fingers grazed as Carter took the mouse from Emily's hand. He quickly skimmed the message that the woman had sent.

"Highfield park. I don't know the area, do you?"

Emily gestured to the computer. "Do you mind?"

Carter leaned back on the stool and stretched out his arms. "This is all very cloak and dagger. Can you tell me what this is really about or will you have to kill me after?"

Emily said nothing. She entered the park's name into Google Maps. A few seconds later, she was staring at a map of Southfields, the pointer hovering over Highfield park. There were several schools in the surrounding area.

"It's complicated," she said, which was not an explanation at all, but it was all she was prepared to offer. As grateful as she was for Carter's help, and regardless of her confused feelings about him, what she didn't need right now was another body to look out for.

"Of course, all will be revealed over coffee take two," Carter said. He blushed a little. "I suppose I can wait until then. . ."

"It'll be worth the wait," Emily said. They were staring at each other again.

Carter's lips parted into a wide smile. "I'll hold you to that."

Emily found herself staring at his mouth. Then her head filled with images of Evan Holt. She stood up, scraping the stool against the floor.

"Thanks for helping me find Anya."

Carter walked her to the door. As they said goodbye, he leaned in closer. Emily hesitated, thanked him again, then made her way back to the car.

"So?" Helen was still angry, but there was also fear in her eyes as they flicked from the rear-view mirror, to the driver window, then back again.

Emily felt guilty for leaving her out here alone. But as she was about to apologize, a terrible realization struck her. Carter had called her this afternoon with news of Anya Copeland's whereabouts. What if she'd answered his call, or listened to his voicemail earlier? Would their plans have changed? Would Evan Holt still be alive? Overcome with nausea, Emily turned and stared out the window.

"Hello, anyone in there?" Annoyed, Helen started the engine. "Did you find her, or what? Where are we going next?"

Emily sat in stony silence. At last, she said, "Right now, we're going to Daniel's. Then tomorrow, you're going to go to work, and I'm going to go and find Anya."

Helen's jaw swung open. "Like bloody hell I'm going to work tomorrow. I'm coming with you."

"If you're in hiding with your child, would you be more intimidated by one stranger showing up, or two?"

"Then I should go and you should stay here."

Emily turned to face Helen, determination making her jaw ache. "I made a promise to Diane Edwards that I would find out what happened to her husband. Tomorrow, that's exactly what I'm going to do. Any evidence I find is all yours. I'm done."

She was shocked by her own words. This afternoon, she was ready to do whatever it took to bring ruin to Valence Industries. But Evan Holt was dead now, and she felt the burden of his murder like a weight around her neck.

"You're kidding, right?" Helen said, the car engine still running. "You can't back out, Emily. You think Jonathan Hunt is just going to leave you alone? He's made it very clear this is personal now."

"We should never have interviewed him."

"So, this is my fault? That's what you're saying?" Helen hit the steering wheel with the palm of her hand. "You think Evan would be happy to hear you're just giving up? Companies like Valence employ people like Jonathan Hunt because they know they're willing to ignore ethics and morals to get what they want. And what they want is more money and more power. When people like us come along and try to expose their crimes, they'll use that money and that power to make sure we disappear. It's not going to stop at Evan. It didn't stop at Max Edwards." She paused, dropped her hands in her lap. "Please, Emily. Don't think for a minute that if you give up now, they won't come for you. You know about TEL. Tomorrow, if you find Anya Copeland, you could know a lot more. That makes you dangerous to Valence Industries whether you quit or not."

Emily's head throbbed. Her heart ached. She wanted nothing more than to sleep. "Let's just wait and see what tomorrow brings, shall we?"

"Whatever it brings," Helen said, pulling the car away from the kerb, "keep looking over your shoulder."

They drove the rest of the way in silence. When they pulled up outside Daniel's place a little after midnight, Helen stayed behind the wheel.

"I'm not staying here," she said, ignoring Emily's concerned gaze.

"But it's late. It's not safe to be driving around alone."

"Believe it or not, you're not the only woman with a man slave." For the first time that night, a wry smile wrinkled Helen's lips.

Emily was about to argue that they would be safer staying together when she tiredly changed her mind. Helen would do as she pleased, whether it risked her life or not. As much as she hated to admit it, it was a trait they both shared.

"I'll be at the office all day," Helen said as Emily climbed out of the car. "Call me as soon as you know anything."

Daniel had already gone to bed, but Jerome was waiting up with a glass of Jack Daniels. When he saw her grey, ashen face, he set down his glass and took her hand.

"Evan Holt is dead," Emily said. "They killed him."

Although she wanted nothing more than to lean on Jerome's shoulder and let the tears come, she remained upright and dry-eyed. Guilt burned her insides like acid.

Jerome squeezed her hand. "What can I do?"

Emily squeezed back. "Exactly what you are doing—I want you to stay away."

"Emily, I—"

"I mean it. You've been through enough."

"And you haven't?"

They both fell silent. Emily let go of Jerome's hand and hugged her ribs.

"Tomorrow, this will all be over," she said. But she knew the words were a lie before they had even left her mouth.

32

HIGHFIELD PARK WAS filled with the screams and cries of children. Emily had been here for an hour, drifting back and forth, waiting for the school day to end. Now, she found a bench to sit on, and observed from a distance as children jostled for turns on the swings and slides, or dangled precariously from climbing frames, while nearby parents kept a watchful eye.

Emily felt conspicuous and out of place, aware of the adults who were casting occasional glances in her direction, no doubt wondering why there was a nervous-looking, childless woman sitting so close to the play area. Ignoring their stares, she pretended to read the book in her lap, while periodically glancing up to watch the children. Taken in by their excitement, her thoughts briefly turned to her teaching days. Sometimes, when her class had been particularly well-behaved, she'd rewarded them with afternoon trips out to the park, to the woods, or to the beach. As the children had laughed and played, she'd handed out the apples that her mother had picked from the trees in her garden. Emily missed those children. She missed her mother. She missed those happy days when everything was in order. But they were all gone now, found only in dreams and memories.

She had dreamt of her mother last night. In the dream, she was a girl again, and her mother was dancing with her on the lawn, spinning her around the apple trees until they were both dizzy and their bellies hurt from laughing. When she'd woken in Daniel's living room, she'd wondered if the dream had actually been a childhood memory. But she could not recall her mother ever dancing with her like that. Not once.

A high-pitched howl drew her back to reality. A little girl had tripped and landed face down on the grass, and she was now dribbling saliva down herself as she wailed for her mother. Emily watched as the woman swept up the child in her arms and cooed soothing words in her ear. When it was clear words weren't going to work, she carried her distraught daughter to the ice cream van that was stationed at the edge of the park.

Emily followed them with her eyes. Her heart missed a beat.

A woman and her young son were approaching the play area. They moved cautiously, as if desperate to go unnoticed. Emily checked the photograph on her phone screen.

It was her. Anya Copeland.

But this was not that same healthy-looking woman whose smiled exuded confidence on Emily's phone screen. This woman was thin and tired-looking, with taut shoulders and a firm grip on her son's hand. Josh. He was squirming, desperate to be set free so he could swing and slide and climb and jump.

Anya stooped to whisper in her son's ear. She straightened up again and looked around the park. Emily dropped her gaze to her book. She glanced up again, in time to see Anya release Josh's hand, then tense her body as he went barrelling forward.

Something extraordinary happened. Whichever direction Josh moved in, the other children shifted in the opposite direction. It was like watching opposing magnetic forces bouncing off each other. And it wasn't just the children who were reacting. Parents darted forward, sweeping their children from the play area, or forming a barrier between them and Josh Copeland.

Emily's gaze darted from Josh to his mother, who watched him like a lioness regarding her cub, but who also seemed keenly aware of the reaction he was causing among the other children. And somewhere beneath that almost aggressive expression, there was despair lurking in her eyes. Her only child had been made an outcast.

Aware that she was watching Anya without discretion, Emily sank back on the bench and picked up her book. She resorted to glancing up every ten seconds or so, watching Josh empty the slide and the spring horses, then look longingly at the see-saw. Emily switched her attention to Anya, who remained at the edge of the play area, ready for battle, determined not to make eye contact with the other adults. But the other adults weren't interested in her. Their attention was fixed on the space between Josh and their children. If the distance closed, the parents would immediately spring up, ready to sweep their children to safety.

As she watched Josh resign himself to playing alone, Emily felt an aching deep in her chest. What were the other children sensing about this boy that she could not? The woman who'd reported seeing Anya had described how Josh had bitten her daughter. Had these children also had their own encounters with him? Emily watched him move away from the see-saw and return to the sandpit, where he scuffed his shoes through the yellow grains. Was there such violence hidden inside that tiny, sad frame? The expression on Anya's face told her that, yes, there was.

Two more minutes passed. Josh gave up on the sandpit, on the hope of being accepted by the other children and returned to his mother. He pointed at the ice cream van. Anya nodded, then held out a hand. Together, they walked away. A chorus of sighs floated over the play area. Emily felt the ache in her chest grow deeper.

Putting her book away, she stood and brushed out the creases in her clothes. Then she began following Anya Copeland.

Her heart raced as she wondered how to approach the woman. There were several ways she could introduce herself, but perhaps only one that would stop Anya from running. And Anya *would* run; she was sure of it. She'd been running since Max Edwards had died. Now Emily was hopefully about to find out why.

She came closer, watching as the ice cream vendor leaned through the window and handed Josh a vanilla cone. Anya paid the man, took Josh's free hand, and led him away.

Emily was closing in behind them. She could hear Josh humming in between taking bites of ice cream. She could see the way Anya was looking left and right, pulling her son along a little too quickly. Emily moved closer, veering to the left until she was walking alongside.

She drew in a breath. It stuck in her throat. *Say something.*

"Anya Copeland?"

It was as if Anya had been skewered by icicles. She froze on the spot, eyes widening, breath expelling from her mouth. Slowly, she turned to face Emily while pushing her son behind her back.

"My name's Emily Swanson, and. . ."

Anya backed away, eyes darting to the sides, skin paling despite the sunshine. Behind her, Josh stumbled and tripped, but managed to hold onto his ice cream.

Emily did not follow. "Please, Anya. I don't mean to scare you. I'm not from Valence Industries if that's—"

In one fluid movement, Anya swung Josh to her side, swooped him up into her arms, then began hurrying away.

"Please, Anya! I want to help you!"

Anya did not look back. She tightened her grip on her son, causing him to complain.

"I'm here because of Max," Emily called out. "I'm here because of what they did to him."

Anya slid to an abrupt halt. Josh stared over her shoulder at Emily, then took a bite of his ice cream.

Emily stepped forward.

"I want to help you," she repeated. "Whatever Valence Industries did, I want to undo it."

She waited, holding her breath. Children's laughter floated on the breeze. Slowly, Anya turned around. Her eyes, which were dark and haunted, fixed on Emily.

"It can't be undone," she said. A single tear slipped from the corner of her eye and splashed on the asphalt, where the sun greedily lapped it up.

33

THE FLAT WAS small and cramped. Furniture and toys that once filled a house were now wedged into just three rooms. Sitting on the sofa in the kitchen/living room, Emily stared at Josh while he watched TV. Anya brought over two mugs of tea, then handed a plate of sandwiches to Josh.

"Here. Go and watch your show in the bedroom." There was no malice in her words, but no warmth, either.

Josh remained seated, transfixed by the kids show, which was painting the television screen in frantic colours. Anya picked up the remote and switched off the TV. Josh blinked, then emitted a disapproving grunt. He looked up, one eye beautiful and cocoa brown, the other an unnerving milky blue.

"Please, Josh. Do as I say. And put your glasses on."

Climbing to his feet, Josh heaved his shoulders, snatched his glasses from his mother's hands, then shot a glare at Emily as he stomped into the bedroom.

Anya closed the door behind him, hovering for a few seconds until she heard the bedroom television burst to life. Frowning, she perched on the edge of the sofa and looked around the cramped space.

"I had to get rid of the armchairs. No room," she said, turning to face Emily. "But I suppose you're not here to discuss the expense of London living. What do you want to know?"

Emily took a deep breath. "As I said, Diane—Mrs. Edwards—she hired me to find out what happened to Max."

"And you went to all that trouble to find me just on the off-chance I might know something?"

A look passed over Anya's face that was somewhere between doubt and suspicion.

"The night of the gala," Emily said. "Max went up to his hotel room at around ten. You left shortly after. But you didn't go straight home."

"Someone's been doing their homework."

"You were seen in the lobby later on. You were upset."

"What can I say?" Anya said with a sneer. "I don't like parties."

The women stared at each other. Emily hadn't expected such a prickly conversation. She could see that choosing her words would be like choosing where to step in a minefield.

"Ms. Copeland. . . Anya. . . What happened that night? Did you and Max—"

Anya's eyes flashed with instant anger. "Did Max and I what? Have an affair? Is that what you've come here to ask?" Laughing, she shook her head. "You've been talking to Charlie Jones."

"Yes, I have."

Anya was quiet, the lines on her forehead growing deeper with each passing second. "Nothing happened between me and Max," she said, finally. "Despite what the rumour mill at E.C.G. would have you believe, I had no interest in becoming one of his extramarital affairs. I'm no homewrecker."

Emily had a sudden memory of Diane Edwards asking about Anya. The way she had carefully chosen her words, had winced as she'd waited for Emily's reply—it was clear now that she'd known, or was at least suspicious about her husband's infidelities. "Max told you about his affairs?"

Anya cocked her head, listening for activity in the bedroom. "He told me about lots of things."

"His alcoholism?"

"Yes. We spent many hours working side by side. We became close. Especially when. . . But I didn't sleep with him." Anya looked to the other side of the room, as if a memory lingered there. "I thought you said you were here to help me, not interrogate me."

"I am, but I need to know all the facts." So, Max and Anya had not been involved in an affair. But Emily had other, more pressing questions that needed answering. "Why were you upset at the gala?"

Anya's eyes darted back and forth. "I can't tell you."

"Anya, please."

The women were silent as cartoonish music floated out from the bedroom.

Trying a different approach, Emily said, "What do you know about Tetraethyl lead?"

Anya's jaw tensed, but she remained silent.

Enough of this, Emily thought. "Miss Copeland, since I've been looking into the death of Max Edwards, I've had my home broken into, I've been followed. One of the people I've been working with—Evan Holt—is dead. The police will say it was an accident, but you and I know better, don't we?"

"Evan Holt?" Anya's eyes were round with fear.

"Did you know him?"

Getting up, Anya hurried into the kitchen area and peered through the window into the street below. Beads of sweat were forming on her brow.

"How did you get here?" she said. "Were you careful?"

Emily nodded. She had planned her journey in detail and had constantly looked over her shoulder. "No one followed me."

"How can you be sure?"

Anya turned back to the living room, her face pale and sickly. Emily was losing her already.

"Please, Anya. If you know something, I can help you."

"You can't. No one can."

"I know that Valence Industries is producing and exporting TEL to developing countries. But I also know Max arranged to meet with Evan Holt to give him evidence of something worse. Evan may be gone, but I'm working with another journalist who can help to expose whatever it is Max found. What *did* he find?"

Anya shook her head, over and over. "I'm sorry. I can't."

"People are dead! Max, Jason Dobbs, Evan Holt, God knows who else. You're the only lead we have left."

Tears splashed down Anya's face. "Is that all I am? A lead?"

"Of course not." Emily softened her voice. "But without you, we have nothing. Max, Jason, Evan—their deaths will be meaningless."

Anya slumped against the kitchen sink, a moan escaping her throat. "Don't you understand? Hurting him was their way of keeping me quiet. If I help you, they'll kill him. They'll kill my boy!"

The bedroom door opened. Josh appeared in the crack and stared at his mother. Anya quickly wiped tears from her face.

"Go inside, Josh. Everything is fine. Go on. Go eat your sandwiches."

Josh remained in the doorway a few seconds longer then retreated. Anya returned to the sofa and perched on the edge. She looked exhausted, Emily thought. Like a woman who hadn't slept in months, who carried the weight of the world on her shoulders. Emily wanted to take her hand and tell her everything would be all right. But she refused to make promises she couldn't necessarily keep.

"What did they do to your son?"

Anya wiped more tears from her eyes. When she spoke, it was through clenched teeth. "The day of Max's funeral, I decided to stay away. Not because of the rumours, but because I was terrified. What happened to Max, then Jason. . . I knew I would be next. It was just a question of when." She clasped her hands together, but they continued to tremble. "I was planning to run. To take Josh and go anywhere they couldn't find us. I was busy packing up the house. I'd told him to stay indoors, to stay where I could see him. I must have turned my back for a second and . . . he was gone."

Anya paused to fight back fresh tears. "I panicked, running from room to room, calling his name. But he wasn't in the house. He was outside. He must have sneaked out to play in the back yard. I found him on the ground, covered head to toe in . . . dust. It was everywhere—his hair, on his skin. And he was having some sort of seizure. By the time the ambulance came, he'd stopped breathing." Anya stared at Emily in horror. "My son died. They resuscitated him, but . . . just for a minute, he was dead."

Emily stared at her, an icy chill slipping down her spine. "What had they done to your son?"

"They'd poisoned him." Anya's eyes grew very dark. "The dust he'd been covered in—it was lead dust. They must have been watching us, waiting for him to come outside."

Emily couldn't believe what she was hearing. Was Valence Industries monstrous enough to do this to a child? Of course they were. She needed only to think about the millions of children who were being slowly poisoned every day from the effects of TEL, while Valence sat back and made a fortune.

"Anya, I'm so sorry. But Josh recovered? He's all right now?"

Anya laughed. Her shoulders sagged. "How long were you watching in the park? He's different now. And I'm not talking about the physical damage he's been left with—the blindness in his left eye, the failing kidney—I'm talking about his behaviour. When Josh was born he was such a good baby. He slept through the night, was always smiling, always healthy. Right through nursery, people were always commenting on what a polite little boy he was. So friendly and sociable with the other kids. Now, those other kids are scared of him. Their parents, too. They're *afraid* of my son."

Anya swept tears from her face. "The doctors say the lead got into his nervous system and damaged his brain. He was a smart boy before, but now everything's difficult. He forgets things. Sometimes I need to remind him what order to put on his clothes. He gets so frustrated with me." She smiled, but there was no joy in it. Only failure. "He has outbursts so violent that even I get afraid of him. *His own mother.* Those children in the park, he's hurt so many of them, but their parents won't call him on it. They can't, you see. Because how terrible it is for a single mother like me to be struggling with a child with such needs. I wish they would. I wish they would shout at him to stop. Or shout at me. Because he knows, you see. Josh knows he's different now. He knows that everyone's afraid of him. Can you imagine how that must make him feel?"

Her voice faltered and Anya fell silent.

Emily's heart ached. She reached out a hand toward Anya, then drew it back.

"I need to know what happened," she said softly. "I need to know what you know. What Max knew. We need to stop Valence from hurting anyone else."

Anya stared at her hands, which now hung limply over her knees. "It won't undo what they've done to my son."

"No, it won't. But we have a chance to stop them doing the same thing to millions of other children."

Anya sat still for a long time, more tears escaping her eyes.

"Now that you've found me, I'll have to move again." She looked up, staring intensely at Emily as if she were trying to see inside her mind. Slowly, she nodded. "Valence Industries knows it's a matter of time before the public find out about TEL. It knows the public will react with shock and outrage. It also knows the outcry will hit its shares. But you have to remember that Valence Industries is a multibillion-dollar conglomerate with hands in everything—chemical processing, fuel, oil, household cleaning, beauty products.

"A few disgruntled shareholders and a public outcry might bruise its reputation temporarily, but it doesn't care. What it does care about is the money it's making from TEL. And Valence know it's not going to last forever. At some point soon, those developing countries will come to their senses and ban the stuff. Or so you'd hope."

"Hope?" Emily repeated. "But surely if they knew the damage it's doing..."

"That's just the thing," Anya said. "Most people in those countries don't have a clue about the damage being done to their kids, and that's because Valence is working really hard to keep them in the dark."

"How?"

Anya looked away for a moment, staring into space. "If you've done your research, you'll know how passionate Max was about the environment. About the job he'd been hired to do. But he quickly realized that sustainability in Valence's eyes isn't about protecting the environment. It's about saving money. When Max found out Valence was exporting TEL, he was furious. He went to Jonathan Hunt and told him he was going to the press. Hunt's response was to create the Clean Water Project and put Max in charge."

Emily leaned forward. "The project was Jonathan Hunt's idea?"

"From day one. Max refused at first, thought about resigning right there on the spot. But the activist in him saw an opportunity."

"By going ahead with Clean Water?"

Anya shook her head. "By bringing the company down from the inside. By the time E.C.G. were brought in and I started working with Max, he was already snooping around their systems. I had no idea about any of this in the first few months. But as we worked together, we became close—close enough for Max to trust me.

"He told me about Valence and TEL but made me promise to keep quiet about it. He was convinced there was more going on besides TEL. There were signs, he said—budgets not quite adding up; unaccounted expenses; mysterious donations. That's when he brought Jason in, to hack Valence's system and take a closer look.

"I only met Jason once, at a bar. He and Max started talking about going to the press. I got scared. I didn't want to know the things they were telling me, but at the same time, I didn't want to be part of Valence's smokescreen." She shook her head, lowered her gaze to the carpet. "I should have quit right then and there. I thought about it, I did. But Max and Jason were so sure they were going to take Valence down that I started believing it myself. Then one night, about a week before the launch, Max showed up at my house. He told me they'd found something big. Something criminal. But there was none of the excitement I'd seen back at the bar. Max was terrified."

"What did he find?" Emily bunched her fingers into anxious fists as she braced herself for what came next.

Anya sucked in a deep breath. "The reason Valence Industries was able to dominate the markets in those countries with TEL was because they were getting rid of the competition."

Emily heard Evan Holts words in her ear: *I want to know why no unleaded alternative has tried to take their crown.*

"How do you get rid of whole companies?" she asked.

Anya ran trembling fingers through her hair. "By arranging accidents, staging career-destroying scandals . . . and by taking care of the people at the top."

Emily stared at her, open-mouthed.

"This is what Max and Jason uncovered," Anya said. "Valence Industries has been bribing government officials in those countries with millions of dollars to fail their unleaded competitors at the testing stage. If there's no suitable alternative. . ."

"There's no one to stop Valence Industries selling TEL for as long as it likes," Emily gasped.

Anya nodded grimly. "Meanwhile, Valence sits back and collects a fortune while the lives of millions of children are irreparably damaged."

Now it all made terrible sense. The countries Valence Industries had targeted were all in states of pandemonium. Civil war, violence, and poverty were a way of life. And so was corruption. Emily raised a hand to her lips. What kind of government cared so little for its people? What kind of government actively took part in destroying the health of generations of children? She was sickened.

"I made the same face when I first found out," Anya said. "Jason hacked into Jonathan Hunt's emails. It was all there—all the exchanges between him and the various mediating agencies who took care of the dirty work. There was never direct contact between Valence and the governments, of course, but each month, payments were sent and competition was disposed of. Max and Jason found evidence of those transactions, too. They made copies of everything. They were going to take it all to Evan Holt the day after the launch."

Emily's mind raced as all the pieces flew together. "Anya, what happened that night?"

"Max came to me, said he needed to talk to me in private. We arranged to meet upstairs in his hotel room. He told me to make sure no one saw me coming, so I made up the excuse Josh was sick, and I left the gala. When I met Max upstairs, he was in a bad way. He told me Jonathan Hunt was onto him, that he'd been called in that morning and questioned about a security breach, that someone had followed him home the night before.

"Max was terrified. But he knew there was no going back. The only choice was to make a move before Valence did—which meant making a move right then and there. He said we had to run. That the only way was to go into hiding, lay low for a few days, then contact Evan Holt again."

Emily watched as Anya's body sank like a punctured tire.

"I panicked. I told him he was going too far, that he was putting us all in danger—that he was risking my son's life. Believe me, I wanted him to bring Valence Industries down. But I was never meant to be part of it. It's all very exciting when you're watching from a distance, but when they come knocking on your door, it's a different matter. Max and I fought. I told him I wanted nothing more to do with what he'd found, that I was going to leave E.C.G. He accused me of being weak." The sting of those words was still smarting on Anya's face. "So, I showed him how weak I was by storming out of his room and going home to my son."

Emily tried to imagine herself in the same position. Would she have made the same decision as Anya? She wasn't so sure. But she didn't have a child to consider.

"And that was the last time you saw Max?"

Anya nodded. "And he was sober. He hadn't touched a drop."

They were both quiet for a moment, Anya haunted by memories and Emily frantically going over everything she'd learned.

"The evidence they found," she said. "You saw it?"

"Yes. At my house that evening. That's why I was so afraid. Max had made a list of names of the people involved. Jonathan Hunt might be at the centre of it all, but he's small fry compared to some of the others. This isn't just about Valence's involvement, Emily. This goes further. Higher. How do you think the company made contact with those governments in the first place?"

Emily caught her breath, then lowered her voice to a whisper. "What do you mean? That *our* government is involved?"

Anya slid her arms around her ribcage. "If you know politics, there are names on Max's list you'll recognize. There's no price too high when your funds are limitless."

Emily's head was spinning. Suddenly the room felt hot and airless. It was all too much. But she finally understood why Anya had run from the hotel room that night—and why she'd been running ever since. Now Emily had come blundering into the Copelands' world, shining a great spotlight on mother and son, putting their lives in danger once more. Guilt stabbed at her conscience.

"What did Max do with the evidence?"

Anya stood up, went to check the window again. "He had it with him in the hotel, ready to hand over to Evan Holt."

"Surely he made copies?"

"I'm sure he did. And I'm sure Valence would have gone out of its way to find them all."

"He didn't give you a copy?"

"He tried. I refused."

Emily asked her about the envelope that Max had given to the night porter. "He didn't send it to you?"

Anya shook her head. "What about Evan Holt?"

"If it was meant for him he never received it."

"Perhaps Valence intercepted it."

It was possible, Emily thought. But that would mean Valence Industries had eyes everywhere. Did the company really have such power? Either way, she was still no closer to finding Max's evidence.

A thought struck her. "How did Valence know that it was Max hacking into its system?"

Anya shook her head. "Maybe Hunt was keeping tabs on him. He would have been suspicious ever since Max confronted him about TEL."

"But to kill him—to know Jason Dobbs was involved and kill him, too—surely that kind of extreme reaction requires hard proof?"

"You underestimate Valence Industries. You shouldn't," Anya said, returning her gaze to the street below. "In some ways, I admire its tenacity."

Emily's jaw fell open. "How can you say that?"

"Because Valence is absolutely dedicated to its cause. It's just unfortunate that what it—what *they*— believe in is a whole world of fucked up. Since when did yachts and second homes have more worth than human lives?"

"We have to get you out of here. Somewhere safe." Emily crossed the room and looked out the window. It was a quiet, tree-lined street made up of Victorian houses and new-build apartment blocks. A handful of people sauntered by. Birds flitted from canopy to canopy. "Do you have family in London?"

Anya pressed her head against the glass, then closed her eyes. "My parents are in Bristol, but—"

"Okay, so we put you on a train. Right away. Right now."

"There's no point in—"

"It's not safe here. So, you take Josh and stay with your parents for a little while. Just until this is all over."

Anya turned to her, desperation in her eyes. "For how long? A few days? A week? Do you even know what you're going to do? You think one person against an entire corporation is going to win? Look at Max, at Jason. Look at my son. You don't even have the evidence you need to bring Valence down."

A small voice behind them made the women turn around.

"I'm thirsty."

Josh was in the bedroom doorway again, staring at his mother and the strange woman next to her.

"We were safe until you came here today," Anya said. Her voice was cracked, defeated.

Emily placed a hand on her arm. "I saw you in the park, Anya—how can you be safe when you live every minute in fear?" She stole a glance at Josh, who was now standing in the middle of the room, staring impatiently at his mother. "Pack some things."

"We're going to see Nanny and Granddad?" Josh bounced with excitement.

Anya opened her arms and he scurried into them.

"Yes, we are," she said, glaring at Emily. "But just for a little while."

"Good," Emily breathed. "That's good."

All she had to do now was to get Anya and Josh safely across London without being seen.

34

HELEN SAT AT her desk going over the story she'd just written; a small, satirical piece for London Truth about the recent tax relief scandal involving several high-profile celebrities and politicians. It wasn't her best work, but with the events of the last forty-eight hours, it would have to be good enough. If it wasn't, her editor would get the subs to rewrite it, just like she'd done with her last article, allegedly to save her from a potential libel lawsuit.

Giving her eyes a break from the screen, Helen leaned back in her chair and stretched out her spine. An image of Evan Holt's dead, naked body assaulted her mind. The room spun. Nausea bubbled in her stomach.

Standing up, she hurried past her busy colleagues and headed to the bathroom. Finding it empty, she dashed into a cubicle and vomited. When she was done, she dabbed her mouth with tissue and flushed the toilet. At the sink, she splashed cold water on her face.

She thought about Evan again—not about his actual death, which was too grisly to have in her head—but about the timing of it. Just twenty-four hours had passed between the theft of Max Edwards' diary from Emily's apartment and Evan's murder. How had Valence found him so quickly? Even if they'd gone through the diary straight away, they would have needed to know who Evan Holt was in the first place to have been able to find him.

Helen had recognized his name instantly, but that was because she was a fan of his work, hoping to one day emulate his success as an investigative journalist. But would Evan have been known to Jonathan Hunt? It was possible, she supposed. His PR people would constantly be on the lookout for names like his. But still...

Helen glanced at her reflection in the mirror and was shocked by what she saw. She'd lied to Emily—there was no boyfriend, and last night, she'd returned to her apartment and bolted the door. She hadn't wanted to be around people; that was not her way of dealing with shock and upset. Her way was to be left alone, to process the event as quickly as possible, then to shut it away somewhere in the back of her mind.

Usually, her method worked. But last night, when she'd finally fallen asleep, she'd been plagued by nightmares of being chased, of getting caught, of being stripped and throttled. And when she'd woken, she'd immediately lunged for the knife hidden beneath her pillow and brandished it at the empty bedroom.

This behaviour was most unlike her. She was supposed to be the tough one. Tougher than her three older brothers. Tougher than her father, who'd said the only job she should be thinking about was settling down and birthing him grandchildren. Tougher than her mother, who said yes to her husband, and agreed with his opinions, and didn't know what she would do without him.

"Get it together," Helen whispered to her reflection.

Her reflection stared back with wide, frightened eyes.

Returning to the newsroom, she sat down at her desk and tried to zone out from the din of clacking keyboards and telephone calls. How had Valence Industries found Evan so quickly? Had Emily unwittingly told someone about him? It was entirely possible. She was, after all, a rank amateur who had somehow managed to stumble upon the story of the year—the kind of story that would not just elevate the profile of London Truth, but would also skyrocket Helen's career. And wouldn't she have earned the step up? If she hadn't directed Emily to Evan, then she would still be stumbling around in the dark, still convinced that Max Edwards had died because of his inability to keep his penis in the marriage bed.

Helen huffed. She should never have texted Emily. She should have contacted Evan Holt herself. Perhaps this whole sorry business would have been conducted a little more professionally. Perhaps Evan Holt might still be alive. *Or perhaps if you hadn't opened your big mouth and mentioned TEL, none of this would be happening.*

A wave of nausea crested in her stomach, threatening to send her running to the bathroom again. No, this was not her fault. She had only been following her impulses like any other forward-thinking journalist.

So why was she the one sitting here, stuck at her desk, writing some pointless article she didn't even care about, while Emily Swanson was off chasing Anya Copeland and probably asking all the wrong questions?

Helen glanced around the room. She would speak to Emily when they met later, and she'd make it clear who was the professional and who was the amateur. And she would demand exclusive rights to the story. Emily would probably whine and complain, but Helen would insist. She had risked her life. Valence could be watching her right now, waiting for her to leave the office so they could drag her down a dark alley, never to be seen again.

Shivering, Helen looked over her desk, toward the smoked glass office doors. *Or they could walk straight in and stick a knife in your gut.* The air grew thick around her, making it hard to breathe.

Yes, she would speak to Emily Swanson, and she would get what she deserved.

"Helen?"

Startled, she spun on her chair. Her colleague, Bill, was staring down at her.

"Are you okay?" he asked. "You don't look well."

Helen straightened. "Jesus, a hundred points for compliment of the week, Bill. Charm like that must work wonders for your wife's self-esteem."

"Okay... Well, a call just came in for you while you were in the bathroom. A Sally Turner? Said something about her landlord giving her an eviction notice. She wants to see you."

Sally Turner was one of a handful of tenants Helen had recently interviewed for a feature on corrupt London landlords. Without any legal cap in place, many landlords were charging extortionate rental prices while providing little to no maintenance management when problems arose.

Sally had been living in the same one-bedroom apartment for the last four years and seen her rent increased each year. She'd also been living with ME, as well as chronic damp and mould issues that were affecting her health. After interviewing Sally, Helen had approached the property owner, who had slammed the door in her face and told her in no uncertain terms to 'go fuck a lamppost.'

"I'll call her back," she said, turning away.

"Is that the rent piece?"

Irritated, Helen turned back again to see the editor-in-chief, Christine Gates, was standing next to Bill.

Bill nodded. "Sally Turner's just been served an eviction notice. Reckons it's because of the interview."

"What's your schedule like for the next couple of hours?" This was directed at Helen, who stared at her computer, then at the office doors.

"Well, I have the tax evasion piece. . ."

"That can wait. Get over to Sally Turner's now and see what's going on," Christine said. "And put some makeup on. You look like hell."

Helen opened her mouth to protest, but Christine was already walking away. Shrugging an apology, Bill retreated to his desk. Helen returned her gaze to the doors and a cold tremor ran down the length of her spine.

"Get it together," she whispered.

Her car was parked at the back of the building. There would be people in the street. Nothing was going to happen.

Logging off the computer, Helen grabbed her bag, fished out her car keys, and made her way to the doors. The corridor was empty; the stairwell, too.

Out in the street, she looked left, then right. It was a little after five-thirty and the pavements were already busy with pedestrians.

Good, she thought. *You see? Nothing is going to happen.* Turning down a narrow, litter-strewn alley, Helen hurried toward the car park. As she walked, her phone started ringing. While she waded through her bag to retrieve it, two young men with buzz cuts and bloodshot eyes entered the alley behind her.

35

THE TAXI FERRIED its passengers through the streets of Southfields. Sitting in the front passenger seat, Emily fixed her gaze on the wing mirror. Rush hour had started. Although Southfields was relatively suburban, traffic clogged the roads. Behind them, a red Nissan was close enough for Emily to make out the passengers—a female driver and a school girl who was busy texting.

Southfields Underground station was just a few minutes away. From there, it was a twenty-five-minute journey to Paddington via the District line.

Emily's palms were already sweating at the thought of battling the swathes of homeward-bound commuters. Having to do it underground would make it a thousand times worse. The only other alternative was to take the taxi all the way, but the rush hour traffic would mean missing the train. Besides, being out in the open felt reckless.

An excited cry from the back seat interrupted her thoughts. Josh had unbuckled his seatbelt and had pressed his face against the side window. He banged on the glass, laughing at the woman who stopped to stare at him.

"Josh put your seatbelt on, *now*." Anya's voice was firm but strained. "I mean it, young man. Or we won't be going to see Nanny and Granddad."

Emily twisted around in her seat. Ignoring his mother, Josh continued to hit the window.

"Hey, boy. Put your seatbelt on like your mother told you," the taxi driver called.

From the corner of her eye, Emily saw Anya return the driver's disapproving stare, then lean across to put a hand on Josh's shoulder.

"Come on," she said in a gentler tone. "You're not being safe and that's making me worried. Don't you want to see Nanny and Granddad? I'm sure they'll have ice cream for you."

"No!" shouted Josh. But he moved away from the window.

"Good boy, now put your seatbelt on. Here, I'll help you."

"No!" Swivelling around, Josh rested his back against the door and pulled up his knees.

Anger flashed in Anya's eyes. "Put your seatbelt on!"

As the traffic lights changed from red to amber, the boy clamped his arms over his chest and shook his head.

The taxi driver swore under his breath. "Lady, I can't drive with your boy jumping around like that."

Blasts of horns filled the air. Just as Emily wondered if she should intervene, the driver turned back to the wheel, muttered something in Turkish, then got the car moving once more. In the back, Josh started banging his head against the window.

Anya unbuckled her seatbelt, grabbed her son by the arm, and pulled him away from the door. He squirmed against her, growling through clenched teeth as she held him down and clicked his seatbelt into place. As soon as Anya sat back, there was an audible *clunk* and Josh was up by the window again, smacking his forehead against the glass.

When the taxi pulled up in front of the station two minutes later, Josh was pinned to his mother's lap, her arms wrapped around his chest. He bellowed in anger, making his body stiff like cement, then throwing his legs out in wild kicks.

"Fucking bitch!" he screamed.

"Out of the mouths of babes," the driver grumbled.

Emily paid him, tipped him generously, then hopped out. The station was busy, but not overwhelmed. The moment he was out of the taxi, Josh stopped screaming. He peered up at the station with wide, excited eyes. Anya surfaced behind him, her face red with stress and exhaustion, and scooped up his hand.

"It will be all right," said Emily, carrying Anya's hastily packed suitcase and checking the station entrance. Anya stared at her as if she'd just announced she could walk on water.

Leading her wards through the ticket barriers, Emily stepped onto the platform. Josh pulled on Anya's hand, straining to run up and down, desperate to see the trains. He didn't have long to wait. The train pulled in and commuters spilled from its doors. They swarmed around Emily, a tidal wave of bodies in sharp suits. Instinctively, she held her breath.

Keep it together. If you lose it, they'll lose it.

Josh was staring at her, then at the train. He wrenched his hand from Anya's grip and held on to Emily's. It startled her; she hadn't felt the grip of such a tiny hand since her school days, and the sensation filled her with intense comfort and fear.

The crowds thinned. Josh ran forward, pulling Emily with him, and jumped onto the train. Anya followed, pausing in the doorway to peer along the platform. She joined them moments later, sandwiching Josh between her and Emily.

The good thing about travel etiquette in and around London was that people kept themselves to themselves. Making eye contact was a sin, while trying to make conversation was tantamount to assault. As the doors slid shut and the train pulled away, Emily watched the other passengers. She was confident they had not been followed—no one in the carriage was paying them any attention, even with Josh jumping up and down on the seat.

Taking out her phone, she checked the time. 5:36 p.m. There was a train leaving for Bristol in just over forty minutes. They would arrive at Paddington with just enough time to buy tickets. The train would be filled with commuters returning to Reading—which was a good thing because more people meant less chance of something happening to Anya and Josh.

"What will you do?" Anya was staring at her intensely. In between them, Josh balanced on his knees and watched the outside world whip past the windows.

Emily stared back. She didn't know what she was going to do. Last night, she had vowed to find out the truth from Anya, to finally return to Diane Edwards and tell her that her husband had been murdered by his employers—even if there was no proof to substantiate that claim. Then Emily was going to walk away. She knew Diane would not be free of her torment, that she would remain trapped inside that tomb of a house. But it didn't matter—

because Emily *would* be free.

So why was she sitting on a train with a mother and son who were now relying on her for protection?

Emily's mouth was dry. She tried to swallow. *What was she going to do?*

The train pulled into East Putney station. More people got on, filling the seats. Emily's watchful eyes moved from passenger to passenger. There were no men in blue coats. But that didn't mean a thing. Her knee bouncing up and down, Emily checked the time again. Then she called Helen.

The line connected. The journalist picked up after a few seconds. "There you are. Any luck?"

"You could say that," Emily said, flashing a glance at Anya and Josh. "Where are you?"

"I've been- - -a job, but- - -you at the office. Can you make it for seven?" Helen said something else but her words were swallowed by pops and crackles.

"What was that?" Emily said, raising her voice. "The line's bad—I'm on a train to Paddington."

"Paddington? Where the hell are you- - -" More pops and crackles. Then Helen's voice came back. "Emily, did you tell- - -Evan Holt being in Max's- - -"

The line went dead. Emily tried Helen again, but the call went straight to voicemail.

"Everything all right?" Anya glanced at her with quizzical eyes.

Emily smiled, but an odd prickling sensation had started at the base of her skull.

As the train headed toward Kensington, it suddenly entered a tunnel and plunged its passengers into darkness. Invisible hands pierced Emily's chest and squeezed her heart. Icy blades sank into her spine.

Breathe! she told herself. *Just breathe, and you'll be fine!* But it was as if all the air had been sucked out of the carriage. The clack of wheels on rails became a deafening roar. The train sped up, hurtling through the underground.

Emily dug her nails into the palms of her hands. Beside her, Josh covered his ears and screamed.

36

"THERE YOU ARE. Any luck?" Helen said, pressing the phone to her ear. At the same time, she reached the end of the alley and pushed open the gate to the staff car park.

The line crackled with interference. Emily's voice sounded far away. "You could say that. Where are you?"

"I've been sent out on a job, but I'll still meet you at the office. Can you make it for seven?"

"What did- -? I'm on a train to Paddington- - -line's bad."

The car park was a small stretch of concrete surrounded by high walls with an open entrance to the road. Nine of the ten parking bays were full. Helen's car was parked front and centre.

"Paddington? Where the hell are you going? You're supposed to be meeting me." Helen's irritation grew. Yet again, Emily was off chasing leads without her. Taking out her car keys, she pushed the unlock button and the car flashed her a hello. After opening the driver door and climbing in, Helen pressed the phone to her ear again. "Emily, did you tell anyone about Evan Holt being in Max's diary?"

The line crackled.

"Emily? Hello?"

Muttering under her breath, Helen tossed the phone into the cup holder and reached for the door. She looked up. Two shaven-headed men were hurrying in her direction. They were young, perhaps in their early twenties, but there was nothing youthful about their eyes, which were hardened and dead, as if they'd witnessed a lifetime of cruelty.

Helen froze. Her heart smashed into her chest.

Then the men began to run.

With a cry, Helen yanked the door closed and hit the locks. She dropped her keys, scooped them up again, then slid the car key into the ignition.

The men were almost upon her. She turned the key and the engine roared to life. Pressing down on the clutch, she shifted the gearstick into first—just as a fist slammed into the side window.

Helen screamed. Her foot slipped off the clutch. The car lurched forward and stalled. One of the men jumped onto the bonnet and pressed his hands against the windscreen, his eyes burning into her as he flashed a wicked grin.

For a second, Helen was paralyzed. Coming to her senses, she started the engine again. Something glinted at the corner of her eye.

The driver window exploded.

Helen's arms shot up to her face as glass rained down. A hand reached in and snatched up a fistful of hair. The man pulled, setting Helen's scalp on fire and wrenching her neck. She screamed and clawed. Her nails sank into flesh. The man yelled but he didn't let go. He tugged harder, lifting Helen from the seat and halfway through the window. The second man watched with amusement as he sat on the bonnet with his legs crossed.

Helen screamed again, thrashing and kicking, digging her nails down harder. She felt her assailant's skin come away and blood seep from his hand. The man yelled, releasing his grip.

Helen was free. The engine was still running. The man on the bonnet was no longer smiling.

Adrenaline surged through Helen's veins as she pressed down hard on the accelerator. The car lurched forward, making the man lose his balance and fall to the side. Helen watched him disappear, his arms and legs flailing, then her eyes found the exit.

"Get going!" she screamed.

Something flashed in the corner of her eye. Twisting her head to the right, she saw the other man running at her, a crowbar swinging from his bleeding hand.

Helen shrieked and hit the accelerator. The crow bar smashed into her shoulder. The wheel slipped out of her hand. The car swerved violently, knocking the man sideways. Then it ploughed straight into the wall.

37

BY THE TIME the train pulled into Paddington Station, Emily was barely holding on. The carriage was full, with limbs and suitcases crammed into every available space. Josh's continual screams and cries had earned Anya several judgmental looks. Meanwhile, Emily had tried very hard not to curl up into a ball and have a full-blown anxiety attack.

But they were here. As the train doors slid open and its passengers spilled out, Emily sucked in a lifesaving breath and signalled to Anya. On the platform, she took in more deep breaths. Her anxiety level dropped from near hysteria to moderate panic, but she was still underground, which wasn't helping.

"Are you okay?" Anya had a worried look on her face.

Emily nodded. "Fine."

"I want to see the train leave!" Josh screamed. He tried to pull away from Anya, but her grip was like iron. Instead, he let his legs go limp beneath him and he dangled like a doll from his mother's hand.

"Come on," Emily said, in between breaths. She bent her knees until she was eye level with him. "There are lots and lots of trains upstairs, much better than this one."

Josh scrambled to his feet and the three of them made their way up steps and escalators, until they were above ground.

Stepping into Paddington Station, Emily felt a surge of relief. She sucked in air, ignoring the taste of engine oil and grease from fast food stalls, and Anya's continued stares.

It was almost 6 p.m. Emily made quick work of buying tickets. Anya tried to pay for them, but Emily refused to take her money; it was the least she could do for bringing trouble to the Copelands' door. A voice boomed from the loud speakers, startling Josh as it announced the Bristol train was ready for boarding. The three of them made their way to the platform.

"Here." Emily handed Anya a piece of paper with her phone number written on it. "Call me as soon as you get there."

Anya folded the paper and slipped it into her bag. She turned slowly and stared at the train.

"It's going to be fine. You'll be safer there," Emily said. Josh glanced up at her with wide eyes.

Anya had a sad, strange smile on her lips. "You don't know that. You don't even know what you're doing."

Hoisting Josh into her arms, she turned to board the train, then stopped. "I lied earlier," she said, without looking back. "We kissed. Just once."

Then she was gone, disappearing inside the carriage with her son. Emily waited on the platform, searching for Anya and Josh through the carriage window. She saw them a moment later, Josh clambering into a window seat to peer excitedly out at the station, and Anya staring silently into space. Two minutes later, a whistle blew and the train pulled away, taking the Copelands to safety. When the train was just a speck in the distance, Emily turned and exited the platform.

Finding a quiet corner in one of the station cafés, she tried calling Helen again. When she didn't answer, Emily hung up, gave it another minute, then tried again. Where was she?

A man dressed in a suit sat down at the next table and set his briefcase on the floor. He glanced casually in Emily's direction.

Emily watched him for a moment, then glanced back at her phone screen. Helen had said something about being sent out on a job—or at least that's what Emily had interpreted from the bad line. It would explain why she wasn't picking up.

On the next table, the man had picked up a newspaper and was reading the front page. But Emily could see him from the corner of her eye, glancing in her direction every twenty seconds.

Getting up slowly, she picked her way between the tables and exited the café. Glancing over her shoulder, she returned to the station concourse and eyed the surging crowds. It was 6:18 p.m. To meet Helen at the London Truth offices at seven—another educated guess—she had no choice but to travel via the Underground.

The thought made her nauseous, but the longer it took her to get to Helen, the longer she was leaving Anya and Josh Copeland at risk; no matter how much Emily had tried to convince Anya, she couldn't be certain they hadn't been followed.

Her eyes found the café. The man was still reading the newspaper, one hand on his coffee cup. But did he just look up in her direction?

Pulse racing, Emily delved into the crowd and made her way to the top of the escalators. The Underground stretched out below like a gaping mouth. *You can do this. You already did it once. You can do it again.* Emily drew in a deep breath, then took one last look back at the café.

The man was gone.

Spinning on her heels, she searched the crowds. It would be impossible to spot the man in a sea of suits. Where was he? Was he watching her right now? Had he seen her put Anya and Josh on the train?

Panic gripped Emily's mind. She stepped onto the escalator, and taking two steps at a time, descended into the Underground.

She headed straight for the ticket barriers, then turned to look over her shoulder. A man stood by the ticket machines, newspaper in hand, looking her way. Emily didn't wait to see if it was the man from the café. Half running along the tunnel, she headed toward the Bakerloo line. She was already losing control of her breathing as she reached another set of descending escalators, and she felt a familiar prickling at the top of her head, signalling the beginning of an anxiety attack

Emily ploughed forward, scurrying down the moving steps, knocking into shoulders and jutting suitcases. At the bottom, she turned and looked up. Was that the man at the top of the escalator? Or was that him a few metres away and walking in her direction?

Breaking into a cold sweat, she turned and dashed to the eastbound platform. Every time she drew in a breath, she felt a terrible weight pressing down on her chest. Every time she exhaled, she felt her lungs constrict a little more. She needed to regain control of her body. Now.

Racing along the platform, Emily breathed in for a count of four, held it for a count of seven, then exhaled for a count of eight. She repeated the pattern, over and over, as she ducked and weaved between the bodies, until she reached the end of the platform. Pressing herself up against the wall, she closed her eyes and waited for the train to come.

In for four, hold for seven, out for eight.

She risked a quick look down the length of the platform. She couldn't see the man from the café, but there were several people here now. *He could be hiding among them*, she thought.

Or perhaps he's just someone grabbing a coffee while he waits for his train home.

A rush of warm air shot out of the tunnel, followed by a low rumble that rapidly grew into a deafening roar. Brakes screeched. The train emerged from the tunnel and slowed to a halt. Seconds later, the doors slid open. Emily raced toward them, pushing past disgruntled travellers. She hurried to the far end of the carriage and waited for the doors to close. For the man to come.

But he didn't.

The doors slid shut. The train pulled away, gathering speed as it plunged into the darkness of the tunnel. Emily pressed her back up against the door and scanned the packed carriage. *You're being paranoid,* she told herself as a cold sweat dampened her neck. But she had every right to be.

She was now in possession of knowledge that had resulted in the murder of at least three people, destroyed a young boy's life, and stood to ruin millions more. But without physical proof that knowledge meant nothing. Who had Max sent the evidence to for safe-keeping?

As Emily continued to slow her breathing, she hoped that she and Helen would soon find out. Because Valence Industries was coming for them with one goal in mind—to silence them for good.

38

PALE AND BREATHLESS, Emily entered the newsroom just after 7 p.m. She was surprised to see a few employees still at their desks, but although the journalists were hard at work, she instantly sensed something was wrong. Her fears were confirmed when she approached the man at the nearest desk and asked for Helen.

"We don't know where she is," he said. Other colleagues turned their heads in Emily's direction. "She went out to do an interview, and. . ."

His voice trailed off. He glanced across the room at a stocky, middle-aged woman with cropped hair.

"And what?" Emily said, following his gaze. The woman was marching over.

She introduced herself as Christine Gates, the editor-in-chief for London Truth. Emily shook her hand. She didn't know whether Helen had told Christine about Valence Industries, so for now, she kept the story to herself.

"Helen's not here," Christine said. She had a brusque manner, but she shared the same worried expression as her colleagues.

"Do you know where I can find her?" Emily asked.

"Helen's car was found outside an hour ago," the editor-in-chief said. "Looks like there was some sort of accident."

Emily froze. "Is she all right?"

"We don't know. Helen wasn't in her car and she's not answering her phone."

The room stretched away from Emily as Christine's voice echoed around her. "The police are on the way. We think she might be hurt. There was blood on the ground."

They had her. Valence Industries had taken Helen. Emily's legs grew weak. She tried to speak, but nothing came out.

Christine whispered something to the man at the desk, who jumped up and hurried from the room. She turned back to Emily and regarded her with a hardened expression.

"I know who you are," she said. "You were at Meadow Pines with Helen. You're the one she wrote about."

Emily's mouth hung open. She nodded.

"Is this a social call, or are you two colluding on something I don't know about?"

"I—"

Christine leaned in closer and dropped her voice to a hush. "Because let's not waste time here. The driver window of Helen's car was smashed in. Bill found a clump of her hair, for God's sake!"

Emily wanted to vomit. Had they killed her already? Or did they have her locked up somewhere, preparing her for interrogation? Torturous images attacked Emily's mind. Then Helen's voice echoed in her memory. What had she said on the phone? Something about Evan Holt. . .

Christine was growing impatient. "Well? Is there something you want to tell me or not?"

Did you tell anyone about Evan Holt being in Max's diary? Was that what she'd said before the call had been cut off? Emily raced through the events of the past week. Besides Helen, who had she spoken to about Evan Holt? She'd told Jerome, who would have more than likely told Daniel. Then there was Lucy Dobbs. Then Anya Copeland.

Another thought entered Emily's mind. Her conversation with Anya had revealed something—that Valence Industries had known Max's every move. It was like the company had inside knowledge—as if someone close to him had been watching and reporting back.

Emily's intuition began to spark. Why were these thoughts converging?

The spark became a fire. Suddenly she knew why.

"I'm sorry," she said. "I have to go."

Before Christine could say another word, Emily bolted through the doors and headed back to the street. If Helen wasn't already dead, there was one person who could lead Emily to where she was being held.

Exiting the building, she paused to look both ways down the street. Safe for now, she pulled out her phone and headed back toward the station.

Jerome answered after a few seconds. "I've been worried about you. Where are you? What's going on?"

"No time to talk," Emily said, glancing over her shoulder. "Listen, what are the chances of me borrowing Daniel's car?"

Jerome laughed. "Are you serious? I'd say slim to none. What do you need it for?"

"To follow someone."

The line was quiet. "On a scale of one to people-are-trying-to-kill-me, how much trouble are you in right now?"

"It's not me who's in trouble. But right now, I'd say Helen was about an eleven—Valence have her."

Emily quickened her pace, pushing her way through the crowds.

"Christ. Have you called the police?"

"They're on their way to London Truth right now. Please, Jerome! Can you ask Daniel? It's urgent."

Jerome's voice was frantic in her ear. "I don't think you should be chasing after these people, Em. They're dangerous. The police will—"

"I'm coming to Daniel's right now. I'll ask him myself."

Anxiety gnawed at her gut. Evan Holt was dead. Anya and Josh were currently on a train to Bristol after she'd promised them safety. And now Helen was missing. Emily was running out of time.

"Fine, I'll ask," Jerome said at last. "But you can't go after these people on your own."

"Helen could die. You can't stop me."

Emily hung up. Then she broke into a run.

39

TIM MARSDEN PULLED into the quiet suburban street on the outskirts of Dartford at 8:48 p.m. Climbing out of his silver Audi coupe, he stopped to erase a greasy smear from the driver window, then strolled up the drive to his four-bedroom detached house. At the door, he fumbled for his keys, almost dropped them, then turned to glance back down the drive. He seemed nervous; as if he expected someone to be standing there. Shrugging off his paranoia, he slid the key into the lock and quickly disappeared inside.

But Tim had been right to look over his shoulder—because he was being watched. Sat behind the wheel of a blue Mazda, Emily watched the windows of the Marsden house. Tim's address had been easy to obtain. The use of Daniel's car had been less so—with him setting a number of conditions that Emily had to agree to before getting her hands on the keys. One of those conditions was currently sitting beside her in the passenger seat.

"For the record, I'm deeply unhappy you're here," Emily said, peeling her gaze from the Marsden house for a second.

Jerome shrugged a shoulder. "I'm not happy I'm here either, but as I said, you can't go after these people alone. Besides, Daniel is very protective of his car."

"Somehow I think you being here wasn't Daniel's idea."

Emily looked back at the house. Jerome followed her gaze.

"What do we do now?" he said. "Do we just walk up to the door and demand answers? Want me to rough him up a bit?"

Emily narrowed her eyes. Now was not the time for jokes. Helen had been missing for almost two hours. Every attempt to call her had gone straight to voicemail. As Emily spied on Tim Marsden's home, she wondered if she should have said something more to Christine Gates. But what could the police do except put Helen's life at further risk? If she *was* still alive.

"You're not going to do anything apart from sit here and stay safe," she told Jerome as she pushed open the door. He didn't protest. "Watch the road. If you see any signs of trouble, let me know."

Jerome's face appeared at the window and he stared at her with worried eyes.

"Be careful, okay?"

Crossing the quiet, suburban street, Emily headed for Tim Marsden's house. He was all she had now. Valence Industries knew Meryl Silkwood did not exist, but that Emily Swanson did. Marsden was the only person who could have told Jonathan Hunt the truth. And now Emily understood why Helen had asked her about Evan Holt—the speed in which Valence had struck meant that it had already known about his involvement before discovering Max's diary. And Emily had been wrong—there had been another person she'd talked to about Evan Holt—and now she was standing at his front door.

Expelling a shaky breath, Emily pressed the buzzer.

A few seconds later, the door opened and a young girl, no older than five, stared up at her with round, blue eyes.

"Is your daddy home?" Emily asked. She had not considered the possibility of Tim Marsden having children. Suddenly she felt guilty for being here, for the threats she was about to make.

The girl continued to mutely stare. Her father's voice rang out from inside the house.

"Megan, how many times have I told you not to open the door? You wait for an adult."

He appeared behind her, his hand reaching out to pull her back. Spotting Emily, he froze in mid-movement.

"Go inside to Mummy," Marsden whispered.

Giving the woman on the doorstep one last look, the girl tiptoed away. As soon as she was gone, Marsden stepped out of the house and advanced toward Emily. They stood, glaring at each other under the halo of porchlight.

"What the hell are you doing here?" he hissed.

"You know why. Where's Helen Carlson?"

"I—I don't know what you're talking about."

Emily examined every centimetre of the man's face. "Helen Carlson—the journalist you saw me with at the plant—she's missing. I know you recognized me. I know you told Jonathan Hunt. Now you're going to tell me where they've taken Helen."

She was surprised by the sudden anger firing from her mouth. But she *was* angry. All the lives that Valence had ruined, all the lives that would be ruined in the future—Emily felt their fury burning through her veins.

Tim Marsden flinched then glanced back at the house. "I don't know where she is, I swear. Whatever's happened to her has nothing to do with me."

"And what about Evan Holt? I told you about him and now he's dead. And what about your good friend, Max Edwards? And Jason Dobbs? Their blood is on your hands!" Emily paused, afraid of the rage boiling inside her.

Tim Marsden stepped back toward his home. "I don't know anything."

"Well, I do." Emily said, closing the gap between them. "For instance, I know that Valence is poisoning millions of children through the sale of TEL."

Tim's face paled. "Exporting TEL isn't breaking any laws."

"But bribing government officials to destroy the competition is." She glared at him, fires burning in her eyes. "That's why Max was killed. Jason Dobbs, too. That's why Anya's son was poisoned, his life ruined—because they found out the truth. And if it got out, Valence would be finished. Jonathan Hunt and whoever else is involved would spend years in prison. Well, they may think they're going to stop it from getting out this time, but how long before someone else finds out what they're doing? They can't kill everyone, Tim. The people at the top will already be planning their way out of this. And you can bet your life that way out requires a scapegoat. When it comes down to it, who do you think they'll choose?"

Tim stared at Emily through frightened eyes. "What did they do to Anya's son?"

He doesn't know. The terror on his face was genuine enough to make her believe it. "They poisoned him with lead, left him with irreparable damage that will mark him for the rest of his life. He's five years old, Tim. How old is your daughter?"

Marsden shook his head. He opened his mouth but Emily interrupted him.

"If Valence can harm a five-year-old without blinking an eye, believe me, it will have no qualms in doing what needs to be done to make this whole situation go away—including hurting its own people."

Tim was staring back at the house again, his jaw clenching and unclenching. Emily held her breath. He turned back to her, suddenly aged and defeated.

"Do you have a car?" he asked.

Emily nodded.

Tim was trembling now. "I'll be five minutes. Keep the engine running."

Giving her one last frightened look, he darted inside the house. Emily returned to the car and ushered Jerome into the back seat.

"What happened?" he asked.

"He's coming to talk to us." Emily peered into the rear-view mirror, checking the road behind. It was a typical middle-class suburban street—whitewashed houses, manicured lawns—the kind of street where children played safely, where nothing terrible ever happened. But Emily did not feel safe here.

Jerome squinted at her from the shadows. "Does he know where Helen is?"

"I don't think he does."

"Then why is he coming to talk to us?"

"I guess we're about to find out."

They were quiet then, both watching the street. Two minutes passed. Emily slid the key into the ignition and started the engine, then pulled away from the kerb, positioning the car in front of the Marsden house. For a moment, she wondered if Tim had made a run for it through the back. Then he appeared on the drive, dressed in more casual attire. As he reached the car, he stared into the backseat and froze.

Emily rolled down the window. "It's all right, he's a friend."

Jerome waved a hand. Marsden eyed him, then checked both sides of the street, before climbing in.

"Where am I driving?" Emily asked him.

Marsden shot one more glance toward his home. "Around."

*

Emily did as she was instructed, reaching the end of the road and heading left onto another identical suburban street. The roads were maze-like, easy enough to get lost in if you didn't know where you were going. They drove in silence. When several streets lay between the car and Tim Marsden's family, he let out a shuddering breath.

"What exactly do you know?" he asked.

Emily wasted no time. "Max found out Valence Industries was bribing government officials to discredit its unleaded competitors, thereby prolonging the legality of TEL and allowing Valence to continue making a fortune while destroying the health of millions of children. He knew Valence was onto him, that he was in trouble. He told Anya Copeland what he'd learned. He had proof—emails, documents—that would incriminate Valence. He was going to expose them. Valence stopped him before he could. Valence took back what he'd found and silenced everyone involved." She paused, taking her eyes off the road for a second. "Someone betrayed Max. It's the only way they could have known what he was planning."

Tim sank into the shadows and cocked his head toward the wing mirror. The road ended in a T-junction. Emily spun the wheel, heading left onto yet another leafy, suburban street.

"Jonathan Hunt came to me." Tim stared out the window, watching houses whip by. "He told me there'd been a breach in security, that someone had hacked the system and potentially accessed sensitive information. I assumed he'd meant one of our competitors. But then I wondered why he was telling *me* about it. I was a nobody in the company, nothing to do with computer systems or security. Then Jonathan told me Max was a suspect, and that given his background, it was possible he'd deceived Valence Industries and was working from the inside to bring the company down.

"At first, I didn't believe it. Max seemed completely dedicated to helping Valence become a much greener company, and he was passionate about the Clean Water Project. But Jonathan Hunt insisted Max was up to no good. That's why he came to me. They needed proof that Max was behind the breach."

"So, they asked you to spy on him?" Emily tightened her grip on the steering wheel. "To spy on your friend?"

"Yes, they did. And I agreed."

"Because they promised you his job once he was gone?"

Tim shook his head. "No. Because I wanted to prove them wrong."

Emily had had enough of driving in circles. She pulled into the kerb, found a space, and parked. In the passenger seat, Marsden swivelled his head from left to right. "What's going on? Why have we stopped?"

Emily unbuckled her seatbelt and turned to face him. "You could have told him. If you'd been a real friend to Max, you could have told him what Hunt asked you to do."

"I couldn't."

"Because you wanted his job."

"Because Jonathan Hunt made it very clear that if I didn't do as he asked, there would be consequences."

Emily paused, narrowing her eyes. "He threatened you?"

"You don't understand how a company as powerful as Valence Industries operates." Marsden shot a nervous glance at the street, then let out a trembling breath. "If it wants something, it takes it—with or without consent—and you'd better not get in the way if you don't like it. If I'd refused, Hunt would have made damn sure I never worked in the chemicals industry again. I couldn't afford to lose my job—I have a kid, a mortgage… So I agreed to watch Max. I honestly believed Hunt was wrong about him. And it was looking that way, too—until a few days before the Clean Water gala."

"What happened to change your mind?"

"We'd been working at E.C.G., ironing out the finer details of the launch. It was the end of the day, but Max and Anya decided to stay behind. I'd got all the way to my car before realizing I'd left my jacket behind. I went back. They were alone in the office with the door open. They were talking."

"About TEL?"

"About me." Tim hung his head and was quiet for a moment. "They were discussing whether I could be trusted. Anya didn't think so. But Max did. He told her he'd trusted me about his alcoholism and I'd never told anyone about it, that we'd worked side by side for years. They must have heard me then, but I left before they could see who it was. The next day, I went straight to Max and told him what I'd heard. That was when he told me about TEL, about the bribery.

He said he'd been working with that Jason guy, that they had evidence and they were going to the press. He said he wanted to give me a heads up before the shit hit the fan. That was what they'd disagreed about—whether they should warn me."

"He was an idiot to trust you," Emily said, clenching her jaw.

Marsden ignored the comment. "When Max showed me what they'd found, I was horrified. As a parent, I couldn't believe what was happening—what they were willingly allowing to happen."

Jerome's face appeared between the front seats. "You don't need to be a parent to see how fucked up this company is. Just human."

"I'm under no illusion of how Valence Industries operates," Marsden said, his chin pressed against his chest. "But I panicked. We were in debt with the bank. I had the mortgage to think about, my family's wellbeing. Max didn't have any of those worries. He'd never had kids. He barely saw his wife. I couldn't put everything I had in jeopardy because of his crusade, no matter how justified it was." He shook his head, then let it hang heavy on his neck. "So, I thanked Max for telling me, and I told him I hoped Jonathan Hunt and the others got everything that was coming to them."

"And then you went straight to Jonathan Hunt."

Tim retreated into the shadows. "I thought they would just fire him. I had no idea that they would... How could I have known? It's not my fault. I didn't have a choice!"

"You had the choice of keeping quiet," Emily said, leaning forward. "Of telling them you didn't know anything."

"And what if Hunt found out I was lying? Who would provide for my family? Feed my daughter and put clothes on her back?"

Unable to look at him, Emily turned away. "They killed Max. You could have warned him. He could still be alive. So could Jason,

Evan. . . Josh Copeland could still have a future ahead of him."

In the backseat, Jerome let out a disgusted grunt.

Marsden threw his hands in the air. "You don't understand what it's been like for me! Every morning, I wake up regretting what I did. Wishing I could go back and tell Max to drop everything and get out. And now I'm stuck there. I can't leave Valence Industries because they won't let me. I know too much. They can give me Max's job, they can throw money at me, but if I try to leave, I'm as good as dead. My family, too."

Emily's fingers hurt. She uncurled them from the steering wheel. Time was slipping away, and Tim Marsden wasn't leading her any closer to finding Helen. But there was still another question he could answer. "What happened on the night of the gala? What happened to Max?"

There was a long silence before Marsden answered. "I'd been waiting for Hunt to call him in. I'd assumed he'd decided to wait until the launch was out of the way—for Max to not be there would have been a PR disaster. The only thing I can tell you is that Max hadn't been himself all night. He was nervous, paranoid even. So I pulled him aside and asked him what was wrong. He asked me if I could be trusted." Marsden hung his head again and sobbed. "I should have just come out with it right at that moment. But by then it was too late. So I lied. I told him he could trust me. But he didn't say anything more, just looked me right in the eye and nodded. The rest happened the way I told you. He left, went up to his room. I didn't see him again, I swear. The next morning, he was gone. And I knew then. I *knew* something terrible had happened to him."

"Something terrible is going to happen to Helen," Emily snapped. "Are you going to be responsible for her death, too?"

"I don't know where she is! Jesus, I'm putting my life on the line trying to make things right here. Do you have any idea what Jonathan Hunt will do to me if he knew I was talking to you right now?"

"Then why *are* you talking to me?"

Marsden was silent. When it was clear he wasn't going to answer, Emily started up the engine.

"You're wasting our time," she said. She pulled away from the kerb and began the journey back to Tim Marsden's house. Inside, her heart was beating out of control. Time was ticking away and they were no closer to finding Helen. As for Marsden, she was too angry to even look at him. Valence Industries may have killed Max Edwards, but it was Tim who had provided the gun. Yes, he'd been protecting his family, but people were dead now. People he could have saved with a simple, anonymous warning.

In the backseat, Jerome tried calling Helen again. "Straight to voicemail."

"Try again." Emily spun the wheel and took a left.

Tim Marsden was silent and still, only moving to point Emily in the right direction. Finally, they pulled up in front of his drive. Emily kept the engine running.

Marsden remained unmoving, staring up at his home. Soft light spilled out from one of the bedroom windows.

"If you had the proof you were looking for, what would you do with it?" His voice floated out of the shadows like a ghost.

Emily stared into the darkness. "I'd make sure it was put in the right hands so that Jonathan Hunt and Valence Industries got exactly what they deserved."

"And what about the people caught in between?"

"If they have nothing to hide, then they have nothing to worry about."

Tim brought his hands to his face. He nodded. "Wait here."

Climbing out of the car, he checked the street then jogged up to his house.

Jerome leaned forward. "Fucking coward! But seriously, Em—what's going on here? How are we going to find Helen?"

Emily said nothing as she watched the Marsden house, waiting for the door to open. Jerome continued to speak, but she didn't hear him. The porch light snapped on. Tim Marsden emerged from the house and began walking to the car. He was carrying something. Emily's pulse raced as she realized what it was.

Then Jerome said, "Who's that?"

Parked on the other side of the road, a black SUV had switched on its headlights. As Emily watched, the back passenger door opened and a man stepped out. Dressed in black, he was tall and muscular, with a shaved head and cold eyes that stared across the street at Tim.

"Oh, shit," Jerome said, his breaths thin and fast. "What is this? What do we do?"

Tim had seen the man, but instead of hurrying toward the car, he'd frozen on the drive like a statue. Dipping his head, the man began crossing the road, heading straight for him.

Heart smashing against her chest, Emily reached for the door.

"What are you doing? You can't leave this car!" Jerome grabbed her shoulder, digging his fingers in.

Emily tried to shake him off. "I have to! Let go!"

She watched as the man reached the kerb, then her eyes shot up to the driveway, where Tim was now slowly backing away. He was going to run, taking his evidence with him.

Emily tried to free herself but Jerome's grip was firm.

"Let go of me!" she yelled.

"You can't go out there!" Jerome cried. "You need to be ready to get us out of here."

Emily spun around and saw the man step onto the grassy kerb. *Of course,* she thought with sudden clarity. *Jerome can't drive!*

"I'll get him," Jerome said, and before Emily could stop him, he wrenched open the door and leaped onto the road.

"Come back here!" she shouted.

But Jerome was already off and running, heading straight for Tim Marsden.

40

THE ONLY THOUGHT that screamed in Jerome's head as he pelted across the tarmac and onto the pavement, was that he was going to die. But what he lacked in self-confidence, he compensated with speed. His sudden appearance had startled the man in black, giving Jerome an extra second of time. Throwing himself onto the drive, he raced up to Tim Marsden.

"Come on!" Jerome yelled, snatching Tim by the arm and glancing over his shoulder to see the man in black running straight for them, while two more men were exiting the SUV.

Tim would not move. He stood rigid, terrified of the shape careering toward them. Jerome yanked his arm, lifting him off his feet. Tim stumbled back—just as the man in black launched himself in the air and collided with Jerome, knocking him to the ground.

He hit the gravel hard and rolled onto his back. Before he could catch his breath, a fist slammed into his cheekbone. Momentarily blinded, Jerome drew back his knees and kicked out. His feet connected with soft tissue and the man doubled over. Another kick took him down.

Scrambling to his feet, Jerome saw the other men dash across the road, heading straight for him. He lunged out for Tim's arm again. Tim pulled away, his shoulders sagging with defeat.

"For Christ's sake!" Jerome bellowed in his face. "Get a fucking move on!"

The man on the ground pushed himself onto his knees, just as the other two reached the drive.

Tim stared at the envelope in his hand. Silently, he held it out.

Jerome snatched it, and giving Tim one last, bewildered look, he turned and ran.

First, he tried for the car, but the men were blocking his path. Then spinning on his heels, he raced toward the house. A path led around the side of the building. He came up to a waist-high gate and vaulted over it in one fluid movement.

Adrenaline pulsing through his muscles, Jerome sprinted down the path, then skidded to a halt in the back garden, which was large and shadowy, and surrounded by tall wooden fencing.

The men were close behind. He could hear them gaining on him. His heart leaping in his throat, Jerome raced across the lawn and reached the fence that bordered the neighbour's garden. He sprang forward, grabbing the top of the fence and swinging himself over, just as two burly figures appeared behind.

He hit the concrete, almost landing on a child's toy car. He swung his head from side to side, looking for an exit. There was no side path back to the street like the Marsden house, but there was a hedgerow separating this home from the next. Behind him, his pursuers hit the fence and began to climb.

Jerome raced on, hurdling over the hedgerow. He landed awkwardly, twisting his ankle and staggering forward. Pain shot up his leg, but there was no time to stop. The next hedgerow came up to meet him and he vaulted over it, landing on his uninjured foot.

Somewhere in his unconscious, thoughts were trying to formulate. Where was he going? How would he find his way back to Emily? What would happen if the men caught up with him?

He cleared another hedgerow, then another, his ankle complaining and slowing him down.

Then he slid to a halt.

He'd reached the last house of the row. Like the Marsden house, there was a side path that led back to the street. But unlike the Marsden house, there was a tall gate that was padlocked and topped with wood panelling that reached high above Jerome's head.

Lungs burning, he spun on his heels. He could hear his pursuers tearing across the adjacent garden.

He stared wildly at the end wall that bordered the street, at the shards of broken glass glued on top; a nasty deterrent for any would-be thieves. Frantic now, he glanced down at the envelope in his hand, then back at the garden.

He was cornered. There was no way out. And now the men were leaping over the final hedgerow and heading straight for him.

41

TIME SLOWED DOWN. Emily saw Jerome snatch the envelope from Tim Marsden's hand, then disappear around the corner of the house. Two of the men chased after him, while the third staggered to his feet. Tim stood still, his limp body that of a man who had nowhere else to run.

Blood rushed in Emily's ears. She wondered if she should get out of the car to help him. But her hands and feet would not detach themselves from the steering wheel and pedals. She watched as the remaining man took Tim Marsden roughly by the arm and frog marched him to the waiting SUV, where he was pushed into the back seat, the door slammed shut and locked behind him.

Then his assailant turned to face Emily and broke into a run.

She watched him racing toward her with clenched fists and burning eyes. Instinct took over. Her fingers shot from the wheel and hit the door lock button. Then as the man reached the driver door, she shifted the car into reverse and slammed her foot on the accelerator. Tires screeching, the car shot backward. The man lurched forward. He chased her a few metres, then slid to a halt.

Emily had to take her eyes off him. With cars lining both sides of the road, she was in danger of a collision. And reversing was not her strongest skill. As she zipped backward down the street, house lights began to light up the dark. Hopefully, someone would witness what was happening and call the police.

Emily peeled her eyes from the rear-view mirror to see the man had returned to the SUV. Behind her, the road was reaching a bend. She turned the wheel sharply, clipping her wing mirror against one of the parked cars.

More vehicles lined the street. But now the street was coming to an end and merging with a crossroad. With the car reversing in a straight line, Emily tore her gaze from the mirror again and searched the pavements. Where was Jerome? Her phone sat in the cup holder behind the gear stick, but there was no way she could take her hands off the wheel. And finding Jerome was not her only problem.

Tires screeching, the SUV skittered around the bend. Dazzled by its headlights, Emily floored the accelerator, bounced off a parked car, then skidded into the crossroad.

Her body on autopilot, she reversed right, slammed on the brakes, shifted gears, and hit the accelerator. At the same time, the SUV entered the crossroads and swerved.

Emily screamed as the sides of the vehicles grinded together, tearing off her wing mirror. Then her car shot forward, leaving the SUV behind.

She was dazed, disoriented, in the midst of a panic attack. Adrenaline pumped through her veins like a jackhammer. She had to get out of the car. She had to stop driving before she killed herself. But glancing in the rear-view mirror, she could already see the SUV catching up to her.

Emily drove on. She had no idea where she was going and every street was identical. For all she knew, she was driving in circles in an endless rabbit warren of suburban streets. And Jerome was out there somewhere, with two of Hunt's men in pursuit.

As the SUV's headlights grew larger in the rear-view mirror, Emily spotted a turning up ahead on the left. She spun the wheel and the Mazda skidded around the corner, then barrelled along the street between rows of parked vehicles.

With a cry, Emily slammed on the brakes. The car skidded in a half circle and slid to a halt. The road had ended in a cul-de-sac. The only way in was also the only way out—and it was now blocked by the SUV.

42

THE MEN CAME over the hedge and hit the ground. Jerome had two choices—to hand over the envelope or to escape over the glass-topped fence. Neither was going to end well.

His reflexes made the choice for him.

Clamping the envelope between his teeth, he turned and dashed toward the fence. Propelling himself forward, he jumped and grabbed the top with both hands.

Blinding pain ripped through his nerve endings as thick shards of glass sliced into his palms and fingers, opening the outer layers of flesh. He screamed through clenched teeth and almost let go.

A hand wrapped around his ankle and yanked his leg. The glass sliced deeper, making him scream louder. But Jerome didn't let go. Instead, he thrashed and kicked until he was free. Then it was as if he had left his body and was floating above it, watching it work of its own volition as it hauled itself over the fence and swung over to the other side.

Indescribable pain brought him rushing back. He landed on the pavement, stumbled, and rolled. The envelope slipped from his jaws.

Lungs heaving, Jerome pushed himself to his feet. His hands were on fire. Pain shot up from his palms to his elbows. He staggered forward. The men hadn't followed. Glancing back at the fence and its row of vicious glass teeth, he couldn't blame them.

Jerome's gaze dropped from the fence to the glistening, black trail on the ground. Horrified, he followed the trail until he was staring at his hands. Blood was pumping from his shredded flesh and raining down on the pavement. On his left hand, the glass had sliced through an artery.

Crying out in shock and pain, he clamped the hand to his chest, then turned on his heels and stared down the road. He had no idea where he was, or how far he had run, or where Emily was right now. But he had to keep moving. It wouldn't be long before those men double-backed and came for him.

Wincing, he stooped to pick up the dropped envelope with the finger and thumb of his less-damaged hand and tucked it under his arm. Then with both hands now pressed to his body, he took off down the street. Terrible images flashed through his mind. What if Emily had been caught by the men? What would they do to her?

He hobbled along, blood soaking his T-shirt, the envelope pressed against his ribs like a brand.

There were lights on in houses. He knew he should knock on a door and ask for help, but he couldn't help wondering how many people would rush to the aid of a bleeding black man, late at night in quiet suburbia.

But now he was feeling light-headed. And had the temperature dropped? He stopped outside of a house with its downstairs lights on. He was about to bang on the door when his phone started to ring. Slowly, carefully, he fished it out of his pocket with two fingers. Blood dripped on the screen and he wiped it clean against his T-shirt.

Emily was calling.

"Are you okay? Where are you?" she whispered, her voice stricken with fear.

"I have no idea. I got away from them, though. And I have your envelope." The street tipped slightly as if Jerome were a ship on a wave. "You need to come and get me!"

"I can't. Are you sure you're okay? They didn't hurt you?"

Jerome took the phone away from his ear for a second and glanced down at his body. The front of his T-shirt was black and sodden. "Nothing I can't handle. What do you mean you can't come get me?"

"Whatever's in the envelope, you have to keep it safe. Take it to the police."

"Just tell me where you are—I'll find you."

"There's no time."

"Jesus, Emily! Stop being so dramatic!"

Through the receiver, Jerome heard a car door open and close, followed by scurrying footsteps and Emily's frightened breaths. The line was quiet for a second. Then Emily whispered, "I'm on Steven's Close. But go for help, Jerome. Don't come here."

"I'll be five minutes."

"Jerome, don't —"

Wiping more blood from the screen, Jerome hung up. He opened the phone's map application, and with what appeared to be his only wound-free finger, tapped in: *Steven's Close.* He waited, feeling dizzy and faint. The map zoomed in. Steven's Close was three streets away, but there was a short cut just up ahead through a series of connecting alleys.

Swaying on his feet, Jerome stared up at the house in front of him. The lights were warm, inviting. Somewhere inside, a family was enjoying an ordinary evening of television and squabbles. He looked back at the road. Emily had been adamant for him not to follow her, to prioritize the contents of the envelope over her wellbeing. Had she learned nothing about him?

Backing away from the house, he returned to the street, and limped along the pavement. His hands continued to bleed, but the pain was beginning to subside, which he suspected wasn't a good sign.

By the time he reached the first alley, he was finding it difficult to walk in a straight line. By the second, he was dragging his body along, leaving a thick trail of blood in his wake. Then cleaning the screen once more, he managed to dial 999.

The operator's calm voice spoke in his ear. "Emergency services. Police, ambulance, or fire?"

"Ambulance, please," Jerome replied as darkness swirled around him. "I do believe I'm bleeding to death."

43

THE SUV TURNED sideways and came to a stop, blocking the way out of Steven's Close. One man stepped out and approached the blue Mazda parked haphazardly on the kerb. He peered through the windows, saw its driver was gone, then walked in a slow, deliberate circle around the cul-de-sac, his eyes moving from front garden to front garden, until he'd completed a circuit. Returning to the SUV, he leaned in through the driver's window and spoke in a low murmur.

His phone rang. Removing it from his jacket pocket, he answered in a deep, gravelly voice. "Where are you? No... Stay where you are. We'll be five minutes."

He hung up, then leaned through the window again and spoke to the driver. He returned to the Mazda and peered in. He spent another a minute scanning each house, looking for exits and ways for a person to escape on foot. Cursing under his breath, he pulled out a switchblade, sank it into each of the Mazda's tires, and stood listening to the hiss of escaping air. Satisfied, he returned to the SUV and slipped into the front passenger seat.

The engine growled. Headlights flashed. The SUV slowly rolled away.

From her position lying flat up against the garden fence, Emily listened to the engine fade. Relief crashed over her in trembling waves. She stood up on quaking legs and saw the SUV reach the end of the road.

Still not convinced she was safe, she kept low and crouched her way to Daniel's car. Air was still escaping from the shredded tires. Swearing, she returned her gaze to the road. What if the men leaving was a ruse to lure her out into the open? What if they suddenly returned? She had nowhere to run.

And now Jerome was on his way, even though she'd begged him not to come. As soon as he arrived, they would find the nearest police station and hand over the envelope. Emily didn't need to look inside to know it was the same envelope Max had given to the porter at the Riverside Hotel on the night he disappeared.

Movement stirred up ahead. Emily ducked behind a car, then peeked over the bonnet. Up ahead, a tall figure emerged from an alley.

Jerome!

Something was wrong. He was stumbling like a drunk, weaving in and out of the road. Emily stood up and waved. Jerome stopped still, swaying dangerously from side to side.

"Jerome? What's wrong?"

As Emily circled the car and hurried toward him, she saw him teeter to one side, then stagger beneath the beam of a streetlight.

"Jerome!" she screamed, running now as she stared in horror at his blood-drenched clothing. There was so much of the stuff she couldn't tell where it was coming from. "Oh My God, no!"

Jerome staggered forward and fell into Emily's arms. They sank to the ground together.

"What happened to you?" Emily cried as her fingers scrabbled for her phone.

With a torn and bloody hand, Jerome held out the envelope.

Got it," he said. Then his eyes rolled back in their sockets and his body grew very still.

44

LIKE ALL HOSPITALS, Darent Valley was brightly-lit and wreaked of disinfectant. As Emily drifted through long corridors toward the cafeteria, she was temporarily overcome by memories of her incarceration at St. Dymphna's Private Hospital. It was terrifying how a simple smell could instantly take her back.

At the vending machine, she pushed coins into the slot and waited for hot, watery coffee to fill a plastic cup. Her body was stiff and lead-like, her mind muddled and distant.

Jerome had lost a lot of blood. He would need a transfusion. Other than that, Emily knew nothing. She'd tried to listen to what the doctor had been saying, but there'd been another voice whispering in her ear; the same voice that taunted her now. *You did this to him. If he dies, it will be your fault.*

The doctor had questioned her about Jerome's excruciating wounds. Emily had mumbled incoherently then sloped away to call

Daniel. He had been deathly quiet on the phone, asking only for the hospital's address, and saying he would be there as soon as possible. Emily didn't want to face him when he arrived.

Emily sipped coffee and winced as the liquid burned her lips. There was a handful of people in the cafeteria, all tired and worried-looking. Choosing a table in the farthest corner, she pushed her coffee to one side, and set the blood-spattered envelope in front of her. She stared at it for a long time, breathing in and out, fighting the urge to burst into tears.

It was Jerome's blood that soaked the envelope—the envelope that he'd almost died protecting. Tim Marsden had surrendered himself to Jonathan Hunt's goons so Emily could see what was inside of it. And what about Helen? All these lives were hanging in the balance.

Their blood is on your hands, the voice whispered in her ear. This *is who you are now.*

Emily turned the envelope over. Tim Marsden's name and address were handwritten on the front. The postmark was dated 29 May—the day after the Clean Water gala, the day before Max Edwards was found dead.

Emily stared in shock—the seal was still unbroken. Tim Marsden had been so afraid of what was inside that he'd left the envelope unopened all this time, hiding it away, hoping and praying its existence would go undiscovered.

But if he'd been so afraid, why hadn't he destroyed the envelope and its contents?

Emily glanced around the cafeteria. Satisfied no one was paying her any attention, she carefully opened the envelope.

There were two items inside.

Emily removed the first—a handwritten letter. Her lips moving silently, she began to read.

Tim,

Something is going to happen to me. Something bad. Tonight, I asked if I could trust you. You said I could. I hope so—because you may be our last chance. They know about me. About all of us. They're coming to take everything we have on them, and they are likely to succeed—which is why I'm giving you this. You already know what's on there. You've seen it with your own eyes. We're trying to get a copy to the press. If they get to us before that happens, you need to make a choice.

Will you stand by and do nothing while Valence Industries destroys hundreds of thou-sands of lives? Or will you bring it all to an end? There's a reporter named Evan Holt. If something happens to me, take the drive to him. He'll know what to do

It's up to you now, Tim. I'm trusting you to make things right.

Your friend,

Max

Beads of perspiration broke out on Emily's forehead. She picked up the envelope and emptied the remaining item into her hand. It was a flash drive. Max had entrusted Tim with the evidence he'd been collecting against Valence Industries. He had believed Tim would finish what he could not. Instead, Tim Marsden had betrayed him yet again by burying the evidence to save himself.

Emily pictured Marsden's haunted face as he was led toward the SUV. He had been afraid; terrified of what the contents of that envelope could mean for his family. That was why it had sat at the back of a drawer, collecting dust. That was why Tim had continued working for Valence, had accepted his promotion without question—he'd been protecting his family.

So why had he suddenly given up? Had the guilt finally broken him? Had the blood on his hands finally soaked through to his heart?

Emily closed her fingers over the flash drive, forming a tight fist. Her thoughts returned to Jerome. To Evan Holt. To Helen. Angry tears fought their way to her eyes.

Tim Marsden had been too afraid to finish Max's work. Now, people were dead or hurt. But Emily was not afraid. She had nothing left to lose.

A row of three old desktop computers sat on one side of the cafeteria, beneath a sign that read: FREE INTERNET.

Crossing the room, Emily sat down at the first computer and inserted the flash drive into the USB socket. As she waited for it to install, she warily eyed the cafeteria users. The drive icon popped up on the screen. She clicked it.

The flash drive contained a single folder titled: MERRY CHRISTMAS. Opening it up revealed further subfolders. Emily clicked on each one, adrenaline pumping through her veins as she pored over their contents.

There were screen grabs of emails, statements of financial transactions, falsified invoices, and a document containing a long list of names and addresses from around the world. Several of the names belonged to high level managers, directors, and CEOs of Valence Industries. Jonathan Hunt's name was right there at the top. There were names connected to foreign companies and governments, and there were names Emily thought she recognized—political figures, here in the UK, whose careers and reputations would be destroyed if their involvement in Valence's wrongdoings was made public.

Emily waded through the list, trying to make sense of what she was seeing. Now she understood why Max had risked his life to uncover the truth—and why Valence Industries had gone to extreme lengths to silence him and the others. Now she understood why Tim Marsden had been so afraid. When Anya had spoken of bribery and corruption it had sounded like fiction, but here was proof, right in front of Emily's eyes; the proof that Max Edwards had fought so hard to bring to light. Now Emily would do it for him.

Removing the flash drive from the computer, she slipped it inside her jeans pocket, then left the cafeteria and returned to the A&E department.

Daniel had arrived. He looked pale and frightened as he approached the reception desk. Emily watched a nurse point him toward a set of double doors. She was about to go after him, when something else caught her attention.

Two police officers had entered A&E. Emily moved closer. She didn't know if they were here because of Jerome, or for some other incident. And she didn't care.

The flash drive felt like a tumour against her leg. She needed to get rid of it, to cut it out of her life.

She had no proof that Valence Industries was responsible for Max's death, but the evidence she did have would bury its key players. Anya and Josh would be taken into police protection.

Perhaps Max's case would be reopened. Perhaps Diane Edwards would be appeased. But there would be no satisfaction in Emily's success. People were dead. Lives were ruined. But it was going to end now—because Emily was about to finish what Max had started.

Her jaw clenched with determination, she marched toward the police officers.

A voice stopped her in her tracks. "Emily?"

Emily turned around. Her eyes grew wide.

Helen stood in front of her. Cuts and bruises covered one side of her face and she had a burgeoning black eye. But she was alive.

"Helen! You're here! I thought that—" Emily ran toward Helen, who flinched in her embrace. "You're hurt. Do you need help? What happened to you?"

Helen's gaze wandered to the police officers at the reception desk. "What were you doing?"

Taking her gently by the arm, Emily moved her away from the rows of people waiting to be seen. "I have Max's evidence," she whispered. "Proof that Valence Industries was bribing government officials to fail its competitors."

"Where is this proof?"

Emily tapped her pocket. "Right here, on a flash drive. It's over, Helen. I'm giving it to the police. Jonathan Hunt and Valence Industries are finished. Anyway, where have you been? How did you know we were here?"

Helen didn't answer. Her eyes moved from Emily's pocket to the police officers at the desk. A nurse was pointing them in the same direction Daniel had headed.

Emily pulled on Helen's arm. "Come on, before they're gone."

Helen refused to move.

"You can't give it to them," she said.

Emily shook her head. "This isn't about getting your front-page story, Helen. It's about protecting millions of people's live."

Helen stared at Emily's pocket.

"You can't give it to them," she repeated.

"I'm sorry, but I have to."

Emily turned away. Helen seized her arm in an iron grip.

"You don't understand," she said, her voice trembling. "They have someone at my sister's house. They're going to hurt her."

Emily stared at her through shocked eyes.

"Give me the flash drive."

"Helen, I can't." She turned back to the reception desk. The police were on the move, heading toward the doors.

"They'll kill her. Please, Emily! You have to give it to me."

Emily stared at Helen's outstretched hand. This couldn't be happening. Not now. Not when it could all be over in a matter of minutes. "The police can send a unit to your sister's house. Valence won't even know."

Helen shook her head. Her eyes were dark and desperate. "They won't get there in time. Emily, this is my sister's life—I'm begging you. Please!"

Angry tears slipped down Emily's face. It was all over. She would not be responsible for another death.

Valence Industries had won.

Emily dug into her pocket and produced the flash drive. "We had them, Helen," she said, her voice barely a whisper. "We had them."

She dropped the drive into Helen's palm and watched it disappear inside a protective fist.

Helen began to walk away.

Emily hurried after her. "I'll come with you."

"No," Helen said, holding up a warning hand. "You can't."

Emily watched her go, drifting past the sick and the injured, toward the exit. A second later, Helen was gone, taking the flash drive with her. A hole opened inside Emily's chest. She wanted nothing more than to fall into it.

Instead, she remained standing for a minute more, exhaustion creeping in as she swayed silently from side to side. Then she crossed the room and made her way through the double doors.

45

EMILY FOUND DANIEL sitting in a small waiting area, along with a handful of other people who were waiting for news about their loved ones. There was no sign of the police officers who'd arrived a few minutes earlier, and she wondered if they were here to see Jerome after all. Daniel stood, staring at Emily with haunted eyes. She felt tears coming, could feel them breaking down her resistance.

"What happened?" he asked, his tone somewhere between terror and fury.

Emily stared at the floor, avoiding his accusatory gaze. Where did she begin? "Your car is—"

"I don't care about the damn car! What happened to Jerome?"

"They were chasing him. He got hurt." Emily risked a glance up and saw Daniel's eyes were growing darker by the second. But now was not the time for hiding behind excuses. "He was protecting evidence. Evidence I was going to take to the police."

Daniel said something angry-sounding in Italian, then threw his hands in the air. "Jesus Christ, Emily!"

Something was happening to her. She felt numb, detached—as if she were in the room but outside it at the same time.

"It's too late now," she said. "I had to give the evidence to Helen. It's all over."

Daniel shook his head. "Helen was here?"

"They have her sister."

Thrusting his hands on his hips, Daniel stared at Emily as if she had lost her mind. "What are you talking about? Helen doesn't have any sisters. She has four brothers."

Emily stared at him, suddenly very much back in the room. "Brothers? But she—"

"Helen called me just after you did. She told me she'd tried calling both of you, but you weren't answering. I told her what happened to Jerome, that I was on my way here."

Confused, Emily checked her phone. It was true—she'd missed a call from Helen an hour ago, about the time she'd been in the back of the ambulance with Jerome.

"But that doesn't explain. . ." Realization hit her like a punch in the gut. At first, she couldn't believe it. Surely not even Helen was capable of stooping so low. Her phone buzzed in her hand. She stared in shock at Daniel, then back at the phone. The caller ID read: UNKNOWN.

"She wouldn't have. . ." Emily began. But when she answered the call, any doubt she had about Helen's deceit was quickly obliterated.

"Good evening, Miss Swanson. You *are* a tricky character to pin down, aren't you?"

At first, she thought the man on the phone was Jonathan Hunt, but the voice lacked his charm and arrogance.

"Who is this?" she asked. Her mind was reeling. Nothing felt real.

"I believe you have something of interest to my client," the man said. "Something they would very much like to have returned."

Emily stared at Daniel, then holding up a finger, she slowly turned and walked down the corridor.

"Come now, don't be shy," the man said. "We know Mr. Marsden gave you something. What I'm proposing is a quick, painless exchange. Then we can be out of each other's hair and put this whole embarrassing event behind us."

"Exchange?" Emily said. "You have nothing of mine."

"Nothing of yours, no. But we have something of value to you. Or perhaps I should say *someone*."

From the confused fog of Emily's mind came the instant realization that Anya Copeland hadn't checked in with her. She and Josh would have reached Bristol over an hour ago. Despite the warmth of the hospital, a terrible chill pierced Emily's heart as she heard a high-pitched squeal in her ear. It belonged to a child.

"Please. . ." she whispered, her voice trembling. "Please, don't hurt him!"

"Oh, I'm not hurting him," the man said. "Young Josh is having the time of his life running around this big old place, aren't you?"

She heard more squeals and whoops. When the man spoke again, his happy, polite tone was gone. "Two hours, Miss Swanson. St. Katharine Docks. Warehouse three. I'll send directions. You know what will happen if you involve the authorities."

The floor was slipping away from Emily's feet.

"I don't have what you're looking for," she said. "Someone's taken it."

"Then I suggest you get it back. Two hours, Miss Swanson."

The line went dead. Emily checked the time: 11:44 p.m. She spun on her heels. The lights bore down on her. The smell of antiseptic became an overwhelming stench, churning her insides.

Two hours. It would take her half that time to get back to London. And then what?

Helen would be on her way to London Truth right now. Even if Emily could get there in time, how was she going to convince Helen to give her back the flash drive?

Racing along the corridor, Emily burst through the double doors, and found herself back in A&E and heading for the exit. Outside, the night air had grown cold. The sky was black and filled with thousands of stars. For a second, she was paralyzed; captivated by their beauty. Then she was waving down a taxi and hopping into the back.

"Where are we going?" the taxi driver asked.

"London. Please hurry."

As the taxi pulled away from the kerb, Emily tried to push down the terror bubbling in her throat. Then pulling out her phone, she dialled Helen's number and waited for the line to connect.

46

THE TAXI PULLED up in front of the London Truth office at half past midnight. Helen paid the driver, who'd been silently eyeing her cuts and bruises throughout the journey, then let herself into the building. It was dark; her colleagues had gone home hours ago. Some had tried calling and had left worried voicemails. People were concerned for her safety. Well, they needn't be, Helen thought. She was just fine.

She'd managed to get out of her car and run as hard as she could, away from those psychopath assholes, and she'd hidden among street crowds and in department stores, ignoring the stares and concerned looks, and growling at those who offered help. She didn't know how long she'd wandered for—an hour or two, maybe more—but at some point, she'd woken up from her shock-induced haze. Night had fallen. The crowds had thinned. She had never felt more alone in the city.

Climbing the stairs, Helen reached the press room and went straight to her desk. Leaving all the lights off, she switched on her computer. Her phone started buzzing. Emily was calling again. She'd already left several voicemails, none of which Helen had listened to

The decision to take the flash drive had been impulsive. After learning from Daniel what had happened to Jerome, she'd made her way to the hospital; partly out of concern, but mostly to discover what Emily had found. After all, Helen had almost been murdered—she had a right to know why. The moment she'd learned Emily was about to hand over Max Edwards' evidence to the police, Helen's decision to take it had been instantaneous.

Somewhere beneath the hardened shell of her conscience she felt a pinch of guilt. She knew what she'd done was wrong—in fact, it was the most awful, underhand stunt she'd ever pulled—but Emily would never understand what Helen was trying to achieve.

This wasn't just about furthering her career. It was about journalism. It was about shining a light on corruption in the world. It was about telling the truth.

If Emily had given the flash drive to the police, they would have investigated, made some arrests, and that would be the end of it. The sale of TEL would go on. Valence Industries would prevail—because the police did not have the power of the press. Only the press could ensure that Max Edwards' evidence was shown to the world. Left to the police, it would be buried under a mountain of red tape and government bureaucracy. So yes, Helen knew what she'd done to Emily was wrong, but she also knew Evan Holt would have done the same thing.

The computer had finished booting. Helen took out the flash drive and plugged it into the USB slot. Once it had installed, she opened the folder and clicked through the files. As she read, she gasped and she swore and she grinned with excitement. It was far worse than she'd anticipated, but far better than she'd hoped.

The newsroom was suddenly bathed in light. Helen jumped up.

"Normally, I don't appreciate late night calls from my staff," Christine Gates said, standing by the door. "But in this situation, despite the fact you look like shit, I'm glad you're all right. Now, would you mind telling me where the fuck you've been, and why I'm here when I should be tucked up in bed getting my beauty sleep."

Helen's shoulders relaxed. She nodded at the screen. "Believe me, when you see what I have, it'll be worth the extra wrinkles."

Sucking in a large breath, she quickly relayed everything she knew about Valence Industries and its criminal activities, including the attack in the car park, and the murder of fellow journalist, Evan Holt.

As the editor-in-chief listened, the lines on her forehead grew thick and deep. When Helen had finished talking, Christine pointed at the computer screen. "How did you get this?"

Helen scratched an ear. "It fell into my hands, it doesn't matter. What *does* matter is what we're going to do with it. We have a chance to get this out there before anyone else. An exclusive, Christine—the biggest fucking story of the year! I could write it up—right here, right now. We could make the deadline for the next issue."

Christine stared at the screen in stony silence. Running her tongue over dry lips, she clicked through the files.

Helen tapped her foot impatiently on the floor. "So? Is this the story that's going to make our careers, or what?"

Christine drew back. Slowly, she shook her head. "No. I'm sorry, Helen. Come on, you know the rules. If we print this story before an arrest is made, we'll be looking at a libel case big enough to bury us six-feet under."

"There's enough evidence here to put Jonathan Hunt away for years," Helen said. "The police *will* make an arrest."

Christine shook her head, over and over. "No. I can't allow it. Even before we get to the lawsuit, this magazine is not big enough or strong enough to go making enemies with the police. You want an exclusive? Go through the proper channels. Broker a deal with the police—the flash drive for first rights to the story. They may go for it, they may not, but it's the only way you'll get what you want."

Helen jabbed a finger at the screen. "I almost died getting this."

"Then make sure the police know about it when you talk to them. I'm sorry, Helen. This story is big. It's fucking huge. Which is why I can't risk London Truth without doing things the right way."

Anger welled inside Helen's chest. She had expected to be championed, commended for bringing London Truth what was undoubtedly its biggest ever story. But instead she'd been met by fear and cowardice. *Fine,* she thought. The magazine didn't go to press for another week, anyway. She would take the flash drive to the tabloids and sell it to the highest bidder. The day after tomorrow, her story would be front-page news. Her name would be everywhere.

"Okay, you're right," she said. "It's not worth the risk."

Christine patted her on the shoulder. "Good girl. We'll get that exclusive—we just need to do it by the book."

Helen wanted to knock the editor's hand away, to tell her to shove her job up her ass. Instead, she smiled and stared hungrily at the screen. It was then that the office doors burst open and Emily Swanson came rushing in.

47

EMILY WAS FURIOUS. As she bounded into the newsroom and caught sight of Helen, it was all she could do to stop herself from launching forward with fists flying. The taxi driver had put his foot down all the way from Dartford, but it had still taken an hour to get here. That left her with one more hour to deliver the flash drive to St Katharine Docks.

She advanced toward Helen. "Where is it?"

Christine Gates stared open-mouthed at Emily, then at Helen, who had returned her gaze to the computer screen and was clicking away on the mouse.

"What's this about?" Christine asked.

Emily ignored her. "You have no idea what you've done, Helen. Where is it?"

Helen finally turned to face her. "Relax. It's right here. And you were right, we should take it to the police."

It was not the response Emily had been expecting, and it only stoked her anger. "Then why did you take it from me? I've just left Jerome in the hospital, not knowing if he's going to live or die!"

Helen shrugged and leaned back on her chair. "Because I did what I thought was right."

"You mean right for you! That's all you've done throughout this entire investigation. To hell with everyone else!" Emily trembled with fury. "Evan Holt is dead because you told Jonathan Hunt we knew about TEL!"

"Evan Holt is dead because Valence murdered him!" Helen snarled back.

Emily stuck out a hand. "I don't have time for this. Just give me the damn drive!"

Helen stared at her, unmoving.

Christine Gates wedged herself between the women. "Now, wait a second. Helen has agreed to take the flash drive to the police. I'll see it's taken care of, so try not to worry."

"So you can get your exclusive? It's too late for that!" Emily stretched out her fingers. "Give it to me."

Helen folded her arms. "You heard what Christine said. We'll take care of it."

Emily glared at the two women. *Bloody journalists!* "They have Josh and Anya Copeland," she said. "They're going to kill them if I don't bring them the flash drive."

Helen flinched but made no move to retrieve the drive.

Christine's hardened expression drooped. "Who are Anya and Josh Copeland? What is she talking about, Helen?"

"Josh Copeland is a little boy who's going to die along with his mother if Helen doesn't give me the drive!" Emily was desperate now, her hands digging into her sides. "Please! I have less than an hour."

There was a moment of terrible silence that stole the air from the room. Slowly, Helen shook her head. "I'm sorry. You're asking me to choose between saving two lives or saving millions. You *know* what the right answer is."

Bitter tears stung Emily's eyes. "You're right. I do know," she said, reaching out her hand again. "Give me the drive."

Their eyes locked. Helen clenched her jaw.

Emily stepped forward.

"For God's sake, Helen!" Christine Gates grabbed hold of Helen's chair, rolled her out of the way, then pulled the flash drive from the computer and handed it to Emily. "Some stories have to wait."

Emily stared at the drive in her hand, relief flooding her body. She thanked Christine, then glowered at Helen.

"You need to take a good look at the people around you," she said, barely able to control the fury burning through her veins. "Because if you keep going the way you are, pretty soon they won't be around anymore. Believe me, it's a very lonely path to take."

Refusing to meet Emily's gaze, Helen shrugged a shoulder. "People are overrated."

Emily backed away, trembling with resentment and pity. "I don't think I ever want to hear from you again."

Spinning on her heels, Emily bolted from the newsroom. The taxi was still waiting outside.

"Where next?" the driver asked as Emily jumped in.

"St. Katharine Docks." She squeezed the flash drive tightly in her hand. It was now 12:57 a.m.

48

ST. KATHARINE DOCKS lay east of Tower Bridge. Heavily bombed during the Second World War, what was once a thriving if not commercially successful part of the Port of London network had since been redeveloped into a popular modern housing and leisure complex, complete with marina.

The taxi pulled up in a nearby empty car park at 1:23 a.m. As Emily fumbled in the dark for her wallet, the driver peered through the windscreen.

"This isn't any place for a woman on her own," he said.

Emily paid him, thanked him for his concern, then she got out and watched him drive away. Darkness swarmed about her as she crossed the car park and headed up a short flight of stone steps. By the time she'd reached the top, her stomach had knotted into a tight ball. Crossing a small footbridge, she descended the steps on the other side.

A minute later, she came upon the quayside. The River Thames stirred in the night time breeze, lapping against the harbour walls, yachts and barges gently rocking on its surface. Modern warehouse-style apartment complexes flanked the marina, along with strips of restaurants and bars, now all closed for the night and shrouded in shadows.

Emily made her way through St. Katharine Docks, following the directions that she'd been texted. As she walked, she listened to the gentle slosh of the Thames and the soft creaks of the boats, but the sounds did nothing to soothe her fear.

Taking a left, she moved away from the quayside and along a cobbled passage. She took another turn and found herself in a wide, open space occupied by several warehouses. It didn't take long to locate warehouse number three.

Her legs trembling beneath her, Emily slipped into the shadows and observed the warehouse from a safe distance. Horizontal windows ran along the top of the building, dull light shining out of them.

Emily squeezed the flash drive, hurting her fingers. It would be easy—she would go in there, hand over the drive, take Josh and Anya to safety, and then it would all be over. She'd go back to the hospital, back to Jerome. Back to her ordinary life, which hadn't been ordinary for a very long time.

Taking a deep breath, Emily held onto it for as long as she could, then let it out. Stepping from the shadows, she walked toward the warehouse.

As she reached the door, she stopped and turned to face the darkness of the garden. She'd heard a noise, somewhere behind her and to the left. And now, real or imagined, she felt eyes watching her.

Emily turned back to the door and grabbed the handle. She froze, unable to escape the feeling that her past and her future were converging in this exact moment. Then she was opening the door and stepping inside.

The warehouse was derelict but it still had power, hanging strip lights illuminating graffiti-covered walls, broken crates, empty boxes, scraps of metal—and in the middle of the cavernous space—a man and a boy. Emily recognized Josh Copeland immediately. He appeared unharmed as he sat cross-legged on a crate, playing with two toy trucks. As Emily came closer, he glanced up and frowned.

The man whispered something to him, then leaving the boy to play, took a slow walk toward Emily. He was tall and slim, with sharp cheekbones and thinning grey hair. Dressed in jeans and a striped polo shirt he looked nothing like the menacing picture Emily had painted in her mind. But hadn't that been Valence Industries' *modus operandi* all along? To mask its cruelty with benevolence?

The man stopped a metre away.

"Miss Swanson, thank you for coming," he said. "And early, too. I do appreciate punctuality. It shows respect for your fellow man, don't you think?"

Emily was silent as she leaned to one side, checking on Josh and glancing around the warehouse. The three of them were quite alone.

"You're not Jonathan Hunt," she said.

The man smiled. It was a warm, inviting smile that made Emily feel strangely at ease. "Indeed, I am not."

"Then who are you?"

"An employee of sorts."

Emily returned her gaze to Josh, who seemed content and at ease, playing with the toy trucks. "Where's Anya. Why isn't she here?"

The man clasped his hands behind his back and continued to smile. "Miss Copeland is quite safe."

"And after I give you what I have?"

"She'll be returned to the safety of her home. Some people have the good sense to hold onto their secrets, Miss Swanson. To take them to their graves." He looked back at Josh, who was uninterested in the adults' conversation. "Of course, it helps when they have an incentive. Miss Copeland has sworn to retain her discretion. And who are we to hold her accountable for the actions of others?"

"You mean she's free to go on living like a prisoner?" Emily said.

The man shrugged. "Miss Copeland is free to live wherever she chooses."

The honesty in his voice was convincing, Emily thought. Perhaps he was telling the truth—after all, why murder a child in cold blood when just the threat of it could easily buy his mother's silence? Emily felt the gentle weight of the flash drive in her pocket, tucked away like a vial of poison. Anya had risked her son's life by trusting her. The woman wouldn't make the same mistake again.

"So, Miss Swanson, shall we keep this brief?" the man said. "Someone here is up way past his bedtime."

Josh shifted his gaze between the adults, then returned his attention to the toy trucks. Emily's hand hovered over her pocket, hesitating as she stared at the young boy. Slowly, she fished out the flash drive.

"Very good," the man said, nodding. "Now give it to me."

"What guarantee do I have that once this is over I'll be left alone?" Emily watched him carefully, analysing every twitch of his mouth and crease of his brow. Inside, her heart was beating like a hummingbird's. Where were the other men? Why weren't they here, taking the flash drive from her by force instead of waiting for her to politely hand it over. Why was she still alive and not face down in her bathroom, the staged victim of an accidental overdose?

The man's smile remained steady and true. "Your silence will be your guarantee. It's as simple as that. You see, it's not the intention of my employers to go around destroying lives, Miss Swanson."

"Tell that to the millions of kids breathing in toxic poison courtesy of your employers."

"But if threatened," he continued, "they will take measures to protect themselves."

"And you're one of those measures?"

"My job is to tidy up, to rectify mistakes."

"Mistakes like Max Edwards? Jason Dobbs?" Emily's voice cracked like glass. "Evan Holt?"

Grinning, the man extended his right hand. Behind him, Josh smashed the trucks together and watched them flip onto their sides.

Emily stared at the flash drive as she held it out. Then she drew it back. "Tell me what happened to Max Edwards."

"As far as I'm aware, Mr. Edwards drowned," the man said, his smile slowly fading.

Emily's fingers closed over the flash drive. "You killed him. First Max, then Jason Dobbs. They knew Valence was onto them. They met at the hotel in the middle of the night, with a plan to lay low for a while before handing the evidence over to the press. But they were too late. You were already waiting for them, weren't you?"

The man said nothing.

Emily's eyes swept the room. "Did you bring Max here? Did you have your men half kill him with alcohol before taking him for a swim?"

She pictured it with terrible clarity: Max Edwards tied to a chair in the centre of the warehouse, one thug forcing his head back, while another poured alcohol down his throat, filling him up like an empty bottle.

The man raised his eyebrows and surprised her by laughing. "You seem to have it all worked out for yourself, don't you?"

He stared at her closed fist. But Emily wasn't done with her questions.

"What will happen to Tim Marsden?"

"Mr. Marsden has already admitted the errors of his ways," the man said. "I'm sure that come Monday, he'll be back in the office, doing what he does best. But really, Miss Swanson, these matters are not your concern. All that's required of you is to give me what's in your hand so that I may return it to my employers. That is all. Nothing more, nothing less."

Emily's skin burned with anger as she uncurled her fingers and stared at the flash drive. It was such a small, indiscriminate object, yet it contained enough power to put untouchable men behind bars, to destroy whole companies, to purify the air breathed in by all those millions of children. If she handed it over, the lives of Max Edwards, Jason Dobbs, and Evan Holt would have been sacrificed for nothing. Valence Industries would continue profiting from the sale of TEL. Children would continue to be poisoned.

But Anya and Josh would not die. They would go on living, even if it was under the watchful eye of Valence Industries. What other choice did Emily have but to choose the living?

"One day, someone else will come," she said. "Someone who will find out the truth about Valence Industries, someone who'll tear it open and expose what it really is to the world."

The man nodded. "I dare say they will. But it won't be you."

Emily held out the flash drive. Her eyes seared into the man as he stepped forward and plucked it between finger and thumb.

"And there we are." He smiled, his eyes glinting. "If you'd be so kind to wait just one minute."

He returned to Josh, then opened a briefcase that was sitting on top of a crate. Emily moved closer to get a better look. There was a laptop inside the briefcase. If she wasn't mistaken, it was *her* laptop. She watched as the man inserted the flash drive, then smiled at Josh like a loving grandfather. As soon as the drive was ready, he patted Josh on the head, and returned his attention to the screen. He nodded, removed the drive, and slipped it inside the briefcase beside Emily's laptop.

He stood, staring at Emily. She stared back. Was that it? The transaction made?

"Please remember what I told you, Miss Swanson. Your silence is your guarantee. If my employers were to find out, for example, that copies had been made of the information you've kindly returned, then they would be forced to react. And I would hate to see any harm come to you. Or to the people around you."

Like a rattlesnake, the man lunged at Josh, wrapping fingers around the boy's delicate wrist and twisting sharply, wrenching him from the ground.

Josh screamed in agony.

"Stop it!" Emily shrieked. "Please, stop it!"

The man let Josh hang there for a second longer, kicking and wailing, then he set him down on the crate. Clutching his wrist to his chest, Josh began a long, drawn-out howl. Emily rushed toward him.

The man blocked her path. "No one else needs to get hurt, Miss Swanson. You may leave now."

Emily was unmoving, desperate to go to Josh, whose frightened wails grew louder. The man's smile was gone, and she saw his true face. He was cold and inhumane; a brutal monster who knew nothing of love and compassion, of human kindness. Staring into his eyes was like staring into the depths of space—there was nothing there but infinite darkness.

"We don't want Josh to get hurt again, do we?" he said through an icy smile.

Emily shook her head, but she stayed where she was, angry tears forming at the corners of her eyes.

"Go on, Miss Swanson. I'll see he gets home safely." The man turned to Josh, who skittered away, whimpering.

Emily's feet betrayed her by taking a step back. She was going to leave him. She was going to leave this child in the hands of a psychopath. But he was giving her no choice.

Seeing the terror on Emily's face, the man called after her. "I'm a man of my word, Miss Swanson. Haven't you learned that by now? Your silence is their safety."

He was quiet and still then, watching Emily retreat to the door. Behind him, Josh continued to cry and stare at Emily with terrified, pleading eyes.

Emily felt like she'd been shot in the chest. The door was behind her. Reaching out, she pushed it open. Tears spilled down her face as she ran out into the night.

She fled. Past the warehouses. Out of the darkness and into the light of the marina. She kept running. Breaths heaving in and out, she raced over the footbridge and through the car park. She did not look back; not until she had reached the road and flagged down a night bus. Behind her, the darkness was everywhere, penetrated by cracks of moonlight that splashed across the tops of buildings.

Emily felt as if she'd been poisoned, deadly chemicals choking her throat and burning her heart. And as the bus rolled toward the city, as tears continued to roll down her face, she wondered if she'd just made the second worst mistake of her life.

49

IT WAS STILL dark when Emily returned to the hospital. She found Daniel still sitting in the waiting room. He stood up when he saw her. Emily braced herself, ready to accept every angry insult he was about to hurl her way. But Daniel did not shout or scream. He merely stared at her with confused, distraught eyes.

"I had to go," she explained. "I had to put things right."

Daniel sat down again. Emily slumped in the opposite chair, feeling suddenly exhausted.

"How is he?"

"I'm still waiting."

"*Still?*"

Daniel nodded. There was no need for more words; the silence spoke for them.

Time passed. Eventually, a doctor arrived with news. Jerome had lost a great deal of blood, resulting in hypovolemic shock. Fast work by the attending paramedics and an immediate transfusion had prevented his organs from failing. He was now in recovery with over a hundred stitches in his hands and possible nerve damage. He would require more rest and further observation, but the overall prognosis was good: Jerome might not be able to play the piano again, but he was alive.

The doctor left Emily and Daniel sitting side by side in the waiting room, relief cleansing them of ill feelings. They waited some more, neither of them wanting to leave until they had seen Jerome for themselves.

Outside, the sky began to lighten. The first rays of sun peeked over the horizon. Morning was on its way.

50

EMILY LEFT THE hospital just after nine. Jerome had been asleep when she'd finally convinced the nurses to let her see him. She'd stayed for just a minute, watching his chest heave up and down, and feeling overwhelmed by equal measures of guilt and relief.

When she returned to The Holmeswood later that morning, she took a long, hot shower, then thought about sleep. But she couldn't. Not yet.

Ninety minutes later, she was standing in the street outside the Copelands' flat, desperate to know she'd made the right decision, and that the man at the warehouse had kept his word.

Mustering courage, she crossed the road and pressed the doorbell. She waited a minute, then tried again.

Emily felt as if she was falling. Hot, frightened tears stung her eyes. She stumbled back to the street and looked up.

Fear turned to relief.

Two silhouettes stood in the window, staring down at her. A mother and her son. Smiling, Emily waved a hand. The silhouettes were unmoving. Then slowly, they retreated into the safety of the room.

*

"Hello, sleepyhead. How are those pain killers holding up?"

"Liquid morphine is a gift from the Gods."

Jerome was half awake and propped up in bed, his heavily bandaged hands resting by his sides. He was still very pale and weak-looking, Emily thought. But he was alive.

"Where's Daniel?" she asked, glancing across the ward.

"He's gone home to get a few things." Jerome's eyelids drooped as he turned to face her. "What was inside?"

"Honestly, Jerome, I don't think now's the time to—"

"Hey, I sacrificed my dream of being a hand model to get that envelope to you. What was in it?"

Emily glanced away. She didn't want to tell him that she'd failed—that the evidence he'd almost died for was now back in the hands of Valence Industries.

"I'm sorry," she whispered, pressing her face into his arm. "It's my fault. I should never have let you come with me."

Jerome closed his eyes. "Stop with the attention seeking already. You're not the one who's short-term future includes having someone wipe your ass." He laughed. The painkillers were clearly working their magic. "I just hope whatever was inside that envelope . . . well, that it was all worth it."

Emily was quiet. Anya and Josh Copeland were still alive. She'd uncovered the truth of what had happened to Max Edwards;

although she was unsure how much of that truth she could tell Diane. The man in the warehouse had been very clear—her silence guaranteed everyone's safety. As for Jerome, she knew he would ask about the envelope again. She would tell him the truth, eventually. Regardless of his feelings, he could be trusted to remain silent. But right now, the truth wasn't going to help his recovery.

"Have they said when you can leave?" she asked him.

"Soon. Mum and Dad are on their way down. They want me to come home with them for a while, until I'm able to use my hands again. Seems best."

"What about the room in Brixton?"

"I guess Mags will have to find a new housemate."

"And you and Daniel will be all right?"

Jerome opened one eye. "Plenty of people have survived long distance relationships. Anyway, this is a very temporary fixture. Just try and stop me from coming back."

"Well, there's always the sofa at mine until you find a new place. It might have a few holes in it now, but it's yours if you want it."

Emily stood and glanced out the window at the car park below. People milled about. She wondered if any of them were here to watch her.

Jerome was drifting off to sleep.

"Emily Swanson," he muttered. "My hero."

51

THE NEXT MORNING, Emily woke around nine, feeling heavy and groggy, and certainly not like she'd just enjoyed twelve hours of sleep. She got up, showered, took her antidepressant, then texted Carter West. She'd been thinking about him last night. Even though she still had her reservations about dating, she did owe him a second chance at coffee. Perhaps this time she would even stay around to answer his questions.

But before she could begin to think of the future, she first needed to put an end to the very recent past.

She arrived at Diane Edwards' house a little after midday. In the kitchen, she accepted the offer of tea and then sat in silence, drumming her fingers against her knees. When they were both seated and the tea had been poured, Emily began her story.

She told a version of the truth: Max Edwards had discovered his employers were engaged in legal but unethical activities that went against everything he believed in. He'd realized that his position had been created not to protect the environment, but to act as a smokescreen. Enraged, Max had attempted but failed to bring Valence Industries' immoral activities to an end. Emily could not confirm for certain how he'd ended up in the Thames, but what she did know was that Max had been acting for the greater good, just as he had always strived to do throughout his life.

And that was it; the most abridged version of the story she could manage without breaking her silence.

Diane Edwards sat at the table for the longest time, staring at the rear garden. Autumn leaves were scattered over the lawn, rust on emerald. Birds flitted from bush to branch.

"I'm sorry there's not much else I can tell you," Emily said, when the silence became unbearable. Even though she hadn't technically lied, she felt wretched.

When Diane finally spoke, her voice was cracked and husky, as if she'd just woken from a long, deep sleep.

"Thank you," she said. She turned back to the garden and her shoulders stiffened. "What the bloody hell was Max thinking?"

A single tear journeyed down the length of her face. She left it hovering on the contour of her chin, then swept it away. When she looked back at Emily, her expression was strangely neutral, as if she had directed all her grief into that single tear and cast it from her body.

"I suppose it would explain why he took to drink after all that time," she said. "Max did hate to be made a hypocrite."

Emily bit her lip and stared at the table.

"That woman. The one he worked with. . . Anya Copeland, was her name, wasn't it?"

"Yes."

"Did they. . ." Diane shook her head, then wrapped her arms around her ribs. "Do I even want to ask this question?"

Emily saved her the pain. "They were colleagues. That was all."

"Colleagues. . ." Diane mused.

"Nothing more. I promise you."

Relief softened Diane's face. She smiled a sad smile, then reached a hand across the table. Emily took it.

"You've gone above and beyond what I've asked of you. I can't expect any more than that. I just wish Max had told me about what he'd found, about what he was going through."

"I expect he was trying to protect you," Emily said. "I think that shows how much he loved you, no matter how distant your marriage had become."

Diane squeezed her hand, then released her. "Well, thank you again, Emily. You've been most helpful to me."

Drowning in guilt and uncertain that she'd been any help at all, Emily nodded.

"What will you do now?" she asked.

Across the table, Diane shook her head. "I'm not sure. Get on with things, I suppose. Whatever that entails. Perhaps I'll start with a walk in the park to think things over. And you?"

"Me?"

"What will you do now?"

Emily opened her mouth, then closed it again. The truth was she had a very good idea of what she would do next, but she was too nervous to say it aloud. Instead, she smiled and said, "Perhaps, if you don't mind, I'll come for that walk with you."

52

THE STAFF OF London Truth were shutting down their computers and calling it a day. One of the benefits of working for a fortnightly magazine rather than the daily tabloids was that, unless a story was breaking, no one stayed late on Fridays. No one except for Helen Carlson. Sitting at her desk, she watched her colleagues go. Some were heading to the local pub. Others were going home.

Bill appeared beside her desk. "Coming for a pint?"

She didn't bother to look up from her screen. "Still busy."

"What's so urgent?"

"Have a nice weekend, Bill."

"Fine," he said, staring at her cuts and bruises. "Suit yourself."

Helen watched him stalk away and leave through the smoked glass doors. Shaking her head, she returned her gaze to the screen.

"You know you're not getting paid right now."

The voice startled her.

She looked up to see Christine standing over her, one arm inside the sleeve of a jacket.

"Are you trying to give me a heart attack?" Helen growled. "Besides, half of the hours I put in are unpaid."

Christine smiled. "Doesn't that tell you something?"

Yeah, to get a better paid job, Helen thought as she moved her hands away from the keyboard and folded them across her chest.

The editor-in-chief was still staring at her.

"I know you're angry," she said. "And you have a right to be. You had a big story at your fingertips—bigger than most journalists will see thirty years into their career, never mind just a few years."

"And Emily Swanson took it from me."

That was what made Helen angriest—losing the story smarted like hell, but the fact Emily Swanson had stolen it from her made her insides burn.

"Think of it this way," Christine said with a pitying look that made Helen scowl. "Lives have been saved. And there are always more stories. More corrupt companies just begging to be exposed. Valence Industries is not unique, and I can guarantee it won't be long before its dirty linen is hung out to dry. Secrets like that won't stay buried forever. Someone will fuck up—and you just have to hope you're in the right place and the right time when they do."

Helen avoided the editor's gaze. She didn't need her pity or her words of advice.

"Have a nice weekend," Christine said, as she made her way through the doors. "You've heard of that, right? A weekend?"

Helen was now alone in the office. The stillness of the room felt physical, like an unwelcome embrace. Stretching out the fingers of both hands, she glanced back at the door. Then she clicked the computer mouse a couple of times, and sat back, staring at the screen.

While Emily had stood there making her demands, Helen had copied the entire contents of the flash drive onto her desktop. Now the files filled her screen, staring back at her. Tempting her.

She could sell the story, make a ton of money, and skip years of churning out shitty stories for shitty magazines. Or she could do as Emily had intended—she could hand the evidence over to the police.

As Helen continued to stare at the screen, Evan Holt entered her thoughts and an awful, twisting pain tore through her stomach. Valence Industries may have killed him, but what if Emily was right? Would Evan still be alive if Helen had kept quiet about TEL? It was possible.

And what about Anya and Josh Copeland? If she sold the story, would she be responsible for endangering their lives, too?

Helen logged off from the computer and the files disappeared from the screen. She would wait a while, a few months, maybe even a year—enough time for Valence Industries to believe its dirty secrets were safe once more. Then she would dig those secrets up again and expose them to the world.

But just like Christine had suggested, she would do it by the book. The Copelands would be taken into police protection, and London Truth would get their exclusive.

Helen smiled. It wouldn't be the huge career jump she wanted, but it would be a jump all the same. Best of all, she wouldn't have to share the spotlight with that rank amateur, Emily Swanson.

53

OCTOBER RAIN WAS turning rusty autumn leaves into pulpy mush. In the streets, Londoners put up their umbrellas and bounced off each other in an endless stream, their summer colours now replaced by drab greys and navy blues as an icy wind chased them along the pavements. Winter had begun its slow approach toward the metropolis.

Emily sat at a desk, watching rain trickle down the glass of the third-floor window, and feeling grateful to be indoors where it was warm and dry. Having slept poorly the night before, she should have been feeling tired, but her nerves were providing a much-needed jolt of energy.

She peered at the other people in the room, noting with some anxiety that she was the only woman. Some of the men were already eyeing her. Why was she here, this thin-framed girl who barely looked strong enough to stand on her feet? Surely she'd stumbled into the wrong room.

Emily stared at the desk, at her new notebook and pen. Her right foot bounced up and down. She brought it to a standstill. At the front, two of the men muttered to each other, then one of them cast a quick glance in Emily's direction. Emily stared right back.

A tall, upright woman, who was dressed in a black trouser suit, strolled confidently into the room. She took a moment to set down her bag and throw her coat over a chair before addressing the group.

"Good morning. My name is Erica Braithwaite. Just to confirm you have the right room, this is day one of IQ Level 3 Award for Private Investigators. Hopefully, you will have provided your real names on the register. If not, I'll have my surveillance team track you down." Her eyes roamed the room and landed on Emily. "Just my little joke. Because you've signed up for the more intense version of the course, I'm assuming you have little to no experience of private investigation. This course will teach you the fundamental basics you'll need to begin your new career—the law, probity, standards, and core investigator competency.

"Once you've completed Level 3, there's a range of other courses to teach you the skills and knowledge needed to become a successful and diligent practitioner within the private investigation sector. So, if you were expecting a crash course in snapping pictures of cheating lovers, or a guide to practical disguises, you have my sincerest apologies and the door is over there. But if you're staying, let's quickly go around the room and introduce ourselves before we look at the course overview. Let's begin with you."

Emily swallowed. Erica Braithwaite was looking at her. And so were the men. Suddenly, she was eleven years old and back at school. One of the men had a smile on his lips, as if he still couldn't believe this little woman was here and not at home washing dishes.

Emily cleared her throat, untangled her fingers, and took in a breath. *In for four, hold for seven, out for eight.* She glanced out the window at the failing rain. Then she stared—not at Erica, but at the men.

"My name is Emily," she said. "Emily Swanson."

AUTHOR'S NOTE

Although *Trail Of Poison* is a work of fiction, environmental racism is very real, with countless documented cases around the world—in both developing and developed countries.

Valence Industries is a fictitious company. However, in 2013 a British chemicals company (who shall remain nameless here) was convicted of bribing foreign officials to continue the sale of Tetraethyl lead (TEL) in unstable countries.

Thankfully, TEL has been outlawed in almost every country in the world. The theory that lead poisoning in children can lead to aggressive behaviour in adulthood has been well documented and researched in the USA, UK, and around the planet. Environmental groups (like the fictitious Earth Conservation Group) continue to work with chemical companies to eradicate the risks of poisoning from lead and other toxins.

ACKNOWLEDGEMENTS

Huge debts of gratitude to my friends and family for their continued support. With special thanks to Kate Ellis for her editorial work, Alasdair Gray, Dutch Hearn, Victor Martinez Cecilia, and of course, to Xander, who always knows what to say when words fail me. To my readers, including my launch team—thank you.

Printed in Poland
by Amazon Fulfillment
Poland Sp. z o.o., Wrocław

49620999R00179